His attraction to her surprised him.

Annie wasn't his type. She was a "nice" woman, the kind a man turned to when he was looking for a permanent relationship. Jett wasn't looking for any kind of relationship, permanent or otherwise. And she was delicate, soft, nurturing—traits that were totally foreign to him. There had never been anything soft in or about his life. As for nurturing, having known little of it in his lifetime, he'd never understood the need for it.

Jett understood sexual need, though. He'd gone without a woman for a long time now. The attraction he felt for Annie was only his body reminding him that he couldn't repress that need forever. His attraction to her was as simple as that.

What wasn't so simple was how the memory of her concern for him last night had made him feel....

Dear Reader,

Whether or not it's back to school—for you *or* the kids—Special Edition this month is the place to return to for romance!

Our THAT SPECIAL WOMAN!, Serena Fanon, is heading straight for a Montana wedding in Jackie Merritt's *Montana Passion,* the second title in Jackie's MADE IN MONTANA miniseries. But that's not the only wedding this month—in Christine Flynn's *The Black Sheep's Bride,* another blushing bride joins the family in the latest installment of THE WHITAKER BRIDES. And three little matchmakers scheme to bring their unsuspecting parents back together again in *Daddy of the House,* book one of Diana Whitney's new miniseries, PARENTHOOD.

This month, the special cross-line miniseries DADDY KNOWS LAST comes to Special Edition. In *Married... With Twins!,* Jennifer Mikels tells the tale of a couple on the brink of a breakup—that is, until they become instant parents to two adorable girls. September brings two Silhouette authors to the Special Edition family for the first time. Shirley Larson's *A Cowboy Is Forever* is a reunion ranch story not to be missed, and in Ingrid Weaver's latest, *The Wolf and the Woman's Touch,* a sexy loner agrees to help a woman find her missing niece—but only if she'll give him one night of passion.

I hope you enjoy each and every story to come!

Sincerely,

Tara Gavin,
Senior Editor

Please address questions and book requests to:
Silhouette Reader Service
U.S.: 3010 Walden Ave., P.O. Box 1325, Buffalo, NY 14269
Canadian: P.O. Box 609, Fort Erie, Ont. L2A 5X3

CHRISTINE FLYNN

THE BLACK SHEEP'S BRIDE

Silhouette®

SPECIAL EDITION®

Published by Silhouette Books
America's Publisher of Contemporary Romance

For Pat Heeter—
you're a great sister-in-law but an even better friend.

 SILHOUETTE BOOKS

ISBN 0-373-24053-8

THE BLACK SHEEP'S BRIDE

Copyright © 1996 by Christine Flynn

Printed in U.S.A.

CHRISTINE FLYNN

admits to being interested in just about everything, which is why she considers herself fortunate to have turned her interest in writing into a career. She feels that a writer gets to explore it all and, to her, exploring relationships—especially the intense, bittersweet or even lighthearted relationships between men and women—is fascinating.

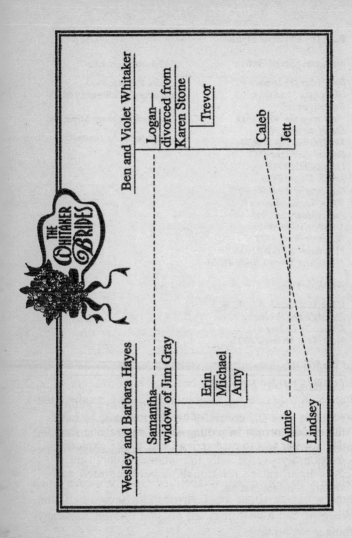

THE WHITAKER BRIDES

Wesley and Barbara Hayes

Samantha—
widow of Jim Gray

Erin
Michael
Amy

Annie

Lindsey

Ben and Violet Whitaker

Logan—
divorced from
Karen Stone

Trevor

Caleb

Jett

Chapter One

Jett Whitaker winced at the pain in his side when he killed the headlights on his rental car and groped in the dark for his duffel bag. On top of everything else, he was about to get soaked. It was a good thirty yards to the back door of the RW Ranch's main house, and the wind was driving the rain in sheets. The storm had pounded with that same ferocity since he'd landed in Austin, nearly three hours ago, reducing visibility to near zero and turning the one-hundred-and-ten-mile drive into its own brand of nightmare.

Most sane people would have waited out the storm. Jett hadn't even considered it. He'd never been accused of being particularly patient, anyway. Fearless, unyielding, aloof. Those were more common labels. Not that he wasted much time worrying about what anyone else thought of him. When he had a goal in mind, he didn't let much of anything get in his way.

Right now, his goal was to hole up at his brother Logan's place and sleep for a week.

The slam of the car's door was swallowed by the roar of rain beating earth. Bag in one hand, key in the other, Jett hunched his shoulders against the deluge and bolted for the blurry glow of the porch light. A dozen strides from his destination, a gut-twisting cough shook his body, the stabbing sensation vibrating through his chest. The spasm nearly doubled him over, but he kept going, cold rain running in rivulets down his collar. He scarcely noticed how wet he was getting. All that registered were the shock waves each step sent through his battered body, causing nerves to scream and muscles to ache.

Taking solace in the fact that he actually felt better than he had a couple of days ago, he shouldered open the screen and forced his concentration onto fitting the key into the lock. It would only be minutes before he could give in to the fatigue clawing at him; only minutes before he could kill the thirst that made his mouth feel as if it were full of hot cotton and he could collapse on something bigger than an airline seat. He'd slept in some damned uncomfortable places in his lifetime. In cars. Under bridges. On metal bunks in barracks. But trying to sleep with his aching six-foot-three-inch frame folded into the space allotted in economy class had been the ultimate torture.

The door swung in, letting out a rush of warm air and the lingering scent of cinnamon. The mudroom was dark, but light from the kitchen kept him from tripping over a pair of small pink rubber boots on the rug just inside. The clank of a pot hitting porcelain joined the sound of running water.

A rush of pure, unadulterated disappointment had him groaning to a halt. He'd been under the impression that he would have the place all to himself. But someone was there.

And having to talk to someone—anyone—was the last thing in the world he wanted to do.

Hoping he could escape without having to answer too many questions, he stepped through the doorway. The bright overhead lights made him wince. Keeping his eyes narrowed while they adjusted to this latest assault, he skimmed a glance over the battered old oak breakfast table that had occupied the near end of the room for as long as he could remember. Logan's new wife, Samantha, had called it "antique," and covered the worst of the nicks and scars with rust-colored mats. A large brass pot of some sort of dried flowers sat in the middle.

That table was the only thing about the room that looked familiar. When he glanced past it, he realized that Samantha had completely redone the place. Unfinished pine and chipped green Formica had been replaced with new oak cabinets and gleaming white counters. A curtained bay window with a cushioned seat opened the wall beyond the table, and a breakfast bar jutted into the large room, cutting it in half.

It wasn't Samantha at the sink, though.

A petite woman with short fawn-colored hair stood with her head turned toward the dish rack. Her head was bent slightly, exposing the long line of her neck below the boyish cut of the hair at her nape. She was fine-boned and delicate, and her dark lashes curved against alabaster skin as she set a skillet on the rack. Her profile reminded him of an exquisitely carved cameo. Dainty. Fragile. Or maybe an elf, he thought, when her pert nose wrinkled and she rubbed it with the back of her soapy hand. He wasn't sure why such comparisons occurred to him, foreign as cameos and elves were to a man who spent most of his time with bulldozers and dynamite. He was sure only that she was too young to be his sister-in-law, and not young enough to be his oldest niece.

An aching body that screamed for sleep, and a room that should have looked familiar but didn't, combined to test what remained of his endurance. Jett knew he was in the right place. He even knew that Logan and Sam wouldn't mind him being there. But he was wondering only whether he could make it back outside to get to the bunkhouse when the room seemed to tilt and the bag containing all his earthly possessions bumped against the wall. The sound it made was little more than a muffled thud, but the woman at the sink went still. Before he could say a word, her head jerked up, her eyes widening when she caught his reflection in the night-blackened window over the sink.

Willing the wave of dizziness to pass, Jett blew out a weary breath as he lifted his hand to let her know he meant her no harm, and silently begged her not to scream. His head wouldn't be able to take it.

Annie Kendall didn't make a sound. She couldn't have if she had to. The instant she saw the reflection of the big, darkly clad man in the glass, her heart had slammed into her throat. But big, dark and dangerous were the only impressions that had the chance to register as she spun around—and caught the glint of metal in his hand.

She wasn't even breathing when the scream in her eyes jerked down the arm of his wet brown leather bomber jacket. Her glance froze there for an instant, the messages in her brain scrambling. The man dripping a puddle around his heavy harness boots wasn't holding a knife or a gun or a crowbar. He was holding a key. Not even Hank, the crusty old foreman of Logan's huge cattle ranch, had a key to the main house. Certainly none of the hired hands did.

Annie's glance lurched back up, recognition slowly seeping through the rush of adrenaline and fear. The tall, broad-shouldered man filling the doorway wasn't hired help, anyway. As she understood it, Jett Whitaker rarely set foot on the place.

Annie had met him only once before. But she would have recognized him anywhere. The youngest Whitaker brother had a lean, hungry look about him that made a person want to back up a step. Or, at the very least, proceed with caution. He was tall and brooding, his tanned features were sharply defined, and his mouth was hard, as if it had never known a smile. But it was his eyes she remembered most. The cool blue-gray of a northern wolf's, they held cunning, intelligence, and a world-weary cynicism that made her think nothing could possibly surprise him.

His eyes were narrowed now, making him look every bit as unapproachable as she'd found him the first time she met him. Or maybe it was the stubble on his face, the days-old growth of beard, that made him look as rough as she suspected he was. Annie didn't care. She was too relieved to have identified her intruder as a member of the family to consider much else at the moment.

"Jett," she breathed, dropping her hand from her heart as she sagged against the counter. "You scared me to death. What are you doing here?"

His dark eyebrows snapped together, either at her question or at the fact that she knew his name. He didn't appear to have a clue who she was.

"I'm Annie. One of Samantha's sisters," she reminded him, since he obviously hadn't found her as memorable as she had him. "We met at Sam and Logan's wedding. A year ago last Thankgiving," she added, prompting him further.

The clues did no good. His incomprehension remained as she reached for the towel to dry her hands, hiding their trembling in the yellow terry cloth. It was still there when she looked back to see him running a distracted glance from the neat cap of short hair framing her face to the loose navy sweater that hung nearly to the knees of her slim corduroy slacks.

It was apparent that Jett still couldn't place her. It was just as obvious that he wasn't going to waste any energy worrying about it.

Looking distinctly weary, he ran his hand down his face. "I didn't meant to startle you, but I didn't think anyone was here. When I called this morning, Hank said Logan and Samantha were going to be gone for a while."

His voice was a sensual rasp, its smoky tones deep, rich, and decidedly edgy.

"They're on vacation," she told him, preferring to concentrate on Hank's failure to mention Jett's call. What Sam had told her about the sixty-something cowhand was obviously true. If something didn't have to do with an animal, it didn't matter. "Actually, it's more of a belated honeymoon. I'm staying with the children while they're gone."

"They didn't take the kids with them?"

"It's their honeymoon," she repeated, thinking that the man was obviously not a romantic. "Erin's upstairs doing her homework. Amy and Michael are in bed."

The furrows between Jett's eyes deepened. "How long will they be gone?"

"Two weeks. They just left for their cruise yesterday."

"And you'll be here until they get back."

He made the conclusion sound as appealing as a toothache. Mentally backing away from the slight, Annie was about to ask how long *he* planned to stay when she saw him wince.

He was lifting his hand even as his eyes squeezed shut. Spanning his forehead with his hand, he pressed his thumb to one temple and his middle finger to the other. A moment later, his hand fell and he quietly said, "Can I have a glass of water?"

The request had her turning to the cupboard. Behind her she heard the squeak of damp leather, the faint thud of his heavy boots on hardwood and the soft plop of his leather duffel hitting the floor. Though she avoided his reflection in the window while she filled the glass from the tap, she knew he was watching her. She could feel his eyes on her back as surely as she could sense his displeasure at her presence.

"Do you want some aspirin?" she had to ask, since the man obviously had a headache.

The sudden quiet behind her made her think he was wondering why she thought he'd need them. A moment later, however, she heard him mutter, "I have some."

He'd stopped less than six feet away. Faced with the middle of his impossibly broad chest when she turned around, she could see that the rain had dampened more than just the collar of his shirt. The front was damp, too. She also noticed an airline ticket peeking from the inside pocket of his open jacket. Between that and the Austin designation of the airline tag on the flight bag he'd dropped at his feet, it wasn't too hard to figure out that he'd just driven in from the airport.

"You're the one married to the navy pilot," Jett concluded, finally placing her. "Is he here this time?"

Annie hesitated. "I'm not married anymore." Wishing he'd found some other way to finally remember her, she held out the glass. "Here."

It wasn't like her to be so abrupt. Especially when someone was only seeking assurance. That was all Jett was doing, after all. Seeking assurance that he wasn't going to encounter anyone else he hadn't planned on running into in his brother's home. That was the only possible reason he would have asked about her ex. Rob hadn't attended the wedding with her, so Jett had never even met the man. But her normal instinct to put whoever she was with at ease had taken a hike about the time Jett made it clear he wished she wasn't here. The only instinct she felt now was caution, girded by a healthy dose of uncertainty.

That feeling increased when Jett's big hand closed around the tumbler. He was shaking.

Her glance darted to his face. His fatigue and irritability had been evident even from across the room. But she hadn't noticed the dark circles beneath his eyes until he came closer. Now, near enough to be overwhelmed by the foot of height and eighty or ninety pounds of muscle he had on her, she could see a distinct grayish cast to his skin. Though a fair portion of his face was hidden by a shadowy growth of facial hair, a sheen of moisture glistened on his cheeks and forehead.

That moisture wasn't rain. He'd wiped that off when he drew his hand down his face a few moments ago. The dampness beaded on his skin was perspiration. Now that she thought about it, that wasn't rain on the front of his shirt, either. His jacket had been zipped when he first came in.

Staring up at him, she watched the strong cords of his neck convulse with the four long swallows it took for him to drain the glass. She'd thought he wanted the water so that he could take something for his headache. All he'd done was down it like a man dried to the bone from heat.

Too quickly to be questioned, concern darted through her. His skin was damp. Yet his lips, chiseled and hard, looked as parched as the Sahara.

"Are you all right?"

"I'm fine. I just need some sleep."

The man was not fine. His eyes had a bright, glassy quality to them, as if he might be running a fever. He didn't even seem able to focus on her as he handed back the glass and started working at his temples again.

"Is there a spare bed anywhere? I'll go down to the bunkhouse, if I have to."

Going for a quarter-of-a-mile walk in the rain was the last thing in the world he wanted to do. The grudging quality of his voice made that abundantly clear. Not that Annie was going to ask him to do anything of the sort.

"The bunkhouse is being painted inside. At least I think it is. I heard Logan ask Hank to see that it was done while he and Sam were gone," she explained. "Something about getting it ready before the rest of the men arrive for some kind of season."

"Calving season," Jett muttered, now kneading the back of his neck.

"Calving season," Annie repeated, forgiving him the frown he slanted at her only because he didn't feel well. She'd lived her entire life surrounded by cities and air bases. All she knew of the nearly million-acre RW Ranch was how to get to the main house from the nearest town, which happened to be twenty-two miles away, and that Hank lived in a tiny trailer down by the pecan orchard.

She also knew that the ranch—this house, in particular—had once been Jett's home. Even if he wasn't so obviously ill, she could hardly ask him to leave it.

"You can have Trevor's room." Logan's eighteen-year-old son was away at college. Since his room was at the back of the house, away from the other bedrooms upstairs, Jett wouldn't be disturbed by anyone. And he wouldn't disturb anyone else. "It's the one at the end of the downstairs hall. I'll go make sure there are clean towels in the bath."

"Don't bother. All I need is a bed."

He bent to pick up his bag, a grimace slashing his features when he hauled upward on its weight. What little color he had promptly drained beneath the collar of his jacket.

Bending hadn't been a good idea. As he swayed like a birch in a stiff breeze, Jett's free hand shot toward the counter to catch himself. The slap of his palm met a quiet hiss when he sucked in an uneasy breath.

Alarmed as much by his unsteadiness as she was by his pallor, Annie reached for the bag. "Let me get that."

"I've got it."

"I can see that. But there's no reason for you to hurt yourself. You nearly—"

"I'm not hurting myself," he cut in, his voice tight with a combination of exasperation and discomfort. Pain was bitten back by the clench of his jaw as he adjusted the weight of the bag on his right shoulder. "Thanks, anyway."

Her assistance so clearly unwanted, Annie stepped back. It was either that or get run over. He wasn't about to admit that he found the weight of the bag a challenge, though Annie suspected that, as heavy as it looked, she would have had to drag the thing to move it herself. Despite the fatigue bearing down on his shoulders, there was still enough purpose in his stride to prove he could make it down the hall under his own steam. But then, as stubborn as he was being, Annie suspected he would have made it on his own if he had to crawl.

She'd only been trying to help because he looked so awful. Instead, she'd only been in his way.

Not caring for the way that made her feel, not caring for him for making her feel it, she headed for the mudroom and the mop. He had left wet boot prints and bits of grass on the floor, the same floor she'd had to mop that afternoon, after ten-year-old Michael "forgot" and walked through every puddle between the garage and the back door. Not that she minded all that much having to redo the chore. Little things she could deal with. It was the bigger picture that sometimes threatened to overwhelm her.

Knowing better than to wonder how much more unsettled her life could get, she attacked the floor with the mop. She had no idea what Jett was doing here. Or how long he planned to stay. She knew only that she wasn't going to ask. What she *was* going to do was enjoy being there with Sam's children and get on with building a new life for herself. That was why she'd come to Texas, after all. To get beyond all that she'd lost and find a way to live with the emptiness that had settled so deep inside her. The opportunity to spend time with her nieces and nephew had been the best thing to happen to her in over a year. At least it had been, until Logan's brother showed up, clearly begrudging her presence.

Her mop was sliding through the last puddle when the sound of something heavy hitting something solid snapped her head up. A split second later, a muffled clatter had her mentally bracing herself.

The sounds hadn't come from the children's rooms upstairs. They'd come from down the hall. Specifically, from Trevor's room.

Fifteen seconds passed. Then thirty. All but holding her breath while she waited for some other sound to come from that direction, Annie propped the mop against the refrigerator and hesitantly passed the solemn old grandfather clock in the wide entryway. Despite Jett's conviction that he could manage by himself, the noise had definitely indicated otherwise.

Since her help had so clearly been unwanted by him, Annie didn't plan to offer it. She just wanted to make sure he hadn't passed out. Or broken anything. A glass. Trevor's stereo. His neck.

She had just passed the long wall with the framed aerial view of the RW outside the door to Logan's office when she heard a deep, painful-sounding cough. Turning into Trevor's room, with its collection of rodeo souvenirs and car magazines, she glanced past the double bed, where Jett's jacket clung to the edge of the multihued blue quilt. Jett himself was leaning against the adjoining bathroom door.

Nothing had broken. At least she couldn't see that anything had from where she'd stopped. His shaving kit had been knocked over, though. Its contents were divided pretty much equally between the beige tile counter and the pine-plank floor. What had her attention, however, was Jett. Specifically, the two dark bruises near his left collarbone, the scratches she hadn't noticed before along the left side of his neck, and the beige elastic bandage binding his ribs.

He'd tried to take off his shirt, but he'd managed only half of the task. He'd unbuttoned it and pulled it from his jeans, but he'd succeeded only in getting one arm free. His left arm was still in its sleeve. The other sleeve dangled off his beautifully muscled shoulder, giving Annie a partial view of dark hair flaring over an impressively wide chest, a narrow waist and a hard, flat abdomen—most of which was covered by the wide elastic tape binding him from just below his arms to a few inches above the indentation of his navel.

She didn't allow herself to look any lower than that.

"What happened to you?"

The breath he drew before he spoke brought a flash of pain to his eyes.

"Cracked a couple of ribs," he allowed, his voice strained, as he pushed himself away from the door.

"I didn't think doctors taped cracked ribs anymore."

"They do in Sucre."

"Sucre?" she repeated, unable to accent the lovely word as he had. "Where's that?"

A faint frown slashed his forehead when he gave his head a cautious, negative shake. He looked confused. Or maybe he was just exhausted. "It's where they took me to patch me up."

He didn't say who "they" were. Nor did he offer anything else about his injuries before another dry, harsh cough racked his body. One fist covered his mouth as he bent forward. His other hand gripped his ribs.

The word he uttered after the spasm again left him limp against the door was as short as it was crude. It was also as pathetically weak.

She understood now why his ribs had been taped. Not wanting to think how that cough must have hurt, but wincing anyway, Annie moved as far as the duffel he'd left on the braided blue rug. To keep from encroaching on his space, and to preserve her own, she stayed on her side of the bag.

"Can you make it to the bed?"

"Yeah," he muttered, but he made no attempt to move. All he did was close his eyes as if the light were suddenly too bright and let his head fall back against the door.

The man looked as if he didn't have the strength to stay upright, much less the strength to walk across the room.

With a resigned sigh, Annie stepped over the duffel. He might not want her help, but he was going to get it anyway.

"Come on," she coaxed, more concerned about him winding up in a heap at her feet than about being where she wasn't wanted. "I'll pick up your things for you. You only need to make it about ten feet."

The expected protest wasn't there. Neither was his cooperation. Jett didn't move so much as a single, impressively honed muscle when she touched his arm to let him know she was beside him. He was still perspiring, his skin damp to her touch. And hot. So hot she could feel the heat of his body radiate toward her even before she slid her arm around his rock-hard waist. In the second it took for her shoulder to slip beneath his arm and her body to fit against his side, that heat seared a path from her neck to her knees.

Not caring to consider that this was as close as she'd come to being held by a man in well over a year, she concentrated only on getting him to move.

"Come on," she repeated. "Let's get you to bed."

"I can get there myself," he insisted, his eyes still closed and his weight still supported mostly by the door. "I'm fine."

"Sure you are." Snow had more color than he did. "Please, Jett, I'll never be able to pick you up if you pass out. You either lean on me and let me help you to bed, or you sleep where you fall. If you fall, it'll hurt."

The threat of more physical pain finally had him easing himself upright. Settling his arm around her shoulder, he leaned far more heavily than he probably liked against her thin frame.

He wasn't leaning on her nearly as much as he could have. But Jett had to admit that it helped to have her steady him. It wasn't that he didn't appreciate the help, either. He just wasn't in the habit of leaning on anyone. Ever. Literally or figuratively. To have to do so now didn't sit well at all. Or it wouldn't have, if he'd had the strength to be upset about it. As it was, he needed what energy he had to get across the room to the bed before another wave of dizziness made him any clumsier than he'd become. Anything left over he would save for the anger he felt toward his body for not being as strong as it usually was—and with himself for having stayed behind to secure his rig when the equatorial rain turned torrential. That move had cost him two cracked ribs and the mother of all colds. He didn't even have the energy to enjoy the feel of the small, soft woman tucked against his side. Not that there was much to feel. From what little actually registered of her curves, she felt as skinny as his ten-year-old nephew.

"You need a doctor," he heard her say as she backed him to the bed and he sank down on its edge.

His whispered "No" lacked force, but not conviction. "No doctor."

Light from the table lamp pooled over the bed. Closing nis eyes against the glare and the hot, gritty feel of his eyeballs, he resignedly allowed her to help him the rest of the way out of his shirt. Her small, smooth hands felt cool against his skin. Vaguely he wished she'd put them on his forehead, so that their coolness could ease the pounding inside his skull. What he really wanted, though, was for her to let him sleep. His eyes were so bleary he could barely focus.

"You've got a fever," she insisted. "You don't get a fever from cracked ribs. And that cough is awful. If you don't take care of it, you could wind up with pneumonia."

"I already have it."

"What?"

The room seemed to tilt, much as it had done when he opened his shaving kit to find his aspirin and he grabbed for the counter to stay upright. "Pneumonia," he muttered, easing himself back. Eyes closing, he sank gratefully into the mattress. "Already have it. All I need is sleep."

"Did they give you anything to take? Any medication?"

"Yeah." The word sounded slow and indistinct, as if he were mumbling from the bottom of a well. That was how he felt, too, as if he were slowly drifting to the bottom of a long, deep hole. "Took it a couple of hours ago."

"When are you supposed to take it again?"

Jett's feet were still on the floor, and his head was near the opposite edge of the bed. From where she stood by his knees, Annie saw his lips move. The motion, however, wasn't accompanied by audible sound.

"Jett?"

This time she got no response at all.

Not entirely sure what she should do, Annie stepped back. The man obliterating the blue quilt's triangular center was asleep, his breathing too shallow and his skin the color of ash. Whatever medication he'd been given either hadn't had a chance to work or hadn't been enough. Considering her alternatives, Annie shot a dubious glance at his bandages and bruises and headed into the small bathroom.

The contents of his shaving kit were scattered everywhere. Wondering if he'd dropped it or knocked it over, she poked though the toiletries on the counter. Not seeing what she was looking for there, she picked up the shaving kit and hunched down by the items on the floor.

Next to her foot lay deodorant, shampoo, and a razor. Picking them up, she dropped them in the leather kit while she scanned the rest of the scattered objects for whatever medication he might have been prescribed. She had a cousin who'd once had pneumonia and coughed so hard that he cracked a rib. Jett could have done the same thing himself. A diagnosis of pneumonia, however, did not explain his scratches, or the bruises on his collarbone and shoulder.

Toothpaste and a comb landed in the kit. So did a shaving brush, the kind she hadn't realized men used anymore. Thinking there was something rather appealing about a man lathering up with a brush, liking the image, if not the man prompting it, she added an unopened bar of soap from a foreign hotel, along with a pair of nail clippers.

The next items within reach were three foil-wrapped condoms.

Annie felt herself hesitate, her fingers hovering over the first of the small gold packets. His present condition notwithstanding, she didn't doubt for a moment that Jett was a normal, healthy male with normal physical needs. There was just something a little unnerving about confronting such blatant evidence of his sexuality. Or maybe what had her feeling so unsettled was how he'd caused her to feel when she helped him to the bed. There was no denying the almost forgotten quickening deep in her belly when she'd felt his body pressed to her side.

She'd ignored the sensation then. Ignoring it now, she picked up the first packet, then the next. Not caring to consider the circumstances under which he would require their use, especially with him stretched out on a bed less than ten feet away, she snatched the last one up, too, and dropped them all on top of everything else. His privacy was being invaded big-time. But then, so was her peace of mind.

She found a prescription bottle by the bathtub.

The label was typed in Spanish. Fortunately, since her understanding of the language was limited to items on a menu, someone had also written on it in English: *Penicillin. Two every six hours.*

"Aunt Annie?" an impatient voice called from the hallway. "Can you help me memorize my lines? This stupid play is in three weeks and I'm never— What's going on?"

Erin, Annie's seventeen-year-old niece, had turned into the doorway of the bedroom and promptly come to a halt. Her long blond braid dangled over the shoulder of the University of Texas football jersey Logan's son had given her, and she had a fistful of pages clutched in her hand. She seemed to have forgotten all about them, as her hazel eyes darted from the man on the bed to where Annie was walking out of the bathroom.

"What happened to Uncle Jett?"

"Other than pneumonia and a cracked rib, I don't know. He didn't say how he got to be in this shape. He just showed up a little while ago."

"Is he all right?"

"I don't know that, either."

Concern filled the girl's eyes as they shifted back to the man draped over Trevor's bed. "He sure doesn't look very good."

Annie was inclined to agree. Setting the prescription bottle on the nightstand, she scanned the compelling angles of Jett's face. Exhaustion and pain had etched the lines fanning from his eyes more deeply, furrowing his brow even in sleep, and making him look older than she knew him to be. He was only a few years older than her own thirty years, but whatever had happened to him had definitely taken its toll.

Or maybe, she thought, it wasn't just his injuries and the fever that made him look so haggard and hard. The lines that had settled into his beautifully carved features looked permanent, as if his life were wearing him out.

"Jett?" Annie quietly said, touching the hard flesh of his unbruised shoulder. He hadn't moved by so much as the twitch of a long, dark eyelash while she and Erin spoke. "Can you hear me?"

"I don't think he's going to wake up," Erin observed.

"Then I guess we'll just have to get him undressed and into bed ourselves."

"Undressed?"

"We can't put him under clean sheets like this." There were bits of grass clinging to his heavy boots, and water from the lawn had wicked up the hems of his pant legs. "He'll rest better without his boots and jeans, anyway."

"What if he's not wearing anything under his pants? Some guys don't, you know."

Annie's frown darted across the bed. "I don't think I want to know how you know that."

"Oh, Aunt Annie," Erin muttered, her tone the exasperated one she usually reserved for her mother. "I'm not a child anymore."

"I think your mom wishes you were."

A frown wrinkled her nose. "Mom just wishes Trevor and I weren't so close. Not that we are," she muttered, the chiding slipping from her voice. "He never has time to come home from school anymore. It's not like we've ever done anything, anyway. At the rate we're going," she added miserably, "we never will."

Erin's last words were mumbled, but Annie knew the girl meant for her to hear them. There had been a time when Annie would have picked up on such a blatant hint, and asked what had prompted such a statement. But that time was gone. She adored her niece and would do anything to help her. After all, she'd been privy to most of the details of Erin's relationship with Logan's son since long before Sam and Logan got together themselves, and she knew Erin was crazy about the young man. But Annie couldn't talk to her about men or relationships or sex. Especially not the last. Not the way she once had. As inadequate as she'd proved to be in that department, she couldn't have been objective if she tried.

Hating the feeling that she was letting her niece down, Annie offered the only thing she could—a sympathetic smile. For herself, all she could do was change the subject.

"You get one boot," she whispered to her niece, rounding the bed. "I'll get the other."

"I'll get them both," Erin told her, turning to pull one of Jett's legs between hers. Looking as if she'd done this before, she gripped the heel and toe of one brown-leather size eleven. "*You* can get his pants."

With the brush of denim against leather, the first boot came off. Not allowing herself time to think about what she was doing while Erin started on the other boot, Annie reached toward Jett's waist. Deliberately avoiding the area where an arrow of dark hair disappeared beneath the waistband of his jeans, Annie slipped her fingers beneath the worn fabric near his side. His hot skin felt smooth against her knuckles, the muscles taut and hard.

Half an inch farther, she encountered what she was searching for—an inchwide elastic band.

"We're safe," she told Erin, and went to work on buckle and zipper while Erin tugged on the second boot.

With both women working on him, Jett finally let out a low, halfhearted moan. He mumbled something Annie didn't understand, and his arm came up to cover his eyes.

She didn't ask him to repeat whatever it was he'd said. Instead, she explained what they were doing, hoping he'd help them a little, and promised they would leave him alone as soon as they got him under the covers.

Either Jett didn't hear her, or he was beyond caring who did what to him. He was like so much dead weight as she and their niece pulled and lifted until they had him stripped down to his white briefs. Once that had been accomplished, they carefully maneuvered his amazingly solid body around to get him under the covers—a task made slightly more difficult by the fact that he didn't *want* to be moved. Judging from his groans, every movement hurt.

They were as gentle as they could be, but Annie felt as if she'd just wrestled her first steer by the time she headed into the bathroom to get a washcloth for his head.

Erin followed, leaning against the door frame while she worried the end of her braid. "He looks like he was in a wreck or something. Is he going to be okay?"

"I was just wondering that myself," Annie admitted over the sound of running water. "He saw a doctor." The prescription and bandages seemed to attest to that much. "I don't think a doctor would have let him go if he wasn't going to be all right," she rationalized. "He probably just needs to take his medicine and rest."

The concern remained in Erin's expression. "Do you think he's going to be embarrassed when he wakes up? Because we had to undress him, I mean?"

Annie's smile was gentle, her tone more certain. "I have the feeling that if your uncle Jett is embarrassed about this, it'll be because he wasn't able to do it himself." The words *macho* and *stubborn* could easily be defined in any dictionary with the name Jett Whitaker. Any Whitaker, for that matter. According to her little sister, Lindsey, who had married Cal, the middle Whitaker brother, last spring, their bullheadedness was practically genetic. "If anything, he should be grateful for your help."

Annie certainly had been. She didn't get a chance to mention that, though. A pained expression suddenly merged Erin's eyebrows.

"Oh, geez," the girl muttered, jerking herself upright. "I forgot to do my math." The tortured look magnified. "We've got a quiz, too. You don't need me for anything else, do you?"

"I thought you wanted me to help you with your lines for the play."

"I'll get Angie to do it with me before the game tomorrow."

Annie would really have welcomed Erin's company tonight. But she could hardly keep the girl from her homework just so that she didn't have to tend Jett alone. So she told her niece to go on, and wondered which one of them looked less enthusiastic. Erin as she headed off for her room and her books. Or herself as she filled a glass with water, picked up the wet washcloth and headed back to the bed.

Chapter Two

The grandfather clock in the entry had just struck 11:00 p.m. when Annie found herself standing outside the door to Jett's room. Everyone else in the house was asleep, and she wanted to go to bed herself. But she couldn't. Her conscience was doing battle with her sense of self-protection, and her conscience, disgustingly vocal as it could be, was winning.

The last thing in the world she wanted to do was to impose herself on a man who didn't want her around. But Jett needed his medicine. It was a sure bet he hadn't wakened to take it himself.

With a certain appreciation of how Daniel must have felt walking into the lions' den, Annie opened the door and peeked inside. She'd noticed before that light bothered Jett's eyes, so she pushed the door in only enough for a footwide strip of light from the hallway to angle across the foot of the bed. The corners of the room lay in shadow, still and quiet.

But she could see well enough as she moved like a shadow herself past the chair at the desk and stopped at the side of the bed.

Jett was curled on his side, facing away from her, as she shook two pills from the bottle on the nightstand. It didn't appear that he'd been resting too comfortably. He'd kicked off his blankets, and the sheet was tangled between his long legs. It sounded as if he were mumbling something, too, the words more like groans than anything coherent.

He didn't turn over when she quietly told him it was time for his penicillin, so Annie reached out and touched his shoulder. She couldn't tell whether he was any warmer than he'd been before. To her, hot was hot. But she could feel the gooseflesh on his skin, and the shivers racing through him.

She leaned closer, her glance scanning his profile in the dim light. A sheen of perspiration filmed his cheek above the darkness on his jaw, but the skin of his shoulder was bone-dry. His fever was rising. Despite the goose bumps, his heat burned her palm even when she withdrew her hand.

"Jett? Can you hear me?" Concern heavy in her voice, she moved back to tug at the covers between his legs. "It's Annie. Can you turn over?"

In the pale light, she saw his forehead furrow, his thick lashes squeezing tighter.

"You're lying on the sheets," she explained, slipping her hand along one heavy calf to ease it aside while she pulled at the sheet with the other. The man was about as easy to move as a stone pillar. "Help me. Okay?"

His only response was a muffled "Cold."

"I know." She was sure he felt that way. His body fairly vibrated with the chills. She could feel them even in his legs as he drew them toward his chest. "I'm trying to get you back under the covers."

What she was doing apparently registered at some level. Jett rolled onto his back, muffling the groan of pain the movement caused him by locking his jaw. As sick as he was, he was still fighting. But at least he wasn't fighting her.

The bedclothes came free. Hurriedly drawing them up, she tucked them around his shoulders and smoothed them over his chest. Apparently he didn't like being that confined. She had no more than started to straighten before one hand flailed out, bumping her arm before falling in a fist on his stomach. His head moved restlessly on the pillow, the words he mumbled finally becoming clearer. She could make out what he said. She just couldn't decipher their meaning. He was saying something about moving rocks and wanting the rain to stop.

The disjointed phrases seemed to increase his agitation. And though he was covered now, he was shivering even harder. Each breath he drew shuddered in and out, rasping in his chest and making his teeth chatter.

"You really need to take these pills," she told him, thinking she'd put the quilt back on the bed as soon as he did. "Can you sit up for a second?"

It wasn't until she repeated the question that it seemed to register. Even then, Jett seemed to have trouble connecting what she said with what she wanted him to do. Looking every bit as disoriented as he'd sounded moments ago, she saw him blink into the semidarkness and try to swipe at the hair sticking to his forehead.

"You need to take this," she repeated, unconsciously pushing back his hair for him. His forehead was damp, the dark locks sticking from perspiration. "It's your medicine," she patiently explained again.

His unfocused gaze shifted toward her outstretched hand. Eyes blinking as if he were trying to force concentration, he struggled onto his elbow and lifted a shaking hand toward the glass. Between the effect of the fever on his equilibrium and the pressure the position put on his ribs, it wasn't two seconds before, sucking air between his teeth, he went back down.

His determination survived even the ravages of a raging fever. Setting his jaw against the pain, he tried to lift himself on his other side. Unable to stand his struggle, Annie slipped her arm behind his neck.

"Just lift your head." Working her arm down his back, she eased him off his elbow. "We can do it this way."

She'd acted before she thought. She'd seen only that he was having trouble, and failed to consider how close she'd have to get to help him. It was too late to back away now, though. He was already sagging against her.

The bed gave a little as she rested her hip on its edge, bracing her arm behind him so that she could support his head with her shoulder. "Hold up your hand."

His fingers were trembling when she dropped the pills into his palm, but he managed to get them to his mouth. She wasn't sure whether the trembling she felt was in him or in her, though, when she touched the glass to his lips and his hand closed around hers to lift the glass higher. It didn't matter. What did was that Jett managed to get the pills down—along with most of the water.

His head lolled toward her when she lowered the tumbler. "Do you want more?" she asked, wondering if he even realized his hand was still holding hers to the glass.

The negative motion of his head was so slight, Annie wouldn't have noticed it, had it not been for the shift in pressure against her chest. He moved his head again, his surprisingly soft hair brushing against her neck.

"No more," she heard him whisper, his breath hot and metallic. "Get me up."

"I don't think so," she told him, wondering how he thought he was supposed to stand, when he couldn't even hold his head up. "You're staying right here."

"It's going to collapse. You've got to get me up."

She'd thought he was awake, groggy but lucid. Now she wasn't so sure. "What's going to collapse?"

The mattress shifted under his weight as he rolled toward her, curling toward her warmth. "You gotta get me up. It's going to go. Dear God," he whispered, the rasp of his voice against her heart half prayer, half plea. "It's going to go."

His words were barely audible, but there was no denying the agony in his voice, or the sheer desperation behind his tortured plea for her to get him out of wherever he thought he was. Tremors shuddered though him, fear and chills mercilessly racking his body. She couldn't imagine what tricks the fever was playing on his mind, what images were flashing behind his eyes. Whatever they were, to him they were very real.

He'd curled his big body closer. One arm was trapped beneath him, but his other had locked around her waist. Delirious, he was seeking whatever warmth he could find.

Annie doubted he even knew who she was just then. But that wasn't important. Her only concern at the moment was that he was far sicker than she'd thought.

"It's not going to collapse," she assured him, trying to alleviate some of his fear, even though she was suddenly fearful for him herself. The man was burning up. "I promise, it won't," she added, though she had no idea what "it" was. "You're going to have to let go of me for a minute, though. Okay?"

She pushed his damp hair farther back on his forehead as she spoke, hoping to soothe him as she eased herself away. As she did, the tips of her fingers slid over something raised and ragged.

Guiding his head to the pillow, she discovered a small flesh-colored bandage stuck at the edge of his hairline. Covered as it was by his thick hair, it hadn't been noticeable before. The bandage was coming off now, the adhesive loosened by the dampness of his skin.

Picking up the edge, she discovered two neat stitches.

Wondering what else she'd missed, almost afraid to look, she ran her eyes down the length of his body. She didn't recall seeing anything else when she removed his pants. But when her glance returned to his face, she found herself searching the shadowed angles more carefully than she had allowed herself to do before.

It was only a matter of moments before she realized it wasn't cuts and scrapes she was looking for. To be honest with herself, she would have to admit she was looking for answers. He was a beautiful man, even bruised and battered as he was. He was also a complete mystery to her.

All she knew about Jett Whitaker was what Sam had told her at the wedding: that he worked heavy construction in out-of-the-way places, that he lived nowhere in particular, and that his contact with his family was sporadic at best. Half the time, his brothers didn't even know where he was.

As she eased her arm from beneath his shoulder, she thought he sounded like a wanderer, a man content to drift wherever his work or his mood took him. Content to be responsible to no one but himself.

She couldn't begin to imagine living that way.

"Don't go." The words were little more than a groan of air past parched lips, a faint plea that was barely audible over the rustle of her clothing as she straightened. She didn't get a chance to tell him she wasn't going far. His hand flailed out, seeking a hold, as if his very life depended on making that connection. The cords in his forearms stood out like ropes as he grabbed at her wrist.

She wasn't prepared for the manacle-like grip that nearly brought her to her knees. He wasn't conscious of what he was doing. She didn't doubt that for a moment. Even injured and laid flat by pneumonia, the man was as strong as a bull. Her soft flesh burned beneath his fingers. Fragile bones threatened to snap. Pain shot up her arm, bringing a startled gasp.

"Don't go," she heard him beg, the plea behind his words rooting her in place as surely as his hold. "God, don't leave me here.

"Don't go," he repeated, though the urgency had suddenly faded.

As if the scene in his head had moved beyond the need to hang on, his hand fell limply to the bed.

"I'm not going anywhere." Shaken as she was, she offered the assurance gently, more affected than she wanted to be by his anxiety. She was a stranger to him. Yet she was his only ally against the demons plaguing him. "I'm going to stay right here until we get your fever down. You're going to be all right."

In his delirium, his response was to tell her they had to get back from the edge. He repeated the phrase over and over. *Get back from the edge. Get back from the edge.* And she told him each time that she wouldn't go anywhere near it. She had to leave him, though. Just for a minute.

The bowl she needed was in the kitchen. The towels he hadn't wanted her to bother with before were in the linen closet. Among the items she'd returned to his shaving kit was a bottle of aspirin, so she grabbed that, too, since it could help bring down his fever. The only high temperatures she'd ever encountered had been in the child-care centers where she'd worked on various air bases. Kids were always either coming down with or recovering from something. But a fever in a child, while it could spike alarmingly high, wasn't usually as serious as that same temperature in an adult.

Wondering if she should track down Sam's thermometer to see exactly how high his temperature was, deciding not to waste the time on it, she began to sponge his heated skin.

The water was barely cool to her touch, but as hot as his skin was, it must have felt like ice to him. Every time she drew the cool cloth over him, he flinched from her or tried to shove her hand away. Every time he did that, she would either catch his hand and lay it at his side or try to avoid it. Sometimes she succeeded. Sometimes she didn't. One side step resulted in her knocking over the glass of water, but she didn't believe for a moment that he was responsible for what was happening. For a solid half hour, she quietly explained why it was so necessary that she cool him down. And for most of that time, he rambled on about whatever it was that was going to collapse, while Annie kept telling him he didn't have to worry anymore. He was at the ranch now. He was safe.

She didn't know if her words registered, but she murmured the assurances anyway as she worked, sponging down one side of his body so the evaporating water could take away the heat, then covering that side to work on the other. If she was alone somewhere and as sick as he was, she'd want to know someone was there for her. She understood all too well how awful it was to be alone and in pain, and she wouldn't have wished that feeling on anyone. Right now, she was all he had.

Annie found that thought incredibly sad.

She couldn't begin to imagine how lonely his life must be, moving around the way he did. But then, she couldn't imagine wanting to be so alone, either. That seemed to be exactly what Jett wanted, though. Even at the wedding, he'd kept to himself, saying very little to anyone. Least of all to her. Even then, she had to admit, he'd definitely made an impression. She'd never before met a man who could keep himself so separate from everyone else, even standing in the middle of a crowd. There had been a presence about him that day that made him seem as commanding as he was remote. A sense of power that had given her the feeling that his control over himself was absolute.

That impression had compounded itself tonight. She couldn't imagine how hard he must have pushed his exhausted body to get to the ranch. It was almost as if he'd refused to let himself give in to the illness and fatigue until it was safe for him to collapse.

That trait was as formidable to her as the man himself. And though there was little else she could relate to about him, she couldn't help thinking that she'd give anything to be that clear-sighted about her goals, to be able to focus so absolutely.

She heard the deep, muffled bong of the grandfather clock as it struck midnight. But it wasn't until after the double notes of the half hour had tolled that Jett's fever broke and his listlessness gave way to sleep. It wasn't an easy sleep. Not until he'd trapped Annie's hand against his chest, holding it there with his own when she started to pull away, did his slumber become restful.

That was all he seemed to want. To hold her hand.

Or maybe it was to have her hold his.

Unable to deny him that small comfort, she sank onto the desk chair she'd pulled to the side of the bed. Barely able to keep her own eyes open, she left her hand trapped where it was, laid her head on her free arm and promptly fell asleep herself.

It was thirst that woke Jett. Thirst and the vague disorientation he sometimes felt when he'd been moving around so much that he'd forgotten where he was. It wasn't the panicked feeling he'd experienced as a kid, the awful fear that would grip his first conscious moments and have him sitting bolt upright with his heart pounding in his throat. Sleeping had never been safe back then. There had always been some junkie wanting to roll him for his meager belongings. Some psychotic wanting to beat him up just because he was convenient. Some pervert wanting worse.

Eighteen years had passed since then. Jett no longer awakened ready to fight. The panic would still, sometimes, be there; that sense of being totally, completely alone in an unfamiliar and alien place. Yet what Jett felt as he blinked in the semidarkness and tried to figure out where he was, wasn't at all threatening.

A woman was in a chair drawn up to the bed, her arm angled on the mattress and her cheek resting on it. He couldn't see her face. Only the top of her head. But her other arm stretched toward him, her hand covering his heart. His own hand lay over hers, holding it there.

It was the delicacy of the hand beneath his that jarred his memory. As small as it was, it felt like a child's—and that reminded him of the slightness of the woman he'd seen standing at the sink in his brother's kitchen. The woman who'd overridden his protests and helped him to bed.

Through the gray fog clouding his brain, he finally remembered where he was, why he was there. Mostly, he remembered the woman. Samantha's sister, Annie. She smelled like soap and something that reminded him of spring. Wild roses, he thought, though he had no idea why. She had a voice so gentle, so soft, he might only have imagined the words he'd heard. Yet he remembered those words. He remembered her telling him he was safe. That she wouldn't leave. And he remembered the feel of her hands, of her cool palm against his brow.

His eyes burned. His mouth felt like sand. But misty tentacles of fatigue kept pulling at him, refusing to let him wake completely and drawing him back toward sleep.

His hand felt as if it were weighted with lead when he lifted it from his chest. He remembered her saying there was water if he wanted it. And he did. Yet that wasn't what he reached for.

The fog in his brain was closing in, allowing only the briefest impression of softness to register when he touched her hair. She had stayed. He didn't know why, but that mattered more than the thirst. A moment later, lulled by a totally unfamiliar sense of peace, he folded his hand over hers once more and caved in to his body's craving for sleep.

"Auntie Annie? Aren't you going to fix us pancakes?"

The loud whisper came from somewhere behind Annie, causing her to wake with a jerk. Her head snapped up. An instant later, she was looking through the back slats of the chair at her youngest niece.

Six-year-old Amy stood in the hall doorway, her flannel nightgown dragging the floor and her sleep-tangled curls billowing like spun gold around her angelic little face. In her arms, his pink tongue lolling sideways, was fifteen pounds of motley gray-and-white-speckled mutt. What Spot lacked in pedigree, he more than made up for in patience. Amy had braided the fur of his long ears with beads.

Realizing that she'd overslept, Annie shoved her own hair back from her eyes and darted a glance to the man taking up most of the rumpled bed. From the evenness of Jett's breathing, it didn't appear that Amy's arrival had disturbed him. Not wanting to disturb him herself, Annie was careful to slowly slip her hand from between his chest and his callused palm. Easing out of the chair, feeling as stiff as a brick, she tiptoed toward the door.

"Who's that?" Amy asked, since she couldn't make out anything beyond a shape in the bed.

Pressing a finger to her lips, Annie nudged her niece into the hall. Her voice low, she whispered, "Your uncle Jett. He doesn't feel good, so let's not wake him up."

"How come he's here?"

"I didn't ask. Let's—"

"Can I see him?"

"Not now, honey. Come on." Curving her hand over Amy's small shoulder, she quietly pulled the door closed. "You'd better get back upstairs and get dressed. You don't want to be late for school."

"Michael does. He said he's not going to school until he's as big as Daddy. Do we still get pancakes?"

Pancakes were the bribe Annie had used to get the kids to go to bed last night. "If everyone hurries," she conceded, her determination to keep her word vying with concern over Amy's pragmatic announcement of Michael's intentions. Sam had warned her that school had recently been added to his list of hated things to do. Along with eating food in any shade of green. "Are he and Erin up?"

Miraculously, they were. Also by some miracle, Michael didn't do anything more than pout when Annie pulled the pillow off his head, handed him his clothes and proceeded to ax every excuse he came up with to stay home—including sticking around so he could see his uncle Jett, after Amy told him he was there. After assuring the boy that his uncle would still be around when he returned from school, Annie raced downstairs to cook the promised pancakes. She didn't have time, though. Erin, who drove herself and the younger ones into town every morning, said they all had to leave in five minutes or she'd be late for her first class.

Annie handed them all breakfast bars on the way out the door.

Having blown breakfast, Annie decided to get an early start on dinner and took a chicken from the freezer to thaw before heading up for her shower. Within half an hour, she was dressed in an oversize black turtleneck and jeans and nursing a cup of coffee as she looked over the list of projects she needed to tackle.

House-hunting was out for the day. She needed a functioning brain to do that, not to mention energy, and she hadn't had enough sleep last night to provide either. She was anxious to find a place of her own, to get settled in and rooted again. With most of her possessions still stored in her parents' garage in Florida and the boxes she'd brought with her residing in the tiny apartment above her sister Lindsey's boutique, she felt like an untethered balloon. She hated that scattered feeling. She needed to be anchored somewhere. In a place that was her own. Lindsey had generously offered the use of the apartment for as long as Annie wanted it, but there was no room for her things and no place for a garden. Even when she had to grow plants in pots on a balcony, Annie had always had a garden of sorts. This time, she wanted a real one. Her search for a house would have to wait until tomorrow, though. She'd postpone lunch with Lindsey until then, too.

Item number two was doable. But before she could settle into the window seat with the last six months' worth of the Leesburg *Independent* and another cup of caffeine, she had to check on Jett. It had been a little after eleven when she gave him his medicine last night. He was due again.

Hoping to find him resting as quietly as when she'd left him, she cracked open the door and peeked into the room.

The pearl-gray dawn leaked around the wood-slat shutters on the window. In that weak morning light, she saw Jett grimace, then lift himself up a little as if he meant to change positions. The movement was scarcely enough to make the sheets rustle, but the strain made him decide to stay where he was—until his whole body jerked with one of the dry, hacking coughs that had interrupted his sleep, and hers, all night.

Annie could almost feel his misery before the chest-rattling spasm subsided. Not sure whether he sounded better or worse, she repositioned the cloth over his forehead and eyes. He looked as limp as a rag, even with his lips set hard against the pain the cough had caused to his ribs. Within moments, though, she saw the tension around his mouth ease. His breathing became more even.

His body was still seeking sleep.

She hated the thought of disturbing him. When he was awake, his chest probably felt as if it were on fire. And the way he winced whenever he moved his head made her think it felt as if gremlins were inside his skull, poking around with miniature cattle prods. She imagined the rest of his bandaged and bruised body didn't feel so great, either.

She really did hate to wake him. She told him that, too.

Last night, it had seemed to take forever to get through when she tried to talk to him. Now, though his shaky focus never quite reached her face, he elbowed himself up enough to get down the juice she'd brought, more because he seemed terribly thirsty than because he wanted to take his pills. But he managed to get the medication down and sink back toward sleep before Spot wandered in to check out what was going on.

Knowing the dog loved to nap curled up next to someone, recognizing the intent in the little black eyes that had zeroed in on the lump on the bed, Annie scooped up the little mongrel on the way out the door and headed for the telephone. She didn't care that Jett had said not to call the doctor last night. She needed to talk to someone who could assure her that he was all right. Or, if he wasn't, to get him help. His color didn't look any better to her this morning than it had last night, his cough was horrible, and he still felt awfully warm. He wasn't staying awake long enough to drink very much, either.

After what she'd gone through with him, he could just humor her on this one. She couldn't handle another night sleeping in that chair.

"He's doing just what he needs to do, Miz Kendall. Sleeping. I want him to stay down a good forty-eight hours after his temperature returns to normal, too. Three days would be even better." Dr. Aloisius P. Weger spoke as if he were in a church as he pulled Jett's door closed. "His temperature is a hundred and one right now, but you should see it coming down in a few hours. I don't think you'll have another episode like last night."

Looking more like a withered old gentleman rancher than a physician, he moved from the closed door of Jett's room to where Annie stood at the end of the hall. One long gray hair spiked up from the middle of each bushy white eyebrow, and the wisp of beard on his chin looked more like a tuft he'd missed shaving than a goatee. But the eyes behind his round silver-rimmed glasses were sharp, and his medical instincts just as keen.

Aloisius Weger was the sort of physician that scarcely existed anymore. The rural doctor—the kind who made house calls. Annie hadn't asked him to come out when she'd spoken with him a couple of hours ago; he'd volunteered. Since he'd be out in her direction anyway, he'd told her, he'd stop by to see what had her so concerned.

She'd felt better as soon as she hung up. At the moment, however, being steered by the elbow toward the front door, she wasn't feeling the reassurance she'd expected from the eccentric-looking physician.

"Two or three days?"

"At least. I don't want him doing much for a few days after that, either." Behind them, the grandfather clock struck twice to mark the half hour. Annie had always liked that sound. The predictability of it. Now, the deep bongs seemed to have a faintly ominous ring. "It'll take him a week or two to get his strength back," she heard the doctor continue. "Being that Logan and Samantha are vacationing, it's good that he has someone here to look after him."

Annie stopped dead in the middle of the large, hunter-green area rug. The doctor, certain of his assumption that she would be Jett's caretaker, kept going, to the carved oak coatrack by the stairway.

Black bag in one hand, he reached for the gray cowboy hat he'd hung there. "The prescription he was given is fine," he went on, taking her silence for attention rather than hesitation. "But I gave it a boost with a couple of injections. The one should help knock the pneumonia. The other'll keep him down for the rest of the day. I took a blood sample, too, to make sure we're not dealing with anything exotic, considering where he's been."

The wing of Annie's eyebrow lifted in a delicate arch. "Where *has* he been?"

"Bolivia."

That explained the prescription being in Spanish. But Bolivia? she thought, only to realize how unremarkable such a place would be to a man like Jett. Men like him, men who needed to wander, undoubtedly found little appeal in normal places like Sioux Falls or Duluth. There was no adventure in anything so close to home. As the wife of a navy test pilot, she'd lived for nine years with a man whose thirst for adventure ruled his life. It wasn't a need that could be replaced by anything else. That need was as deeply ingrained as the need men had always had to conquer land and other men, and to populate the earth with their own progeny. Specifically, sons.

Annie mentally closed her eyes against that thought. They were talking about Jett. Not her ex-husband. And children weren't something she should think about at all anymore.

"Did he say what happened to him? How he got the bruises, I mean?"

"Apparently he fell. That's how he said he cracked his ribs, anyway. Two of them. Hairline, from what I gather. Talking made him cough, so I didn't get any of the details. The cough that comes with pneumonia can be mighty painful," he explained, his concern clearly with his patient. "That's why I knocked him out. He'll rest better if he's not hurting, so see that he takes the pain medication I left in there for him with his supper. You can untape him when the cough eases up."

Annie felt her heels dig into the green pile. It was one thing to take care of Jett when the need was immediate. Taking care of him once he was fully conscious was another matter entirely.

"Was he upset that I'd called you?"

"He wasn't too happy about it," the doctor admitted. "But you were right to be concerned. I wouldn't worry too much about him now, though," he went on, patting at his shirt and pants in search of his keys. "As long as he stays down, gets plenty of liquids and finishes those prescriptions, he should be fine. I must say, he has to have the constitution of an ox. I can't imagine how he made it all the way here without collapsing."

"Perhaps it's because he also possesses the stubbornness of a mule."

The doctor's eyes lit with a smile. "If he does, he comes by it honestly. I never knew anyone as hardheaded as a

Whitaker. And I've known every one that set foot in these parts in the past sixty years.''

When Doc Weger, as he'd introduced himself, had first arrived, his priority had clearly been his patient. Now, his patient attended to and preparing to leave, he allowed himself to notice what he'd been too preoccupied to observe before. As he ran an appreciative glance over the new oak wainscoting and deep green-and-cream-striped wallpaper in the open entry, an odd little smile tipped up the ends of his thin white mustache.

''Last time I was in this house was a couple years after I delivered that boy,'' he mused in his deep, smooth drawl. ''Once Violet—the boys' mother—took to bed, it was as if this house started dying with her. When she was gone, it just started decaying right around the people still living in it. I never thought I'd see it looking like this.''

Sam had done wonders with the rambling old ranch house. Having seen it when her sister married Logan, and having thought at the time that it definitely needed a woman's touch, Annie could attest to the transformation herself. It was a wonderful place now. Warm and inviting. But it wasn't the doctor's appreciation of her sister's remodeling skills that had her interest.

''You delivered Jett?''

''Delivered most everybody around here under the age of forty,'' he told her, looking more humbled by the accomplishment than impressed by it. ''That includes all three of the Whitaker boys. As I recall, Jett was a scrawny little thing. Never as big as his brothers, even when he got older. Not that you'd ever know it now,'' he qualified, clearly thinking of the size of the man he'd just examined. ''I took care of their mother, too, until she passed on. Good woman, Violet. Those boys might not have had it so rough if she hadn't died. She never did get her strength back after she had him, though. Just pushed herself too hard."

The kindly doctor shook his head, looking amused by her surprise at his candor.

"I'm not telling tales out of school," he assured her, wanting her to know that the integrity of his Hippocratic oath was still intact. "You stay around long enough, you'll hear about most of the families around here. If you want to know anything about anyone in Leesburg, all you've got to do is walk into The Café and start talking to Louella. If she doesn't know what's going on, check with Essie at the bakery or Harry at the barbershop. The Whitaker family was what you might call notorious in a lot of ways. The boys seem to have settled down now since marrying your sisters. Except for that one in there," he amended, hitching his thumb toward the hall. "From what I gather talking to him, he came here because he had nowhere else to go to recuperate."

With that, he glanced at his turquoise-studded silver watch and knitted his already wrinkled forehead into a frown. "Give my regards to Samantha and Logan," he said, wiggling his hat down tight on his head. "And call me if Jett isn't any better by this time tomorrow. Y'all have a good day now, ya hear?"

Under any other circumstances, there would have been a smile on Annie's face as she thanked the old country doctor for his help and watched him depart. The man didn't walk. He strutted. But she was too preoccupied with thoughts of Jett to be amused by much of anything just then.

She wasn't so sure she'd wanted to know that he'd been raised without a mother. In a way, it explained a little of his roughness, even if it didn't alleviate it. The doctor's description of him as a *small*, motherless child only compounded the impression. Picturing him as scrawny, however, was simply beyond comprehension. A mental image of him scowling at her was far easier to conjure.

He wasn't too happy about it, the doctor had said when she asked how Jett had reacted to her calling him. As uneasy as that made her, she did have one thing working in her favor: Jett would probably be out for the rest of the afternoon.

He was out for most of the evening, too. He slept through the children's arrival home from school, through homework and the battle for the television's remote control and, after Annie peeked in to see if she should take him a tray, through supper. She was beginning to wonder if he was ever going to wake up when Amy, her budding Florence Nightingale, surfaced from one of her tiptoeing trips down the hall.

"Auntie Annie, I couldn't hear anything in Uncle Jett's room," the child began, since sounds of life were what she'd been listening for each time she and Spot made the trip. "But I saw Uncle Jett's light on under the door, and when I opened it up he was awake. He wants to see you."

Chapter Three

Jett wasn't in bed. He was in the bathroom. Annie could hear the splash of water and the squeak of the faucet being turned from behind its partially closed door when she walked into the bedroom with his supper. Not knowing whether she should be more concerned about how stable he was on his feet or about what mood she'd find him in, she set the tray on the nightstand. The clink of the spoon in the bowl joined the faint groan of the bathroom door as it swung in.

Jett didn't seem to notice her standing by his bed. Wearing nothing but bandages and briefs, his rich brown hair spiked up on his head and another day's growth of facial hair darkening his jaws, his concentration was focused on the knots in his muscles. Balanced against the door frame, he lifted his hand to the back of his neck and rotated his head to relieve the stiffness there. He'd been in bed for over twenty hours, the last eight sleeping so soundly that Annie had actually checked twice to make sure he was still breathing. After sleeping that hard, she figured, he probably felt as if he'd been hit by a truck.

Or so she was thinking when he caught sight of her and went stock-still.

"Amy said you wanted to see me." Watching his hand fall in a fist at his side, she motioned to indicate the bowl of steaming chicken and dumplings. "I brought you some supper. I thought you might be getting hungry."

For a moment, he said nothing. He just stood there, dominating the space and looking totally unapproachable as his glance fell away. She hadn't been sure what to expect from him. But it had never occurred to her that he might feel as awkward as she did.

"Thanks," he finally mumbled, his voice thick and rusty from sleep. "Do you know what time it is? I can't find my watch."

"It's a little past seven. In the evening," she added, stifling the impulse to ask how he felt as he made his way toward the bed. Though he still looked lousy, she was certain he'd just insist he was fine, the way he had when he first arrived last night. "Your watch is on the dresser."

"What's it doing over there?"

She'd taken his watch off his wrist so he wouldn't accidentally hit her with it. She saw no point in mentioning that, however. She didn't know what he remembered of last night. How he'd thrashed around. That he'd asked her not to leave him. That he'd held her hand.

None of that mattered.

"I put it on the dresser so it wouldn't get knocked from the nightstand. Do you still need this quilt?" she asked, noticing that he wasn't drawing it up with the rest of the blankets as he eased himself against the headboard. Reaching across his legs, she pulled it toward her to take it off if he wanted, or smooth it if he didn't. "I can put it back on the quilt stand if it's too heavy. You got kind of cold last night."

"You can take it."

"What about this?" Fishing the cloth that had been on his head from the folds of the quilt, she held it up.

"You can have that, too."

There was a certain security in motion. Focused only on what she was doing, rather than on who she was doing it for, she lugged the quilt from the bed, folded it and laid it over the rack by the maple dresser supporting Trevor's rodeo souvenirs. The washcloth she carried into the bathroom. Bringing a fresh glass of water back with her, she handed it to Jett along with his pills, then automatically reached toward his head.

Realizing what she was about to do, she promptly froze.

She'd been about to brush his hair back from where it had tumbled over his forehead and see if his temperature was still down. It was something she had done so often, so freely, last night. Sometimes, while he was rambling, she had stroked her hand over his brow, hoping the gesture would soothe, reassure. As often as not, she had found an odd, indefinable reassurance herself in the contact. But touching him when he was aware of her every movement wasn't the same as touching him when he was barely conscious.

Jett was definitely conscious now. Acutely aware of his quiet scrutiny, Annie curled her fingers into her palm and stepped back. Despite the fact that he still looked awfully pale, his eyes were clear—and clearly assessing.

He'd known what she was about to do. He'd also looked quite curious to know whether she would do it.

Clearing her throat, she glanced toward his supper.

"You haven't had anything but juice and water in at least twenty-four hours, so try to get some of this down, okay?

And take this, too,'' she added, uncapping the new bottle of pills the doctor had left for him. "It's for your pain."

"I told him I didn't want any pain pills. I don't like the way they make me feel."

"You should take them anyway," she said encouragingly, not particularly surprised by his attitude. Anyone who exerted as much control over himself as he did wouldn't willingly turn that control over to anyone or anything. She could only imagine how he felt about last night.

"The doctor said you'll rest better if you aren't hurting so much." She held the bottle toward him so that she could shake the tablet into his hand. "The more rest you get, the quicker you'll heal."

The argument did not have its intended effect. Casting her an amazingly level look, he popped his penicillin and downed it with the glass of water. There was no way she was going to get him to take the other medication, though. Eyeing her evenly, he took the bottle from her and set it on the nightstand, along with the empty glass.

"I asked you not to call a doctor. It wasn't necessary."

"You *told* me not to call him," she corrected, quietly matching his challenge. "And it *was* necessary. You'd told me about the pneumonia and your ribs, but you have those bruises—"

Annie cut herself off. Jett might have a problem with seeking another person's help. Heaven knew he'd made that clear enough earlier last evening. But she had no compunctions about it. Not when someone was sick. And she was not going to justify what she'd done by telling him she'd been worried about him.

She didn't have to. He seemed well aware of what her silence implied.

He knew she'd taken care of him. She wasn't sure how much he remembered, but she saw something shift in his eyes. Something she was sure he would have guarded more closely if his reserves of energy hadn't been so sorely depleted. It looked a little like curiosity, and a lot like gratitude, and as his glance moved slowly over her face, she felt the tension shimmering in the air change quality.

Her throat tightened as his glance moved lower. Gratitude faded. Curiosity did not. From the faint pinch of his brow, it looked as if he were trying to imagine how she was shaped beneath the soft, baggy turtleneck tucked into her jeans. Her hand moved to her throat, as much to ease the knot there as to block his view. He didn't seem to notice. He'd already moved on to skim the curve of her hip, the flatness of her belly, and now he was staring at the hand curved by her thigh.

He lifted his own hand toward hers, then pulled it back, much as she had done with him only minutes ago. It was almost as if he were recalling her touch.

At the thought, a strange, almost foreign sensation of warmth pooled low in Annie's stomach.

Touching Jett as she had last night, there had been precious few moments when she wasn't aware of him. Of the power in his sinewy muscles. The strength. The beauty. But until this moment she hadn't been aware of her own body. Of her own shape and form and feminine textures. Jett made her aware of them now. Just by looking at her. And while she had no idea what he thought of what he saw, she was conscious of herself in ways she found totally unexpected, and nearly forgotten.

"Why did you do it?"

Her voice had lost its strength. "Do what?"

"Stay with me last night."

Because I know what it's like to be alone and ill. Because, for a while, I felt as if someone really needed me.

"You had a fever."

He knew that. He remembered parts of the night all too well, and her answer wasn't the one he'd sought. But Jett didn't push. He wasn't sure what he'd wanted to hear, anyway.

"You asked me to stay, too. You were afraid something was going to collapse," she hurried to explain, certain from the way his eyes narrowed that he couldn't picture himself having requested such a thing of her. "You kept saying you didn't want me to leave. Your fever was awfully high," she said, providing a perfectly logical excuse for his ramblings. "I'm sure you didn't know where you were or who I was. But you asked me to stay, so I did."

His skepticism faded to a frown of recognition. "The ledge," he muttered, and wearily pushed his hair back from where it had tumbled over his forehead. The moment he encountered the bandage she had replaced last night, his scowl deepened.

She didn't understand what he meant, and her expression mirrored his. "The doctor said you fell."

"I did."

"Mind telling me what you fell from?"

"The edge of a canyon."

Annie hesitated. "You fell down a canyon?' "

Jett rubbed at his temple, more irritated with the ache in it than with the event that had caused it to hurt in the first place. "It was a thousand feet down to the river. I only went down about a hundred. A ledge stopped me."

Only a hundred? she thought. "Is that something you do a lot? Hang your toes over the edge of insanely high spaces?"

He wanted to let it go. To forget the whole incident. It was over. Done with. And the last thing he wanted to do was recall the hours he'd spent wondering if every second was going to be his last. What little bit of a conscience he had, however, prodded him to admit that the woman watching him with such unabashed curiosity in her pretty but sad brown eyes was probably entitled to at least as much of an explanation as he'd had to give the Latin version of Nurse Ratchett who'd taped him up.

"Depends where I'm working," he said defensively, thinking he'd have told her he occasionally found himself a few thousand feet under the ground, too, but he wasn't feeling that conversational. "It had been raining for days and the ground was saturated. We'd cleared the area because it had started coming down even harder, but I went back to secure some equipment. The next thing I knew, the crane I was working on was tipping over and I was scrambling for something to hang on to. After that, all I remember is waking up on a ledge that was making like a melting iceberg. It took them a while to get to me."

It was no wonder he kept saying he wanted to stop the rain. "How long is a 'while'?"

"Thirty hours, give or take. Guess that's why I got the pneumonia."

He added the latter with a shrug that somehow made the entire incident sound as inconsequential to him as a fender bender in a parking lot. Amazed by his attitude, more surprised that he hadn't been hurt any worse, Annie tightened her grip around her middle. "Why did they leave you there for so long?"

This time the shrug was in his voice. "Same reason no one else wanted to go secure the equipment—it was too dangerous."

It's going to go. It's going to collapse.

The words he'd uttered over and over last night came back to Annie as she watched him lock his jaw and try to sit a little straighter. He was acting unaffected, but his subconscious had still been dealing with the incident all night as it replayed bits and pieces of that horrible scene in his mind. It would have been traumatic enough to experience such a fall. To be alone for so long, hundreds of feet above a river with nothing but a crumbling ledge of rock to keep him from falling the rest of the way, would be enough to drive some people out of their minds.

It gave her the chills just to think about it. "You could have been killed," she whispered.

"Suppose so," he muttered. "But I wasn't."

Annie blinked in disbelief. His pragmatism was astounding. So was his gift for understatement. He pared everything down to bare bones, omitting the details most people would have tripped over themselves to share. Yet his spare account revealed just enough to make her think he wasn't terribly impressed by his ordeal.

She knew better than that. She'd been with him last night, soothed him when he clung to her. Whether he consciously admitted it or not, it had most definitely made an impression. She couldn't begin to imagine the terror he'd experienced in the thirty hours he lay injured on that ledge. But what she had an even harder time understanding was his apparent lack of concern over his own mortality.

"Do things like this happen often in your line of work?"

He seemed puzzled by her question. Or maybe what puzzled him was her interest. "Some jobs carry a higher risk than others," he admitted, looking as if she ought to know that. She'd been married to a test pilot, after all. "But they're usually the ones that pay the best, or are in the more interesting places. Next time I'll be more careful."

"You're going back?"

He didn't seem to comprehend her bewilderment. "I'm not going back to that job. But not because of what happened. I won't go back there because I'm sick of the rain.

After I've rested up for a few days, I'll find one someplace drier. Saudi sounds good."

Annie turned to his tray, removing the napkin to hand it to him. The man was barely able to sit up, yet he was already talking about moving on. In a way, she supposed, she could sympathize with him. She desperately wanted to get on with her own life. Her idea of moving on, however, bore scant resemblance to his. What she wanted—needed—was to settle in somewhere, establish a routine, plant petunias. She had the feeling Jett would break out in a cold sweat at such a thought.

That she could relate to him at all gave her pause. That she actually admired his pragmatism would have given pause to anyone who knew her. She had always been the sort of person to analyze situations and consider consequences, which was why her sisters said they could always rely on her for the right advice. At the moment, though, Annie would have given just about anything to know how Jett could so easily shrug off an incident that would have altered most people's lives. Or, at least, their outlook.

She didn't have time to ask. The commotion coming down the hall cut off the question the moment it formed.

Spot's high-pitched bark preceded him through the door.

Amy was right on his tail, pleading with him to come back.

"Michael's teasing us," the little girl lamented, dropping to her hands and knees to fish the dog out from under the bed. "He said Spot looks stupid."

Aware that Jett's head still hurt from the way he flinched at the noise, Annie headed around the other side of the bed, in case the little mutt came out the other side. "Let's be quiet for Uncle Jett, okay?" she asked, lowering her own voice so the child would imitate it.

"Okay," came the loud whisper. "He called him ugly, too."

"Michael likes Spot, Amy. Why would he say that?"

"I dunno. But he hurt Spot's feelings."

Spot's feelings might have been hurt, but the promise of a doggy treat had him scooting out from under the dust ruffle in no time. Scooping him up in her arms, the little girl nuzzled his neck, then turned serious brown eyes to the big man watching her from the bed.

From the way Jett eyed the uneven braids hanging on either side of the dejected dog's head, Annie was pretty sure he could tell the little girl what had prompted her brother's comments. Jett said nothing, though. Clearly preferring not to get involved, he closed his eyes and leaned his head back again.

In her innocence, Amy didn't realize that he'd just closed her out. She saw only that he was very tired.

"Do you want to hold him, Uncle Jett? Auntie Annie says holding puppies makes people feel better. Maybe he'll make you feel better, too."

Jett didn't appear at all convinced of the benefits of the child's suggestion. If the way he dubiously watched the little girl was any indication, he also didn't seem too comfortable with the presence of pigtailed people in the three-foot range. Though Amy innocently accepted him as family, he didn't act terribly familiar with the concept of "uncle."

Annie wasn't particularly surprised. Until Logan married her sister, Jett's extended family had consisted solely of a teenage nephew he rarely saw. She could also understand that he wouldn't feel up to dealing with small children and their pets. She wasn't about to let him hurt Amy's feelings, though. His brooding silence had already turned Amy's hopeful smile upside down.

"I think what Uncle Jett needs," Annie told Amy, running her hand over the child's silky hair, "is to take his medicine and eat his supper. And you," she added, smiling at the upturned little face, "need to get ready for bed. If you head upstairs right now, you can use my bubble bath."

The enticement of bubbles had Amy brightening considerably. Within seconds, she was bouncing out the door with the dog in tow, all the while telling Spot that he could take a bath with her.

Certain she'd get no argument from Spot, Annie called out that Amy was *not* to put the dog in the tub and told her she'd be upstairs in just a minute.

There was no time now to return to the conversation Amy had interrupted. Turning back to the man so guardedly watching her, Annie figured it was just as well. If she were to ask Jett how he managed to so easily shake off what had happened, he would probably just give her some variation of the same thing everyone had told her—about how a person needed to get back on a horse when she'd been thrown. What everyone else didn't realize was that, when she stood up and dusted herself off after all that had happened last year, she'd found not only that the horse had taken off, but also that she'd been shaken so badly she had no sense of direction.

"Do you need anything else?"

Not sure what had just robbed the animation from her eyes, Jett shook his head. "You'd better go save the dog."

The luminous dial of Jett's watch indicated it was two o'clock when he picked it up from the nightstand. Except for the sliver of light leaking from the bathroom, the room was dark. The house, quiet. Each time he wakened before, he'd been vaguely aware of children's voices. The distant ring of the telephone. The muffled drone of the television in the living room. Sounds of life, of activity. At the moment, he heard nothing but the settle and creak of an old house that had been settling and creaking for a hundred years.

The watch clinked against a glass when he set it back on the nightstand. Two o'clock in the morning. Heaven only knew what time his body clock was on. Having slept for well over twenty-four hours, he knew only that he was awake, and that he was hungry. The food Annie had brought him last night had been just enough to revive his appetite.

The bedclothes rustled when he carefully sat up and lowered his feet to the floor. The room didn't tilt this time. Encouraged, thinking only of the gnawing sensation in his stomach, he pulled on the jeans someone had washed and left on his duffel and made his way to the door.

He had just stepped into the dark hallway, his bare feet soundless on the hardwood floor, when he noticed a blue-white glow spilling from the kitchen. Thinking it must be some sort of night-light, he followed it past the old grandfather clock ticking solemnly in the entry and stopped by the refrigerator. Someone had left the stove light on. The stove, too. A small dot of red light glowed like a demon's eye from the panel above the oven. On one of the two front burners sat a pan with something white steaming inside.

The step he took toward the stove was canceled when he caught movement at the far end of the dark room.

The light pooled around the stove didn't illuminate the area beyond the breakfast bar. It was dark over there. Still, he could see Annie curled up in the window seat. She looked like a wraith to him, or an angel, dressed as she was in a pale nightgown that covered her from neck to toes and draped down the side of the seat. She sat with her knees drawn up and a mug cradled in her hands, her attention on something beyond the parted curtains. Her thoughts had to be light-years away for her not to notice him standing there.

Never allowing her eyes to leave whatever she was watching, she raised her mug and took a sip.

She must be having a restless night, Jett thought, which explained the milk on the stove. He'd never tried the remedy himself, but he'd heard somewhere that it was supposed to help a person sleep. Personally, he preferred a shot or two of something that singed going down. But he wasn't about to begrudge a person whatever worked for her. Heaven knew he'd spent his share of nights counting ceiling tiles.

He should have said something to let her know he was there. Instead, he moved into the shadows and back down the hall. Going back to sleep on an empty stomach was no big deal. He'd been hungry before. What he wasn't accustomed to was someone taking care of him. If she knew he wanted something to eat, she'd probably fix it for him herself, and he didn't want her doing that. The last thing he wanted was to feel more obligated to her than he already did. As he eased himself back down on the bed, cursing the aches the movements brought, he told himself he didn't want to know why she was having trouble sleeping, either.

He was up again four hours later. Between Erin hollering from upstairs that she couldn't find her new sweater and the scramble of feet over the floor of the bedroom above him, the dead would have risen.

But it wasn't the preschool free-for-all that had Jett searching for his clothes. His body just couldn't take staying prone any longer. After thirty-some-odd hours of sleep, and the drugs having had a chance to work, he was feeling almost human. The downside of that development was that he was now far too aware of how small the room was, of how close its walls were.

He hated being closed in, being confined. He always had. Now that he felt more like himself, he was restless again. That in itself made it impossible for him to stay down. He was a long way from being recovered, though—a point he faced, with considerable irritation, when, halfway through his shower, he realized he could use only his right hand to soap his hair. He'd taken off the elastic bandage, and raising both arms made him feel as if he were being kicked in the ribs. Still, showered, shaved and aching in fewer places every day, he felt a far sight better than he had when he arrived. He'd be even better once he got his hands on something to eat.

The quiet that had settled over the house was deceptive. He'd thought the kids were gone, because he hadn't been able to hear them for the past several minutes. But they were only quiet because they were being fed. He realized that the moment he turned into the kitchen.

The windows were still dark with the gloom of the dreary winter morning. Yet the kitchen itself was bright and warm, inviting him in with the scents of hot bacon and rich coffee. Annie stood at the table, her back to him as she set something on it, and Logan's two youngest stepchildren were attacking plates of pancakes steaming in front of them. The boy he remembered as Michael was eating, anyway. The little girl was feeding hers to the dog begging beside her chair.

The moment Michael saw his uncle, he smiled around the fork he'd just stuffed into his mouth. Seeing that smile, Annie turned and looked up.

Jett watched her go still, a look of surprise sweeping her delicate features. Something about the expression made her look impossibly young just then, impossibly innocent. Or maybe it was the lack of artifice about her that gave him that impression. Her short and gleaming hair feathered back from a face devoid of makeup, and the navy sweater she wore over a pale blue turtleneck was so big for her that she looked like a waif dressed in hand-me-down clothes.

With a quick blink, her eyes jerked from his clean-shaven face to the middle of his gray sweatshirt. "You're up," she said, smiling as she skimmed her eyes past his smooth jaw before placing the syrup on the table. "Feel like joining the kids for breakfast?"

Michael, a blond, brown-eyed bundle of typical prepubescent male, sat taller to impress the leaner version of his adored stepfather. "Hi, Uncle Jett," he mumbled through a mouthful of pancake. "I got a tarantula like the ones you saw in Mexico. Well, not exactly like 'em," he amended, swallowing. "I got it down by the wash. Wanna see it?"

Amy's head popped up. "No! Auntie Annie, don't let him bring the spider down here. He'll chase me with it."

"Not now, Michael," Annie calmly informed the boy on her way to the refrigerator.

"Maybe later," Jett muttered, reluctant to get pulled into anything, even though he was a little surprised at the kid's memory. He hadn't had much to do with the kids when he was here before. But Michael had trailed after him because he knew his new uncle worked in places that tended to have a lot of insects. The kid seemed to have a real thing about bugs.

"How about after school?" Annie suggested to them both. "You'll have plenty of time then."

"I can stay home and show it to him." A hopeful look flitted over Michael's deceptively angelic expression. "You said he's going to have to stay in bed for a couple more days, so I can keep him company, too."

"You're not staying home from school, Michael. Go ahead and sit down, Jett," she added, well aware of the way Jett frowned at what she'd told the boy. "I'll make you some pancakes as soon as I finish their lunches. Do you want coffee?''

Sitting down to a meal had never occurred to Jett. He'd fully intended to eat whatever he grabbed standing at the sink. If he wanted to be more formal about it, he'd sit on the stool at the breakfast bar. Either way, he wasn't prepared to join what he'd just walked in on. He didn't care for family meals, and there was something entirely too domestic about sitting down with those kids, with her, and eating breakfast before the little ones went off to school.

The hearth-and-home aspect of the situation wasn't the only thing that had Jett feeling so uncomfortable—though he had been the first to admit that the cozy little scene held about as much appeal for him as another cracked rib. He knew nothing about the attraction other people found in family. The closest he'd come to seeing a working concept of the institution in action was the month he'd stayed on the ranch following Logan's wedding. Then, feeling even more like the outcast he'd always been, he'd made himself as scarce as he could.

That was what he needed to do now, too, he told himself, more aware than he wanted to be of the woman making peanut-butter-and-jelly sandwiches at the counter. And he would indeed make himself scarce—just as soon as he filled the void in his belly.

He headed for the rack of mugs under the cabinets.

''I'll get it,'' Annie told him, reaching for a mug herself.

He was perfectly capable of getting his own coffee. Annie, however, had already grabbed the coffeepot. A moment later, having just done what he'd suspected she would do last night if she knew he was hungry, she held the heavy mug out to him.

''Do you want milk or sugar?''

Conscious of the way she avoided his glance, he slipped his fingers around the thick handle. "Black is fine," he muttered, frowning as much at what she'd done as at the faint shadows her restless night had left beneath her eyes. Then, he breathed in—and he wasn't thinking about her eyes at all.

They stood three feet apart, close enough for him to catch a hint of the freshness clinging to her skin, her hair. It seemed odd to him that something so gentle could hit so hard. Breathing in her soft scent was like being blindsided. Or maybe what hit so hard was the memories her scent prompted. Memories of how her cool fingers had felt drifting over him, of how freely she had touched and soothed him. There had been nothing at all sexual about what she had done. Nothing in the least suggestive. She had only been caring for him because he had a fever. Yet, now, thoughts of how it would feel for her to touch him more intimately elicited a reaction that had nothing to do with bringing a temperature down, and everything to do with raising it.

She had a waist he could span with his hands, hips shaped so sweetly he ached just thinking how it would feel to cup them, and the fullness of her bottom lip fairly begged to be kissed.

He hadn't moved. But Annie had already aimed a small, uneasy smile at his chest and was turning back to her task. He didn't doubt for a minute that his presence in this house made her uncomfortable. She was just too gracious to be obvious about it. Heaven only knew how she'd feel if she knew he was wondering how her body would fit his.

Jett raised the mug to his lips, welcoming the hot bite of the brew. His attraction to her surprised him. She wasn't his type at all. His brother's sister-in-law was a lot like his brother's wife. A "nice" woman, the kind a man turned to when he was looking for a permanent relationship. He wasn't looking for any kind of relationship, permanent or otherwise, and to him Annie was an alien being. She was delicate, soft, nurturing—traits that were totally foreign to him in any form. There had never been anything soft in or about his life. As for nurturing, having known little of it in his lifetime, he'd never understood the need for it.

He understood sexual need, though. He'd gone without a woman for a long time now. The attraction was only his body reminding him that he couldn't suppress that need forever. His attraction to her was as simple as that.

What wasn't so simple was how the memory of her concern for him last night had made him feel.

The scrape of a chair pulled his glance toward the table. He'd been aware of Amy staring at him with a frown on her face ever since he'd come in. Now, syrup at the corner of her bow-shaped little mouth, she walked slowly toward him and tipped her head back.

"Are you really as stubborn as sin?" she finally asked.

Annie coughed. Faint spots of color tinting her cheeks, she hauled Amy to the sink, to either wash the syrup from her face or gag her, and called out to Erin and Michael. "Come on, kids. Make sure you've got your homework. You're going to be late."

The sudden flurry of movement had everyone but Michael gathering up coats, books and lunches. Erin came flying through a moment later, greeting Jett with a smile that looked either shy or embarrassed. Then, at Annie's gentle coaxing, even the recalcitrant Michael was being hustled out the door.

"Don't forget that I'm staying at Lindsey's tonight," Erin reminded her aunt as cool, damp air rushed in from the outer door. "The bus gets to the ranch road about four."

"I'll pick up Michael and Amy," Annie promised, as much to save herself having to clean muddy boots, clothes and kids as to save them a half-mile walk. "Do you have a play rehearsal tomorrow night, too?"

"Every night for the rest of the week. Oh, and I told Lindsey I'd help her out at the boutique on Saturday. I'll spend the weekend at her house, too. If that's okay," she added, hesitating when Annie's head involuntarily turned in the direction of the man behind them. "You don't need me here, do you?"

At Erin's less-than-enthusiastic question, Annie made herself smile.

"I hadn't thought about you not being around to keep an eye on your brother and sister. While I'm out with Realtors," she said, since Erin had obviously forgotten. "But that's okay," she added, hating to mess up anyone else's plans when hers could be rescheduled. "I'll just do my stuff early so I can be back by the time the kids get home. As busy as you are this week, it makes more sense for you to stay in town than drive back and forth so late at night."

"You sure?"

Annie allowed only a moment's hesitation before bolstering her smile. "I'm sure."

At that, Erin grinned, smacked a kiss to her aunt's cheek, told her she was the greatest and bounced out the door. What Annie hadn't mentioned was that she now had to reschedule the appointment she'd made with a Realtor for tomorrow afternoon.

From where Jett leaned against the counter, he heard the outer door close. It seemed to him that Annie sounded more than a little inconvenienced by Erin's defection, but that wasn't his concern. Nor was that why he was sticking around. He still needed breakfast. Two minutes ago, he would have grabbed something and cleared out along with the kids. He was still going to get out of there for a while, but not before he came to an understanding with his little angel of mercy.

Chapter Four

Jett had a way of watching Annie that made her feel like a specimen under a microscope. He missed nothing and noted everything. Yet he didn't give a clue as to whatever conclusions he'd drawn. His eyes were narrowed on her now as she headed for the stove. Cool blue, assessing, and as unreadable to her as the hieroglyphics in a pharaoh's tomb.

Wondering what she was supposed to do with him now that he was up, other than feed him, she turned the griddle on again and gave the batter an extra stir.

"Do you feel up to having eggs with your pancakes?"

With more caution than grace, Jett slowly pushed his six-foot-three-inch frame away from the counter. "You don't need to do that."

"Do what?"

"Wait on me. You've got enough to do around here. Just tell me where you keep the cereal and what food you don't want me into and I'll get out of your way."

"This is your brother's and my sister's home," she quietly informed him. "Nothing here is mine for me to tell you to stay out of. And I'm not waiting on you. I'm just getting your breakfast. If you want cereal, it's in the pantry over there. You've got your choice of pastel-colored teddy bears or oatmeal. Would you rather have one of those?"

Jett unfolded his arms. The woman had completely missed his point. He'd just told her she didn't need to take care of him, and all she'd been interested in was establishing his rights to the pantry and what was in it.

Looking as if she'd expected his frown, she turned back to the griddle.

"I didn't think so." Batter hissed as it met hot iron. "If you want to rest on the sofa in the living room after you eat," she went on, making a row of perfect four-inch circles, "I'll change your sheets. I took care of the clothes you had on when you got here, but if there's anything else you need washed, just give it to me and I'll throw it in, too."

"Look," he began, taking the bowl from her so he could have her full attention. It landed with a soft thump on the counter. "I meant it when I said you don't need to wait on me. You don't need to do anything to my bed. You don't need to do my laundry. You don't need to feed me. It's not that I don't appreciate it," he admitted, though appreciation was the least of what he was feeling, standing close enough to see the fine grain of her skin. "I can just take care of my own things."

Skimming a glance past his chin, she lifted the spatula toward the grill. "Does that mean you don't want these?"

"Yes, I want those," he muttered. The tangy scent of sourdough was as tantalizing as the soft curve of her neck. He couldn't remember the last time he'd had real sourdough pancakes. And he certainly couldn't remember anyone cooking them just for him.

"I'm not resting in the living room, either," he added, wanting to set the entire record straight. "I'm going for a ride."

Annie had turned back to flip his pancakes. If he didn't want her doing things for him, that was fine. She'd suspected he wouldn't accept help from her much longer, anyway. She did, however, have an obligation to tell him what the doctor had said. Not that he didn't suspect it already, thanks to Michael.

"I don't know if the doctor mentioned it to you or not— or if you remember it," she added, because he hadn't been in the greatest shape yesterday morning. "But he said he wanted you to stay down for at least two days after your temperature returned to normal. You were still running a fever yesterday."

"I'm not staying in bed for two more days."

"You don't have to stay in bed," she pointed out, with the patience she would have used on a small child. "You just have to rest. Riding wasn't in the doctor's orders.'"

"It's been pointed out to me before that I don't take orders very well."

"Even when they're for your own good?"

She shouldn't have challenged him. Or perhaps what she should have done was take a closer look at him before now. Despite the evenness of his deep voice, tension coursed through him like an electric current. Like lightning seeking ground, that tension telegraphed to her as he steadily held her eyes.

"I've been taking care of myself long enough to know what's good for me and what isn't. Unless you have an idea of how to keep me from climbing these walls," he added, his glance slipping slowly, deliberately to her mouth, "I'm getting out of here for a while. I don't care what the doctor said."

He refused to release his visual hold. Shaken by what he'd implied, more unsettled by how she seemed to absorb the frustration coursing through him, she broke that hold herself. "I just thought you might not want to overdo."

"Don't worry about it."

He turned away then, too, snagging his mug from the counter to refill it. His body was rigid, his broad shoulders bunched with the tension that demanded his escape.

He'd never answered her about the eggs. Having no desire to poke at a hornet's nest, Annie didn't ask again. She simply dished up the pancakes and set the plate on the breakfast bar, where he stood rubbing the back of his neck.

When she passed by with the butter and syrup a moment later, his jaw was locked so tight Annie wondered how he could swallow. Every bite he took would undoubtedly settle like lead in his stomach. Her own stomach had a knot in it the size of a small fist.

That knot felt as if it had doubled to the size of a softball by the time she'd made two more trips past him to carry the children's dishes to the sink and wipe off the table.

Jett stabbed the wedge of pancake. He wasn't ignoring her. He was just busy being irritated with himself while he made short work of a short stack and downed his coffee. All he'd wanted to do was make her understand that she wasn't responsible for his care and feeding. But he'd done it with all the finesse of a bull elk.

He'd never been known to tiptoe around anything he had on his mind, but it hadn't been necessary to dismiss her concern so bluntly. It was just that there was as much threat as appeal in the idea of her being concerned about him, and he didn't want her to make any difference to him one way or the other. Not that she did. Or would.

Annie was scouring the griddle when he carried his plate to the sink. Stopping behind her and just enough to one side to see her profile, he held the empty plate out to her.

The top of her head was dead even with the top of his shoulder. Watching her tawny hair shimmer in the overhead lights, he breathed in the scents of lemon from the dish soap—and the fresh, almost imperceptible fragrance of wild roses.

For all its innocence, that scent was positively lethal.

"Did you have enough to eat?" she asked, taking the plate from his with her soapy hand.

He cleared his throat. "Yeah. Thanks."

"You're welcome."

There were other thanks he could have offered. Should have, considering the sorry shape he'd be in right now if not for all she'd done. But he wasn't at all sure how he felt about any of it, and he hated the confusion that made him feel.

Ignoring the dull ache in his ribs, he headed for his room to retrieve his heavy Sherpa jacket, then went back to the mudroom for the black Stetson he'd left hanging on one of the pegs the last time he was there. After taking Logan's oilcloth riding coat from one of the other pegs lining the room and pulling it on, Jett stepped into the late-February drizzle. He couldn't stay in the house another minute. Not with her in there.

He was feeling as stiff and prickly as a piece of barbed wire and desperately in need of something physical to do. The only problem was that his physical self wasn't up to his mental needs at the moment.

The thought did nothing for his mood.

The last time he'd been at the RW, he'd spent his days on the range repairing fence and chasing down strays, or out in the barns helping Logan with the breeding. Evenings he'd ridden out to the old tumbledown shack overlooking the

Pedernales River, coming back when all the family stuff was over and everyone else was in bed. Except for the ride, none of those were options now. Even the ride itself was questionable. He'd barely been able to wash his hair. Heaven only knew how he'd lift a saddle onto a horse.

Hoping Hank or one of the hired hands was around, deciding he'd go bareback if he had to, Jett changed direction and headed for the barn. There was a greater likelihood of finding one of Logan's men in there than in the stables this time of the morning. On his way, he stopped at the pump, fished out the bottle of penicillin from the front pocket of his jeans and popped two of the capsules. Though Annie clearly questioned his judgment, he had no intention of setting himself back again. He'd get over what had gotten him down, recover his strength and get back to work. In the meantime, though his depleted energy wouldn't allow for much progress today, he had a project to work on to keep himself from going stir-crazy. With any luck, it would also get his mind off the woman watching him from the kitchen window.

From where Annie stood at the sink, she saw Jett stop at the pump for a moment, then turn toward the breeding barn. A gray mist hung over the land, blurring the trees and the stark white outbuildings that formed the heart of the RW Ranch's cattle operation. Watching Jett's tall, dark figure through that hazy mist, Annie's first thought was that he shouldn't be outside in such damp weather. Her second thought was that he'd made it abundantly clear his welfare was no longer any of her concern. She was not to worry about him.

Thinking that somebody needed to, she watched him head down the wide graveled road to the workyard. Try as she might, she couldn't shake the thought of how his eyes had lingered on her mouth just a few short minutes ago. She'd seen that same interest, that same heat, in his eyes last night.

She couldn't remember the last time a man had looked at her that way. She couldn't remember, either, the last time she'd experienced the warm sensation that had fluttered low in her stomach. Not that it mattered. Though she was far more curious about him than was probably wise, she didn't believe for a moment that Jett Whitaker was actually interested in her.

Jett was still gone when Annie left to pick up Michael and Amy at four o'clock. But while she and the kids were fixing an after-school snack, she noticed a large piece missing from the apple pie she'd made yesterday. Not long after that, she discovered Jett's hat back on its peg in the mudroom and the door to his room closed.

His door stayed closed all evening. Not until long after she went to bed did he venture from his room. It was well after midnight when she heard him prowling around downstairs—which meant she had to do her own nocturnal pacing upstairs, without the benefit of warm milk.

His door was closed again the next morning, but he left after he heard her and the children leave for the two-minute drive up to the highway to catch the school bus. When Annie returned to dress for her rescheduled meeting with the Realtor, the scent of toasted bread and the still-warm toaster told her he'd fixed himself a quick breakfast before he departed again. Otherwise, she might not even have known he'd been there.

He did make an appearance that evening, however. His cheeks ruddy from the cold and bits of twig and dried leaves clinging to his jacket, he walked in the back door just as she and the children sat down to supper. He stayed only long enough to hang up his hat and jacket and decline her invi-

tation for him to join them. Thanking her anyway, he said
he'd get something to eat later and headed off for a shower
and bed.

His schedule was the same the next day. He disappeared
while the children were gone and Annie was alone, then returned to fend for himself and get some sleep. The moments they spent in passing were marked mostly by her quiet
"Hi" or his "Thanks" for the food she left out for him. To
keep him from telling her she didn't have to feed him, she
told him that a diet of toast and cold sandwiches wasn't going to help him regain his health, then added that since she
was cooking for the kids, anyway, dishing up another serving was hardly a problem. He seemed to accept that. Still,
he clearly preferred to avoid their company. Hers in particular. But then, she had known from the moment she first
met him that all he wanted between him and her was distance.

That was why Annie hardly expected to find herself alone
with him the next morning.

In the early part of the day, the winter sunlight was
brightest in the dining room. Specifically, on the eastern
side, where it shone through the airy white Priscilla curtains draping the big multipaned window. Annie had pushed
aside the lace runner and was working at the end of the long
mahogany dining table. Trying to work, anyway. Her pen
had just run out of ink. Tossing it aside, she rose to get another. As she did, she turned—and found herself facing the
third button on a blue flannel shirt.

Jett stood less than two feet away, his hands on his hips
and his very large, very solid body blocking her route to the
door. Startled to find him there, she sucked in a quiet gasp
and instinctively grabbed the chair to keep her balance. As
she did, she bumped the edge of the table, and the stack of

lists near its edge fluttered to the antique rose area rug beneath it.

Jett's faint frown followed them down.

"How do you do that?" she insisted, the pounding of her heart in her throat making her voice little more than a whisper. The man had practically turned into a phantom—mostly unseen, often unheard. "Don't you ever make noise?"

His frown intensified, deepening the masculine lines carved in his cheeks. "I thought you heard me," he explained, sounding as if he hadn't realized she was concentrating so intently. His boots silent on the thick rug, he moved toward the sheets of yellow notepaper that had settled around one of the table's claw-shaped feet. "I was just looking for the newspaper."

She had it. She would have told him that, too, had she not just realized what he was about to do.

She scrambled to pick up her notes. "I can get those."

"So can I."

"Really, Jett, you don't need to bother."

Being his usual stubborn self, Jett wasn't listening. He crouched down just as she did—which immediately brought her close enough to feel the warmth radiating from his body. The clean scents of soap and shaving cream clung to him, and his dark hair was combed straight back from the rugged angles of his face.

Belatedly realizing they were reaching for the same piece of paper, she snatched her hand back and looked up.

Another moment and his hand would have landed on hers. She had the feeling Jett was as aware of that as she. He was also aware that she'd deliberately sought to avoid that contact.

His eyes bored into hers, narrowed, questioning.

Her own glance faltered as her heart kicked against her ribs.

"Get the one behind you," he said, his voice tight.

She immediately did as he'd suggested, which gave Jett an unrestricted view of the back of her gracefully bent neck. In the beam of sunlight pouring through the window next to them, he could see the downy hair on the skin just above the collar of her sweater, its baby-fine softness almost inviting him to touch. It would feel like velvet, he was sure. And her hair would feel like satin. He'd noticed before how her hair curved just above her nape, but until the sunlight hit the smooth strands, he hadn't realized how many shades of umber and gold were in it.

Paper crackled when Jett reached back to gather the sheets nearest him. He hadn't been this close to Annie in two days. He wished he could say it had been that long since he'd thought about her.

Coming to get the paper had only been an excuse. What he really wanted was to find some way to repay her for what she'd done for him, so he could stop feeling obligated to her. He hated feeling he owed somebody. That was why he never willingly allowed an obligation to be created. He did owe her, though, and the feeling had nagged at him ever since he'd walked away from her the other morning.

Something else had nagged him even more. He had yet to fall asleep without being teased by a memory he couldn't completely recall—the memory of what he'd felt when he awakened and found her holding his hand. Whatever that feeling had been was something he'd never experienced before. Or since. As tantalizing as it was, it eluded him completely.

Unlike his curiosity about her.

She'd once touched him so freely. Judging from what she'd done moments ago, he had the feeling that if he touched her now, she'd probably bolt.

To test his theory—or maybe it was just to once more feel the softness of her skin—he reached over and took her hand to help her up.

Sure enough, the moment his fingers closed around hers, she pulled back. She started to, anyway. He wouldn't let her go. Aware of the tension in her hand, he stood, bringing her up with him. Even then, he didn't release his grip.

Her hand looked like a child's in his, small, delicate. But it was the faint bruise peeking out below the cuff of her sweater sleeve that held his attention. Stuffing her notes between his side and his arm, he turned her hand over and pushed the fabric up to reveal three parallel bruises above the fragile bones of her wrist.

This time, when he felt her pull back, he let her go.

He didn't like the thoughts that rushed into his mind. But he'd seen bruises like that before. A lifetime ago. On the skinny arms of a frightened young boy.

"Who grabbed you?"

He didn't miss the hesitation in her eyes before she lowered them and tugged her sleeve down.

"It doesn't matter. It was an accident."

"You don't get marks like that by accident."

He didn't question how quickly his protective instincts had been aroused. Until that moment, he hadn't been aware he had any. He just picked up her hand again, undoing what she'd just done by uncovering the bruises again. She didn't pull back this time. She didn't get to voice whatever it was she started to say, either.

The tip of his finger rested below one of the long purple marks striping the inside of her wrist. "Those were made by fingers." He drew his finger down, lightly skimming her racing pulse. "That was a thumb."

He scarcely noticed the way her pulse leaped at his touch, or how intently she was suddenly watching him. He was too busy containing the resentment and rage that hadn't been buried as completely as he thought. Whoever had grabbed her had been strong. Far stronger than she.

She wasn't married anymore. That didn't mean her ex-husband hadn't come after her lately. Or that she didn't have a boyfriend. If some man was in the habit of abusing her, that could certainly explain why she'd shied from contact with him a few moments ago. She'd done the same thing the other night when she brought him supper. If she made contact, she was fine. But if someone reached for her...

Sick at the thought of anyone roughing up anyone so small, his voice grew tighter than it had already become. "Did your ex do that?"

Annie's eyes went wide. "No! No," she repeated, sounding a little less horrified. "Rob would never have... No," she insisted again, astounded by Jett's suspicions.

"Your boyfriend?"

"I don't *have* a boyfriend." Amazed by the depth of anger flashing in his eyes, the admission hardly mattered. "It really was an accident." Her voice grew quieter. "It was the fever. It made you delirious."

Jett went still, his eyes locked on hers. His entire body had gone tight as a fist within the past few moments. Now, in the space of a heartbeat, the anger in his expression turned inward, changing to something that completely drained the force from his voice. "*I* did that?"

Her smile was soft, forgiving. "You didn't mean to."

He'd had no idea he'd done such a thing. "Dear God, Annie." He didn't know what else to say. "I'm sorry" would be as inadequate as the phrase inevitably was. "Is that why you wanted to pull away from me just now? You think I'd do something like that again?''

Annie couldn't begin to comprehend the emotions clouding Jett's expression. She knew only that she had never seen anyone look so stricken. The idea of hurting someone in such a way was anathema to him. The idea that she would think him capable of deliberate cruelty appeared as if it would destroy whatever sense of himself he possessed.

It was surprising enough that what she thought mattered to him. That it should matter so much saved her having to answer what he'd first asked.

"It never occurred to me that you would," she had to tell him, wondering if he had any idea how much of himself he had betrayed in the past few moments. "It isn't like you did it on purpose. That's why I didn't tell you what happened when you first noticed the marks. It wasn't important.''

She had no idea what had triggered his initial reaction to the bruises. But she felt certain it had nothing to do with her. The rage that leaped into his eyes had been too quick, too unsettled, to be mere sympathy. Yet there was no denying his concern—or the gentle way he'd touched her when he traced his finger along her wrist. There was compassion buried beneath that hard, solitary shell. Unexpected, but all too real. Yet already that too-brief glimpse inside his soul was being replaced by something less revealing. With the tightening of his jaw, his guard slipped back into place.

She hadn't realized how formidable that guard was until she saw him without it. That he'd allowed her that glimpse touched her far more than she wanted to admit.

"Did I do anything else?''

"Nothing you need to worry about. Just forget it. Okay?''

"I'm not going to forget about it," he countered, feeling even more indebted to her than he had, and liking it even less. "At the very least, I owe you for taking care of me that night. I just don't know how to pay you back."

"You don't have to pay me back."

Ignoring her, he shoved his fingers through his hair. As he did, he exposed the ragged and red inch-long gash near his hairline. "I don't know what nurses get an hour, but maybe I could pay you or something."

"You're not going to pay me." The offer wasn't quite an insult, but the man had a real knack for keeping people from getting too close. "You're part of my sister's family. Both of my sisters," she added. "Family doesn't keep track of who owes who what."

"Maybe I do."

"Well, I don't. Consider it a gift." With a frown, her glance shifted to his forehead. "What happened to your stitches?"

Jett scowled right back. "I took them out."

"Of course you did," she murmured, eyeing him evenly. "Does your side still hurt?"

"Not really."

"That must mean it does." A knowing light entered her eyes, teasing him with its warmth and defying him to be angry. "The night you got here, you were in a lot worse shape and you insisted you were fine. If you ever admit to being in pain, I can probably assume you're near death."

Jett didn't like being so easily read. He still didn't know why she'd pulled from him the way she had, and he wasn't too crazy about the way she'd dismissed his offer to settle up. But he was too distracted by the unexpected smile in her eyes and the quick change in her manner to worry about any of that at the moment.

She had her hand stretched out in front of him, palm up. "May I have my notes now, please?"

Ignoring her request, he shifted his attention to the papers she was waiting for. Across the top of the first yellow page, in her small, neat script, were the words *To Do,* followed by, *Buy house, Move furniture from storage, Utilities* and *Move checking account.* The second page held the heading *Leesburg Independent.* Listed beneath that were *Local organizations, School activities and sports, Local politics* and *Recipes.*

"What are you working on?"

He had just uncovered the list marked *Goals.* Before he could read it, she rescued all her notes from his hand. "I don't think you're that bored."

If Annie hadn't snatched her notes back, Jett might not have pressed. But she had seemed a little too anxious to keep him from seeing the rest of whatever it was she'd written for him to let it go.

"I didn't ask because I'm bored. I asked because I want to know."

His narrowed eyes moved from the pages she'd turned facedown next to her coffee cup to the papers on the table. All fifty-two of last year's local editions were spread over it. Closest to him was yesterday's want ads. "What is all this?"

"The want ads are for houses. Everything the Realtor showed me yesterday was either big enough to house a small battalion or on the verge of collapse."

"You're moving to Leesburg?"

"You say that as if I shouldn't."

"What you do is your business. It's just that there's nothing here but a Podunk town, land and cows."

"And my family," she expanded, thinking it rather sad that he couldn't see that he had the same. Or, if he could, that it seemed to make so little difference to him. He had a brother and sister-in-law in Leesburg; the same, plus nieces and nephews, at the ranch. He had next to nothing to do with any of them. "My sisters and I haven't lived in the same place for over eighteen years. Even when we did, we moved every couple of years, because Dad was in the military. Sam and Lindsey have finally made real homes here. That's what I want, too." She paused, too curious not to ask. "Don't you ever miss being home? Or having one?"

The look he gave her was deceptively even. "No."

"No? Just like that?"

"Just like that," he repeated flatly, then gestured toward the older newspapers. "What are you doing with those?"

There had been a time when Annie would have found his unequivocal denial sad. Part of her still did. But there was a larger part—an unfamiliar, frightened part—that actually envied his ability to feel so little about something so basic. That was what she wanted so badly to learn to do. To feel nothing for everything that had once mattered so much.

"Research for my new job," she hurried to say, suddenly grateful for the change of subject, blatant though it had been. "I'm supposed to start work a week from Monday at the *Independent*. I'm only going to be the inside office person, but if the editor gets desperate, maybe I can do a story once in a while." She pulled out the list headed with the name of the newspaper, shrugging as it landed on the table. "I'm trying to figure out what sort of stories to look for."

"If you're that unenthused about the job, why are you taking it?"

The question threw her. So did his perception.

"I didn't say I wasn't enthused about it."

The sound he made was halfway between a chuckle and a snort. "You didn't have to. When a person is starting something new, a little anticipation is usually in order. Why take a job you have so little interest in?"

Had anyone else asked such a question, Annie would have waved it off with a smile and the assurance that she was most definitely excited about her new position. After all, it would be the expected thing to do. She had a new beginning—of course she should be excited about it. But something about the man quietly watching her told her he didn't give a damn about "should." There was something just a little freeing in that.

"It's not that I'm not interested," she contended, afraid to consider just how much of her life had been restricted by what had been expected of her. What she'd expected of herself. "I was a journalism major before I married Rob. Working on a paper is something I always wanted to do. I've just never done it before."

"If it was something you always wanted to do, why not?"

Because there was something I wanted far more.

At the thought, she crossed her arms over the little knot of anxiety pushing under her heart.

"We'd planned to start our family right away," she told him, skimming over the fact as if the years of trying to get, and stay, pregnant hadn't been like riding the worst sort of emotional roller coaster. Few who hadn't suffered the ordeal could truly appreciate the distance between anticipation and disappointment. "So I never went to work. I spent most of my time volunteering at air base preschools."

"So where are they now?"

"They?"

"Your children."

Her glance faltered, the light in her eyes going out so quickly Jett wondered if he'd only imagined the pain that shot through them before she unwound herself and turned away. With her back to him, she began to straighten an already neat stack of papers.

"We never had any," she said, in a voice so quiet he barely heard her. She gathered her notes, stacking them, too. "You wanted the newspaper." At the reminder, she reached for the sections under the want ads. "I think it's under here."

She had barely started to lift the paper when Jett put his hand on top of it to keep it in place. Ignoring her puzzled glance, hating the way she froze when his arm skimmed hers as he reached past her, he turned over the list she'd been so anxious that he not see.

The one marked *Goals*.

It was not at all what he would have expected of her. She apparently had only two. On the first line, she'd written *Pick up*. On the one below that, *Move on*. The words had been traced over so many times that the paper was nearly cut through.

"These are your goals?"

There probably wasn't another person on the planet to whom she would have felt comfortable admitting such a thing. She didn't exactly feel comfortable admitting them to Jett, either. But she needed to know how to reach those goals. And of all people, Jett should understand.

"I've been thinking about something you said the other night," she explained, hugging her arms around her middle again. "About the way you accept what happens to you. Is it really so easy for you to just pick up and move on when something sets you back? To not let what happens make any difference?"

Jett felt his jaw tighten, the reaction instinctive. There had been no challenge in her question. Annie wasn't criticizing, or judging him for the way he chose to live his life. All he saw in the depths of her golden-brown eyes was interest.

"Why do you want to know?"

"I just thought that if I could understand how you did it, maybe I could do it, too."

The simplicity of her admission caught Jett as unprepared as her question. It also left him with the feeling that she was struggling with something she couldn't seem to get past, the thing that had robbed her of her vitality and left her . . . afraid.

"There's nothing complicated about putting one foot in front of the other," he told her, not particularly proud of his technique, even less sure it would help her. A man did what he had to do to survive. Walk. Run. Crawl. At one time or another, he'd done them all. "What takes practice is learning to not look back."

"How much practice?"

She looked very much as if she needed his answer. That she needed anything from him at all should have had him backing off. He was the wrong person for her to come to for advice. For anyone to come to, for that matter. Instead, he found himself wishing he knew what to say to take the desolation from her eyes.

"I don't know for sure, Annie. But I've been at it since I was fifteen."

Chapter Five

Annie didn't get a chance to ask Jett what had happened when he was fifteen. The phone interrupted. Even if it hadn't, Annie had the feeling Jett had volunteered about all he'd cared to. By the time the first ring ended, he'd shoved his fingers through his hair and stepped back. Halfway through the second, he'd said he had to go and headed for the door.

She had received the answer to her question, though—and she found his solution as disturbing as the ease with which she'd turned to him for advice. She would never have let on to either of her sisters that she harbored far more anxiety than enthusiasm about her move there. She was having to create an entirely new existence for herself, one without all the elements that had held her previous life together. The prospect scared her silly. But whenever she talked with Sam or Lindsey, she kept her fears to herself. She didn't want them worrying about her any more than they already did—

and she couldn't bear to hear one more time that she should stop worrying herself because everything would work out just fine.

With Jett, though, she'd been free to seek the advice she needed. He was as unlikely a confidant as she would ever find, but he had recognized her fear. In some tacit way, he had understood. Just as she was beginning to understand him.

It was with that thought that, several hours later, Annie popped the lid on the breadmaker and dumped the raw dough on the counter. Ever since Jett had left this morning, she had been replaying their conversation, and coming to the same conclusion. He had said there was nothing difficult about putting one foot in front of the other, about moving on. The hard part was learning not to look back.

White flour drifted like smoke over the dough as she brushed it from her hands and began to form balls for rolls. She couldn't help but think that moving around as he did with his work was how Jett avoided whatever he'd left behind. When something went wrong, he simply moved on to a new place totally different from the last. Maybe he even moved on before something could go wrong, or before a situation got too complicated. She could certainly see him doing that, expert as he was at keeping his distance.

The only problem with his solution was that being on the move made it impossible to establish roots or routine; Jett undoubtedly regarded that as a plus. To Annie, it was his solution's biggest drawback. She needed stability far too much to ever find the solution to her own needs in wanderlust.

With a sigh of frustration, she stretched off another piece of dough and wadded it into a ball. There was still a lot to be said for putting one foot in front of the other and not looking back. It was learning how to do the latter part that presented the problem. Or so she was thinking when she heard the kids come through the mudroom door.

Michael and Amy had wanted to walk home from the bus stop this afternoon, so Annie had agreed to let them—provided it wasn't raining and they stayed out of mud puddles. From the looks of Michael as he threw down his backpack and yanked off his jacket, either the puddles had all dried up, or he'd actually listened. There wasn't a speck of mud on him anywhere. He had, however, managed to grind dirt and grass into the backside of his jeans.

"Where's Amy?" she asked, wondering what it was about boys and dirt that made them so inseparable.

"She's coming," Michael mumbled, throwing his jacket on the floor, rather than over its peg.

Annie was about to tell him to pick it up and try again when he turned. The moment he did, she forgot all about the jacket and about telling him he was supposed to stay with his sister when they walked.

She'd expected his blond hair to be tousled and windblown. She'd even expected him to be dirty. She had not, however, expected him to look as if he'd done battle with a bulldog.

He was holding one hand over his right eye, and the neck of his baggy purple shirt was ripped.

"Michael! What happened to you?"

"Nothing," he muttered as the back door slammed open again and Amy came running in.

Ducking his head as Annie started toward him, Michael picked up his pace and scooted right past her.

"Michael, come back here. Let me see you."

"Michael got in a fight," the little girl panted. Her cheeks pink from running, and quite out of breath, Amy dropped her raspberry-colored backpack on the floor and began pulling off her coat. "Billy Hewlett hit him."

Michael didn't respond. He'd just kept going, head down and hiding his eye as he marched himself through the kitchen and the entry and straight up the stairs. Annie, brushing her hands off on her sister's barbecue apron, was right behind him.

Right behind her was Amy.

Right behind Amy, yapping at his young mistress for ignoring him, was Spot.

The door to Michael's room slammed before Annie made it to the top of the stairs. The angry click of the lock came an instant later.

Too concerned to be deterred, Annie tried the door anyway. When all the knob did was rattle in place, she called out again. "Let me in, Michael. I need to make sure you're all right."

"Go away."

"Not until I'm sure you're okay. I know you've hurt your eye. Are you hurt anyplace else?"

"No." Several seconds of silence were followed by a sullen "Leave me alone."

There was far more injured male pride in his wavering voice than disrespect. Already, at the tender age of ten, testosterone demanded that he suffer his wounds alone.

"I need to see you for myself," Annie insisted anyway. "Let me in so I can make sure your eye isn't going to fall out or something. Okay?"

Silence.

She hadn't seen any blood. Taking that as a positive sign, she relaxed her approach. "Can you at least tell me what happened?"

"You wouldn't understand."

"How do you know? You haven't tried to talk to me yet."

"You're not a guy."

He had her there.

Amy tugged her sleeve. "Uncle Jett is."

Annie glanced down at the sweet-faced child hugging her squirming pet. Jett was, indeed, a guy. There were a couple of problems with that particular solution, however. The most immediate being proximity.

"I don't know where your uncle Jett is, Amy. He doesn't usually show up for another hour or so."

Her button nose wrinkling in confusion, Amy pointed in the direction of the long polished banister. "But he's right there."

Annie's head jerked to the stairway. Jett stood at the bottom, a denim jacket hanging open over his faded jeans and his dark hair dented by the black hat he held clinched by its brim at his side. Wherever it was that he went on his rides, it seemed to be doing him as much good as bed rest, and he appeared to have spent time in the day's sun. His face had more tan to it, making the lines fanning from the corners of his eyes more noticeable and turning his eyes the clear blue of a summer sky.

She'd been attracted to spit and polish all her life. From her father to her husband and the couple of boyfriends in between. Refusing to wonder what it was about Jett's rugged look that she found so appealing, Annie curved her hand over Amy's shoulder.

"What are you doing back so early?"

"I need something from Logan's office." His dark eyebrows lowered. Though he looked as if he'd rather not ask, he did anyway. "What's all the commotion about?"

Annie's glance darted to Amy. Turning her around, Annie knelt in front of her and undid the rest of the buttons on her coat. "I need to talk to your uncle, honey. Be a good girl and get an apple and some peanut butter for a snack, and I'll be down in a few minutes."

"For Michael, too?"

"For Michael, too."

"Is he all right?"

"He'll be fine." Annie offered the assurance along with a quick hug. "We'll take care of him. Okay?"

The little girl's quiet "Okay" didn't sound terribly convinced. But she did as she was told and headed down the stairs. Annie followed, hesitating two steps above Jett while Amy wandered on to the kitchen with Spot trotting faithfully behind her.

"Michael has locked himself in his room and won't come out," she quietly explained to Jett, her voice low. "Amy said he got into a fight. He needs you to talk to him."

"Me?" In deference to the child behind the door at the top of the stairs, Jett kept his voice down, too. He did not, however, bother to remove the reluctance from it. "Why?"

"Because you're a guy. His uncle," she added, hoping he wouldn't rely on the fact that he was actually the children's stepuncle to absolve him of responsibility.

Jett didn't seem to care about the finer points. Looking as if he wished he'd kept on going when he came in, he shook his head and turned on his boot heel. "I don't know anything about kids. I sure as hell don't know what to say to one who's just gotten into a fight."

"Weren't you ever in one?"

His jaw locked.

"Come on, Jett," she coaxed. "You said you owe me."

Her words stopped him in his tracks.

She lost some of her height advantage when she moved down the steps. To make up for it, she tipped up her chin. "If you really want to pay me back, this is how you can do it."

Feeling as if he were being turned against his will, Jett faced the quiet determination in Annie's eyes. That glint of steel surprised him a little, small and delicate as she was. Or maybe what it did was disarm him. Standing with her hands on her hips and her chin in the air, she reminded him of a little banty hen protecting her chick. She would do whatever it took to see that her charge was cared for—so she'd called him on the one thing she knew he couldn't ignore.

Exasperation tightened his mouth. "Annie," he began, finding it odd how simply saying her name eased the edge in his tone. "I'm the wrong person for this."

"You're the only person for this right now. You don't have to know anything about kids," she explained, not sure what he doubted more just then, her judgment or himself. "This is a guy thing."

"A guy thing?"

"You know what I mean." Fighting exasperation herself, she motioned back up the staircase. "Just find out if he's all right, will you? He was keeping his right eye covered, so I know there's something wrong with it. And ask him what happened. He needs you to talk to."

Jett didn't believe for a moment that he would do the boy any good. But he would do what she asked. He wouldn't be happy about it. But he'd do it. Only because he owed her.

A little resentful of that fact, he brushed past her on the stairs. Taking the steps two at a time to get the ordeal over with, he paused by the door at the top, then knocked and asked if he could come in. It took a few seconds to get a response, but he finally heard the click of the lock and the door cracked open.

Annie was right at his elbow.

Seeing her, Michael started to close the door.

Jett's big hand stopped it.

"Come on, Michael. Let me see that." Pushing the door in, Jett reached out and eased his fingers around the boy's wrist to pull his hand away. Air whistling between his teeth, he shook his head. "I'd say you're going to have a real beaut, pal. Get us a piece of steak, Annie."

"How about an ice bag?"

"Steak's better. Just make sure it's cold and dry." He tipped the boy's head back, his big hands gentle as he checked out the small scrape above Michael's eyebrow. "We'll need some tweezers and iodine, too."

She was being dismissed. That was blatantly obvious from the way Jett arched his eyebrow in her direction when she moved closer to see the scrape herself. The perception was compounded by the fact that he didn't say another word until she turned around to do as he asked.

She was at the door when Michael plopped down on the edge of his bed and wrapped his arms around a Houston Rockets pillow. One last glance and she saw that Jett had tossed his jacket over the chair he'd pulled out from Michael's cluttered desk and turned the chair to straddle it.

It wasn't until she was out of sight that she heard his quiet "Are you all right?"

Annie hurried down the stairs, checking on Amy before heading first for the freezer, so she could thaw the requested steak in the microwave, then to the medicine cabinet. Though she personally doubted the advantage of steak over an ice pack, she was glad Jett had shown up when he had. Otherwise, it could have been another hour or two before he came back to the house and Michael opened that door. She had no idea where Jett spent his days. He wasn't with Hank or the ranch hands. She knew that much because the foreman had come to the house a few hours ago looking for him. All she knew was what Hank had told her himself. Jett saddled up the same horse every morning and headed east. Since he could ride for fifty miles in that direction and never leave the RW's boundaries, he could be going just about anywhere.

With the thawed steak on folded paper towels and a side of ointment and tweezers in hand, Annie reached the top of the staircase just as Michael was telling Jett that Billy Hewlett had been picking on him for weeks. Michael swore that he'd never done anything to Billy. Why would he? The kid was a sixth-grader and twice his size. "The only reason I shoved him back when he shoved me this time was because I was sick of what he was saying."

"What was he saying?" Jett ventured, caution heavy in his voice.

Michael's tone, low and petulant, dropped a notch. "He said I can't call Logan 'Dad' because he isn't my real father."

Annie was an arm's length from the door. When she heard the hurt beneath the child's bravado, it was all she could do to make herself stop.

Every instinct she possessed told her to march right past Jett, pull her nephew into her arms and tell him that that little brat Billy had absolutely no business saying such a thing to him. But a feeling that was equally strong kept her right where she was. This was between Michael and his uncle. She'd made a point of that herself with Jett. She just hadn't expected that he'd have to deal with something so unfamiliar. From his hesitation, it was apparent that he was on totally foreign ground.

Or so she thought.

"Billy doesn't know what he's talking about," she finally heard Jett say. "He's just being a bully, and a bully needs to make other people feel bad to make themselves feel big.

"As for what he said about Logan," he continued, then suddenly fell silent.

Annie couldn't see him. She could hear the rustle of clothing, though, the sound making her think he might have pushed his fingers through his hair while he searched for the words he needed.

When he started speaking again, whatever hesitation he'd felt was gone. "Any man can make a baby, Michael. What counts is how a man treats a child. Logan treats you like a man should treat his son. And you seem to think of him as your father. Next time Billy starts in on you, just tell him that what he thinks doesn't matter to you in the least, and walk off. If he comes after you, you just be quicker than he is and get out of his way. Any idiot can throw a punch. It takes a real man to walk away from a fight."

Annie quietly moved to the doorway, her glance darting from the boy on the bed to the big man straddling the chair in front of him. She didn't know if Jett was even conscious of how he'd placed the chair like a barrier between him and Michael. Or how generous and wise his words had been. But she knew he greatly underestimated his ability to ease the mind of a young, impressionable boy—where his relationship with his stepfather was concerned, anyway.

Michael was still contemplating his uncle's words when Jett glanced toward her, then stood up. Noticing her himself, the boy let out a sigh and tipped his head back to look up at Jett.

"It'd sure be easier if I was big. I'll bet nobody ever picked on you."

"You'd lose. Come on. Let's get this on your eye before it swells shut."

It hadn't occurred to Annie that Jett intended to take care of Michael himself. Yet that was exactly what he did. She had scarcely moved close enough to get a good look at what was going to be truly a Technicolor shiner when Jett took the palm-size, inch-thick steak from the paper towels she held. Covering Michael's puffy, reddened eye with it, he guided Michael's hand up to hold it in place. Then, looking as if he'd done this all before, he tipped the boy's head back and turned it to the overhead light.

"You only lost the top layer," he advised him encouragingly. "But you've got gravel in it." With a glance toward Annie that said the damage really could have been worse, he took the tweezers she held out. "Did you take a header when he belted you?"

Though Annie was listening to Michael while he reluctantly admitted that was exactly what had happened, it was Jett who had her attention. Specifically, his hands. They were a workingman's hands. Big, callused and rough. Much like the man himself. Yet there was a gentle quality to his touch, and an improbable delicacy about the way he handled the small tweezers to remove the tiny bits of dirt and rock from the raw wound.

This was a man who operated massive machinery, who moved boulders and mountains and dug holes in the earth. Yet he had the touch of a surgeon.

Struck by the incongruity, she let a curious glance drift to his profile. There was strength in his features, a nobility about them that spoke of integrity. There was honor in him, too. Had there not been, he would have ignored the obligation he'd insisted he had to her and walked off when she asked for his help. But she had the feeling he would deny the existence of such traits. Just as he would deny the compassion she'd glimpsed this morning, and the sensitivity he was showing now.

Michael's head was tipped back, one hand holding the meat in place while Jett searched out pieces of gravel. "There was somebody who picked on you when you were a kid?"

"Sure was," came Jett's deceptively easy reply. He dropped another bit of grit into Annie's outstretched palm and zeroed in on another. "I had more black eyes than you can count. I was about your age, too. Only I was a lot smaller than you.''

Abject disbelief swept Michael's expression. The man towering over him was the size of a small mountain. ''No way.''

A faint smile touched Jett's mouth. It wasn't much of one, as smiles went. But it was enough to tell Michael that he was flattered by the disbelief—and to let Annie know that, should he ever manage a smile for real, the effect would be devastating.

''You know that tractor down by the storage barn? I couldn't reach the step without boosting myself off the shovel arm until I was twelve.''

Apparently convinced that the man wasn't pulling his leg, Michael focused on him with his unimpeded eye. ''Is that how you used to get away from him? By talking your way out of it and being quicker?''

''Mostly by being quicker. This guy never listened when you talked.''

''I guess he caught you, though, huh?''

Jett's guarded glance met the boy's, then moved back to the scrape. ''Lots of times.''

''That must be where you learned about the steak, huh?''

''Yeah,'' Jett muttered, then handed Annie the tweezers. ''Where's the iodine?''

The man was far better with children than he'd thought. Wondering if *he* realized that, she held up a tube of antibiotic ointment. ''That stuff stings. Use this.''

Annie wasn't quite sure what to make of the indulgent look Jett leveled at her before he took the tube and the adhesive strip she'd also brought. But she did know that he felt her presence was no longer required when he turned back to Michael and said he could take it from there. Sure that he could, Annie told Michael to come down for a snack if he was hungry. Then, feeling it was only right, she invited Jett to supper.

"There's something I want to do before the sun goes down," he told her, tearing the wrapper on the adhesive strip with his teeth. "Thanks, anyway."

That was the first time he'd had a reason other than that he was going to bed for refusing to join them for a meal. But she remembered that he had come back to the house for something specific and she had sidetracked him. Hoping he still had time to do whatever it was, and trying not to be too curious about it, Annie headed back to her rolls.

Annie had wiped the peanut butter off Amy and the table and sent her in to watch television with Spot when Jett walked into the kitchen a few minutes later. Glancing up from the pan of rolls she was forming, she watched him drop his jacket and a long roll of yellowed paper atop a stool on his way to the sink.

"Michael said he isn't hungry," he told her, taking a glass from the cabinet. "He wants to stay in his room until supper."

The message delivered, Jett turned on the tap.

Setting the walnut-size ball of dough next to two others in the cupcake tin, Annie let her glance drift over his broad back. "You know, Jett," she began, needing him to know how much he'd helped, "what you said to Michael about Logan had to put his mind at ease. The kids had it really rough when they lost their dad and had to move from California. Logan has filled a big gap in their lives."

She knew Jett heard her. But his only response was the tightening of his mouth before he turned off the water.

"And your advice for handling Billy," she continued, only to cut herself off. She didn't want to sound as if she hadn't expected such wisdom from him. "I'm just glad you were here. I'm sure Michael is, too."

Jett had turned his head slightly, listening, but not looking at her. Something like skepticism pinched his brow. A moment later, his attention on the pattern of the glass he'd just filled, he offered a quiet "Thanks."

"It's no wonder he hasn't wanted to go to school lately," she went on, thinking Jett looked as if he didn't believe he'd done all that much. "I know Sam and Logan didn't know about what was going on."

"It's not the kind of thing a boy's likely to mention."

She didn't suppose it was. It seemed to Annie that males were genetically disposed to keep their hurts to themselves. By the time they were grown, some of them had even numbed themselves to feeling hurt at all.

Or maybe, she thought, watching Jett drain the tumbler of water, what they did was refuse to admit they felt it.

"It'll be another week before Sam and Logan get home. Do you think we should call the principal? Or that boy's parents? We can't let that little creep Billy do this to him again."

Jett felt himself hesitate. *We,* she'd said, as if they were somehow in this together.

Feeling the tension in his body change quality, he set the glass in the sink and turned to face her. Upstairs, he'd tried very hard to ignore the effects her proximity invariably had on him. He had yet to get within a dozen feet of her without wanting to feel her hands on him again. What he wanted even more was to feel her body against his, to mold her to him, to make her feel what he felt just watching her now. The entire time she stood at his elbow while he worked on Michael, he had consciously fought thoughts of how it would feel to slide his hands under the predictably loose shirt she wore and discover all there was to know about her feminine shape.

He hadn't succeeded in those efforts, though. Ignoring her was impossible. Even now, he wanted to walk over to her, ease her into his arms and taste the sweetness of her tempting mouth. But he wouldn't. She would shy from his touch as surely as she had this morning. Aside from that, he had no business wanting a woman who was a natural with kids, who chose medicine because it didn't sting, and who managed to look totally captivating with flour on her apron and bread dough in her hands.

"Well?" she prodded, obviously waiting for him to make up his mind.

This was his chance. The one that up until a few days ago he would not have hesitated to take. All he had to do was tell her he'd done what she asked, that they were even now, and leave it at that. The fact that his opinion actually seemed to matter to her shouldn't have made any difference at all. But it did. And it felt kind of good to know she thought he might have actually helped the kid upstairs.

"I'll ask him what he wants. Maybe he'll just want a chance to see if he can handle it on his own."

She didn't look entirely sold on that idea. "You don't think I should call the principal in the morning so Billy can be talked to? If that boy is so much bigger and he really has it in for him, Michael won't have much of a chance without someone to defend him."

A glint like light bouncing off polished steel flashed in Jett's eyes. "Give him a while. If that kid really has it in for him, the best thing for Michael to do is learn how to take care of himself. There won't always be someone around to defend him."

Be quicker than he is and get out of the way.

That was the advice Jett had given Michael. Sensible, certainly. Enlightening, too, considering that the man giving it could probably make mincemeat of any moron wanting a fight. She appreciated his nonviolent approach. She could even appreciate why they didn't see eye-to-eye on the matter of calling the principal right away. The male wanted to give the child a chance to prove himself; the female wanted to protect. What she didn't understand was the sudden hardness in Jett's voice.

It was the same steely edge she'd heard yesterday, when he'd seen the bruises on her wrist. He'd identified the marks as if he were personally familiar with that telltale pattern. Recalling that now, she also remembered what he'd said after he'd admitted to Michael that there was someone who'd picked on him, too, when he was Michael's age.

I had more black eyes than you could count.

"Who was the kid you told Michael about...the one who gave you so much trouble?"

If he was surprised by her question, he didn't let it show. "It wasn't a kid. It was Ben."

"Ben?"

"My father. Look," he muttered as the color drained from her cheeks, "I've got to go." A quick glance out the window behind him, and he swore. The sun was lower than he'd thought. "Tell Michael I'll be back in a couple of hours."

"Jett?"

He had already picked up his jacket and the rolled-up paper and started toward the door. The step she took put her directly in front of him.

He didn't expect what he saw in her face. It wasn't pity. He couldn't have handled that. It wasn't even shock, though he figured someone of her sensibilities might find his earlier years . . . regrettable. What he saw troubling the depths of her eyes looked more like pain.

That she should feel something like that for him touched a part of him he hadn't even known was alive. Or maybe, he thought, aware of a sensation that was more heat than weight, it was her fingers curling over his forearm that made him feel that way.

"Your father?"

He didn't want her concern. But he couldn't bring himself to step back from it, either. "It was a long time ago," he told her, not sure how he could crave something he'd never known before. "It doesn't matter."

"Oh, Jett. Do you really believe that?"

"What good would it do if I didn't?" Soft as a caress, his glance skimmed her face. "It wouldn't change anything. If I let it bother me, I'd just be giving him more power."

"Giving? Isn't your father—? I mean, I thought both of your parents were gone."

"They are. I just mean there's no sense giving the circumstances control. What happened . . . happened. It's over and done with."

His words were harsh, his expression was not. Refusing to ask any more questions about what he chose to forget, she searched the hard, handsome lines of his face. He wasn't shutting her out, as he so easily could have done. But he wasn't really letting her in, either.

"This is one of those things you never look back on, isn't it?" The flatness of her voice made her words a statement.

"I guess you could say that."

Her smile was sad, almost wistful. "I wish I could be like you."

Soft, unwittingly provocative, her voice skimmed along Jett's nerves.

"You don't know what you're wishing for, Annie." She couldn't possibly. "You don't want to be like me."

Oh, yes, she did, she thought, drawn by the strength in him. He didn't believe in giving more power to people or circumstances that had hurt or harmed in the past by letting them ruin his future. However he managed it, he simply relegated the past to its proper place and got on with the present.

Had it not been for the dull roar of a vehicle pulling up out back, she might have told him she admired him for that, too. Now, aware that someone would be at the back door any moment, she pulled her hand back from his arm and stepped away.

Chapter Six

The magnificent animal Jett had ridden to the house stood saddled and snorting at the long hitching rail at the far edge of the lawn. A few feet from the beautiful horse, one of the ranch's Jeeps sat idling while Hank headed at a bowlegged lope toward the back door.

Annie met him there, opening the inner door as he pulled his perpetually unlit cigar from beneath his grizzled mustache and snatched his battered dirt-brown hat from his balding head.

"Ma'am," he muttered, nodding politely through the screen. "Sorry to bother you, but I saw the bay Jett's been riding tied up over there and figured this is where he must be. You mind getting him for me?"

"I'm right here."

Annie hadn't realized how close Jett was until she started to step back from where she was blocking the door. He was right behind her, his hand settling on her upper arm as she backed into him. Flush against her, apparently thinking only to invite Hank in, he reached past her other shoulder to push open the screen.

He was only there for seconds. Just long enough for Hank to give his hat a thwack on his thigh to rid it of a puff of dust and take hold of the wood-framed door himself. But those seconds were all it took for Jett's hard length to sear her from the nape of her neck to the curve of her backside, and for her to go as still as the afternoon air.

Jett must have felt her stiffen. His hand fell the moment Hank pulled the screen door wide. He stepped back, looking to Annie as if he wished he'd been thinking more about what he was doing than about what the old guy might want.

What *she* wanted was to understand why, even now, she could feel his heat humming through her. Feeling more unsettled by the second, Annie aimed a faint smile toward Hank, skimmed it past Jett's chin and slipped through the kitchen doorway to leave the men alone.

"You're harder to find than a tick on a sheepdog," Hank muttered, too busy scraping the mud from his boots to notice the tight set of Jett's jaw. "I've been all over hell's half acre trying to track you down. Saw the horse you've been riding and figured I'd best get up here before you took off again.

"I got a problem up on that feeder stream in section four," he went on, stepping inside to prop himself against the clothes dryer. With a snort, he stuffed his cigar back in his mouth, now that the lady was gone. "That rain we had a few days ago swelled it up and washed an orchard's worth of branches downstream. Now it's all dammed up and barely a trickle's getting through. Logan's got three hundred head running in that section, too."

"You want me to help you clean it out?"

"Hell, no. You just got to where you could saddle your own horse yesterday. Can't picture you out there lassoing stumps and dragging 'em out. What I need is for you to keep an eye on things down at the stable. One of the mares looks like she could foal here in the next day or two. I don't expect it'll happen tonight, but in case I don't get back before morning, I'd appreciate it if you'd check on her once in a while. Logan's been looking forward to that particular foal. Empress throws some of his best cutting stock.

"I know he trusts you with his horses," he added, the ten years he'd spent on this ranch giving him considerable insight where his boss was concerned. "I wouldn't be asking, otherwise."

Jett glanced down at the rolled plat map in his hand. What he had wanted to do could wait. All he'd wanted was to satisfy his curiosity, anyway, and he always did what he could for Logan when he was around. After what Logan had done for him, it was the least he could do.

"I don't remember which one Empress is. I'll follow you now and you can show me which mare you're talking about. I noticed a couple of 'em down there that're about ready."

Jett was going to stay at the stable for a while. At least that was what Michael told Annie after Jett chased him up to the house because it was past his bedtime. Michael didn't say what else they'd talked about, though, and Annie didn't ask. The boy was tired and, after what he'd gone through that day, she figured the best thing for him to do was go straight to bed. She could find out from Jett what the verdict was on talking with the principal when he came back to the house.

Only he didn't come back. When nine o'clock rolled by, then ten, and there was still no sign of him, Annie decided to head for the stable herself. She really did need to know what to do about Michael in the morning. As she pulled her sweatshirt jacket around her and stepped out into the cool night air, she also had to admit that she was a little concerned about Jett.

She knew he'd told Hank he would keep an eye on a horse. After all, it had been impossible not to overhear everything the two men said. But it hadn't sounded to her as if the man had meant for him to spend the night in the stable. Jett was usually back inside long before now, closed up in his room, sleeping. He was showing little evidence of the illness and injury that had brought him here, other than favoring his left side once in a while. But it had been less than a week since he'd arrived so sick he could barely stand. He needed his rest. Not that she was going to tell him that. He'd made it clear enough that she was not to concern herself with his welfare. That didn't mean she couldn't take turns sitting with the mare for him. Not that she knew a thing about horses.

Gravel crunched beneath her feet as she left the house's big, grassy yard and headed down the wide road that led to the heart of ranching operations. Her way was lit by huge halogen lights atop twenty-foot poles that seemed to attract every moth for miles. Probably for the heat as much as for the light, she thought, shivering.

It was cool out. Not icy-cold, as it would be in northern climes this time of year. Spring was already arriving in Texas. But it was cool enough to make her wish she'd put on something heavier than the single layer of fleece covering her cotton sweater.

She didn't know if the stables were heated. The only thing she knew for certain about the ranch was that the huge white barn on the far side of the acrewide workyard was the building that housed Logan's prize bulls, and that the horse corral and stable were at the opposite end of the complex.

What the buildings in between were for was anyone's guess. She never came down here. The one time she had, when Logan had given them all a tour the day after the wedding, she'd found it all pretty overwhelming. After all, she'd been a navy brat, raised around concrete, military housing and homes in the suburbs near navy bases. She'd been an officer's wife, which had simply meant more of the same. She knew PXs and city supermarkets and how to buy the freshest fish from shops at the beach. What she knew about beef cattle was limited strictly to the cuts at the meat counter.

She could, however, tell a whinny from a moo. The soft nickering of a horse told her she was headed in the right direction.

Jett saw Annie coming long before she saw him. He stood just inside in the open doorway of the darkened stable, protected by the shadows as he watched her approach. She was looking around as she walked, her shoulders hunched against the cold and her hands jammed into the pockets of a dark jacket that reached her knees. The chill breeze ruffled her short hair, the bright vapor lights picking out the strands of gold to form a halo around her head.

An angel called Annie, he thought, his lips pressed in a grim line. Tender of the ill, defender of the underdog. A woman of compassion and beauty. And she wanted to be like him.

The woman was operating a card short of a full deck. So was he, for letting her get to him.

He took a step back, retreating farther inside, but still watching her as she reached the railings of the first corral.

He didn't know why he'd admitted what he had to her about Ben. It certainly wasn't anything he'd ever told anyone before. Not even Logan knew how bad things had become those last couple of years. By then, Logan had been in college and was never around. Only his brother Cal had known. Cal, two years older, bigger, but still a kid himself. Cal had defended him, and Cal had helped him get away.

Jett could feel the tension creeping up the back of his neck. He wouldn't be thinking of any of this if he'd just kept his mouth shut. If Michael had pressed him on who the "kid" was, he'd simply have told him it was a jerk named Ben and let it go at that. But, like this morning when he and Annie had been in the dining room, something about her slipped right past his usual defenses. He didn't know what to make of her. Or of himself when he was with her. He just knew that he didn't trust what he felt. It was seductive and dangerous. And he knew better than to let down his guard.

Annie was twenty feet from the low rectangular building when she drew to a halt. She had reached the periphery of the yard lights, and the stable itself was dark. Looking around uncertainly, wondering if she had somehow missed Jett and he was already back at the house, she started to turn back. Just as she did, she saw a shape step from the shadows.

She knew by his size and by the way he carried himself that it was Jett. With the brim of his Stetson pulled low and the collar of his denim jacket turned up, she could see little of his expression. She didn't have to to know that his jaw was set hard. She recognized the tension in his stride, and in his stance when he stopped in front of her.

Unable to avoid absorbing that tension, she felt her smile falter. "It was so dark, I wasn't sure you were still down here."

"Horses like it quiet when they're getting ready to foal. They do better when they think no one's around." His voice was low, his explanation terse. "What are you doing down here?"

He never was in a good mood when he was tired. That much she knew for certain about him. Fairly sure that fatigue was at least part of his problem now, Annie pointedly overlooked the dismissal in his tone.

"I came to see what you and Michael decided. And to relieve you for a while," she added, hearing a deep, guttural grunt from inside the stable. "I don't know anything about horses, but if you'll tell me what to watch for, I'll come get you when it happens. This night air isn't doing your lungs any good."

Jett opened his mouth, then promptly closed it again. Had he not been distracted by the nature of the noises coming from inside the open doorway, he would have been in a better position to assert the defensiveness that usually served him so well. He didn't want it to matter that she was willing to sit in the dark and the cold for him so that he could get some rest. He didn't want it to matter, either, that despite his insistence that she not worry about him, she worried, anyway. Right now, he had a more pressing concern.

"Michael doesn't want us to do anything yet," he told her, his attention on the sounds coming from behind him. "And I need to stay here. I heard her water break a few minutes ago. She just went down."

Annie didn't ask what he meant. All she'd needed to hear was the part about water breaking to know that a birth was imminent.

"I thought Hank said she wouldn't be ready for another day or two."

"That's the way she looked to me, too." The brim of his hat shadowed his face completely when he turned to head into the stable. "She was fine when I first checked her, but she was pacing her stall when I got back a few hours ago."

"Can I come with you?"

Preoccupation outweighed invitation. "Suit yourself."

Jett's thoughts were clearly on the horse. There was no sense of urgency about him, though. Certainly there was none in his stride, even if it did take her two steps to every one of his to keep up with him.

Following his solid shape through the cavernous-looking doorway, Annie discovered that the stable wasn't quite as dark inside as it had first appeared. Heat lamps at the back of some of the stalls gave off a faint orange light, creating eerie shapes that danced along the low raftered ceiling. Those shapes turned to substance when Jett stopped at one of the stalls and flipped on its light. Though the buttery glow was mostly confined by the stall's floor-to-ceiling plank walls, the pale light spilling into the wide aisle was enough to reveal the stable's other occupants, craning their massive heads over their gates.

The scents of hay, horses and liniment blended in an earthy perfume. Breathing it in, finding it far less unpleasant than she'd thought she would, Annie stopped outside the gate Jett had opened.

She was not at all familiar with horseflesh. But the mare on the floor of the stall was huge. She was also absolutely beautiful. Her shiny, sweat-slicked coat was a rich chocolate, and her long mane and tail a darker shade of the same. A marshmallow-colored blaze swept up her noble forehead. Lying on her side, her head toward the gate, she took up all but a few feet on either side of the stall. Yet, as big as she was, there was still a delicacy about her that made Annie think she was far more fragile than she looked.

Or, maybe, Annie thought, straw crunching under her feet as she stepped inside the wooden walls, it was only the mare's vulnerability at the moment that made her seem that way. Her distended belly was huge, the look in her eyes wild as she strained with the contractions.

Thinking it might not have been such a good idea to come in here after all, Annie glanced to where Jett had crouched down to check the mare's progress. "Can you do anything for her?"

"There isn't anything to do." Without shifting his glance, Jett pulled off his hat and tossed it onto a wool blanket in the corner. "The mare does it all herself. Empress is an old hand at this. Aren't you, girl?" he murmured to the horse. Frowning at whatever he was looking at, he absently ran his hand over her rump to soothe her. "Logan said she's the best brood mare he's ever had."

The horse lay panting, nostrils wide. Her whole body seemed to vibrate with the rapidly drawn and exhaled breaths.

Suddenly conscious that her hands were covering her own stomach, Annie crossed her arms and stepped closer. As she did, the mare lifted her head, following her movement until Annie stopped a couple of feet from her muscular shoulder. Unsettled by her presence, but in no condition to do anything about it, the horse let her head fall to the straw.

To get out of her view, Annie moved toward her rump and crouched down, too. "Do you want me to rub her back?"

Pure confusion swept Jett's face. "What for?"

"It helps with the pain. That's where contractions start," she added, when he just kept looking confused. "It does in humans, anyway. Isn't that where they start in horses?"

"I can't say I've ever heard anyone mention it." The look he gave her said he wasn't sure why it would matter, either. "Their water breaks, they lay down, and five minutes later they've delivered a foal."

"Five minutes?" She spoke more in awe than in disbelief. "It can take a woman hours."

"Yeah," he muttered. "I've heard it can be pretty rough."

Annie's glance slid back to the mare. "It can," she murmured, tentatively touching the horse's sleek hide. Labor hurt. What did guys know, anyway?

At her quiet words, the quality of Jett's frown underwent a subtle change. Watching curiously, he saw Annie draw a few hesitant strokes along the mare's long back. She didn't seem afraid of the animal, just unfamiliar with it. It was only moments, though, before whatever hesitation she felt succumbed to her need to help and her small hands were massaging the contracting muscles. It wasn't what she was doing that held his attention. Or even thoughts of how she seemed so quick to offer comfort when she thought it was needed. It was the empathy behind her actions. That, and what she'd said. It sounded to him as if she were familiar with the pain of labor herself. Yet she'd said she didn't have any children.

The implications of that thought gave him pause. But the layers of self-protection that callused his heart had him turning back to the mare.

The furrows in his brow deepened.

Annie caught his concern. "Is something wrong?"

"Yeah, there is. As much as she's dilated, I should see forelegs and a nose by now." Shucking off his jacket, he tossed it over by his hat. A moment later, he was rolling the sleeves of his flannel shirt up to his elbows.

"There's a supply room on the other side of this stall," he told her, his tone suddenly urgent and clipped. "The light switch is inside the door on the left. Right next to it is a metal cabinet. Look in the drawers and see if you can find a box of plastic sleeves."

"Plastic sleeves?" she echoed, rising to her feet.

"They're kind of like long gloves. It'll say what they are on the box."

The other animals seemed to sense a change in the atmosphere as Annie hurried out of the stall. Agitated whinnies and the sounds of restless pacing joined the groan of door hinges as she pushed her way into the supply room and snapped on the overhead light.

Within thirty seconds, she'd handed Jett the box.

Thirty seconds after that, he had pulled one of the cellophane-looking "gloves" up to his shoulder and was kneeling behind the mare again. He reached forward, concentration written hard on his face. "I should be able to feel forelegs. And the nose should be...aw geez," she heard him mutter.

"What's wrong?"

His only response was a muttered oath.

"Jett?"

"I can't feel any hooves."

The horse gave another deep grunt, straining hard, eyes wild.

"Or a head." He swore again. "I'm not sure what I'm feeling in there. Either the head's tucked under, or it's coming breech."

Annie's worried glance darted from the veins bulging on the mare's head to the grim line of Jett's mouth. "Do you know what to do?"

He didn't answer. All he said was that they had to hurry as he stripped the sleeve off inside out, threw it onto the straw and grabbed two leads from a hook outside the stall. The only thing in their favor was the fact that Empress hadn't been pushing for very long. A horse couldn't take a lot of pain before it went into shock. If she started to hemorrhage, they'd lose her for sure. And the vet was twenty-two miles away.

Quicker than Annie could have imagined possible with Empress tossing her head as she was, Jett had the leads clipped to her halter and was tying off one end on a metal ring by the gate. The other end he secured around one of the four-by-fours that anchored the feed bin in the corner. Annie saw him wince when he then twisted around to pull another sleeve from the box, the movement reminding him that his ribs weren't yet healed, but he didn't slow for more than an instant.

"What are you going to do?"

"See if I can feel its hind legs." The fresh plastic sleeve crackled as he stuck his arm into it. "Maybe I can pull it out backward. You're going to have to hold that rope down when she tries to get up," he told her, pointing to the one angled toward the gate. "Lean on it if you have to. Stay behind her and away from her forelegs. And try to keep her calm."

Under any other circumstances, Annie would have appreciated the absurdity of his last instruction. Instead, feeling his tension, her own fear for the mare and her foal and a panic she didn't want to name, she sank into the straw by the horse's neck and tried to do as he'd asked. As quickly as Jett had taken command of the situation, she would just have to trust that he knew what he was doing.

Just to be sure, she had to ask. "Have you done this before?"

There was a moment's hesitation before Jett's tight "No." He'd never done this himself. But he had once seen it done with a calf. During the years he'd lived on the ranch, he had been around enough foalings and calvings, not to mention litters of dogs and barn cats, to understand that Mother Nature could usually do a fine job of getting the next generation here on her own. Once in a while, though, something went wrong. When it did, if man couldn't figure out what to do fast enough, another law of nature took over. The mare would rip herself apart trying to give birth. And the foal would die.

Once he'd told her that, Annie didn't ask any more questions. Anxiety pitted in her stomach, she grabbed at the rope when the horse struggled to pull herself away and tried not to think about what Empress was going through. The beautiful mare looked positively frantic, her huge head rearing up, then falling back down as she strained to push and Jett held the foal back to keep it from tearing her. She could see the strain in Jett, too, along with a certain detachment she desperately wished she could manage. He worked methodically, slipping his hand along the unborn foal the moment Empress stopped pushing, his face a study in concentration as he sought to save mother and offspring.

Annie knew the moment he found what he was looking for. Though tension remained in his features, he allowed himself a short, relieved breath. "I've got a hoof. If I can just get its mate and get the legs straightened out, we're halfway there."

Annie wasn't sure what all Jett did while she stroked and soothed the mare. But whatever it was worked. Empress gave another mighty push, and two long, slender legs emerged, tipped by two little hoofs. With Jett's assistance, a slick and shiny backside came next. Moments later, a wet and perfectly formed little colt was lying on the thick bed of hay, its tongue already licking in search of a meal. It even came complete with a knicker and a whinny. The equine version of baby's first cry.

"Unhook the leads. Just pull down the catch on the swivel hook," he added, when Annie looked uncertainly at the leather straps and metal rings of the horse's halter. "The one on her right first."

With Empress trying to shake her head, it took Annie three tries to get the hook undone. When she did, she immediately understood why Jett had wanted the right one undone first. It was the shorter tether, and it wouldn't have allowed the horse to reach her foal—which was precisely what Empress wanted to do.

The restraint was no sooner gone than Empress was scrambling to her feet, her great head swinging toward the little bundle trying to get its long, skinny legs beneath it. With a snuffle to its tiny black muzzle, she seemed to say, "So you're what gave me so much trouble," and dragged her long, pink tongue along the foal's neck to clean it.

With a shrug of his shoulders to loosen the knots, Jett leaned back on his haunches and stripped off the sleeve. Dropping it on the soiled straw, he drew the first easy breath to enter his lungs in the past ten minutes. Empress had made it back to her feet, just like the old trouper she was, and her new colt looked bright-eyed and healthy. It even bore his mother's arrowhead-shaped blaze on its forehead and matching stockings on its legs. That would please Logan.

Hands on his knees, Jett rose to his feet. Other than to stand up, too, Annie hadn't moved from her spot in the straw. She stood where she'd knelt, smiling at Empress tending her foal. He didn't doubt for a moment that she felt as relieved as he did. But the color had yet to return to her cheeks, and her paleness made her dark eyes look huge. Even though her lips were softly curved, there was sadness in her expression, an almost haunted quality that made her look far too vulnerable.

He wanted to ask if she was all right. But if she said she wasn't, he wouldn't know what to do to help. That he would want to was something he didn't have time to consider. Instead, thinking she looked as if she could use something to take her mind off whatever had put the shadows beneath her delight at the new foal, he snatched up one of the old towels he'd brought in with the blanket.

"Want to help her out?" he asked.

"How?"

He held out the rectangle of worn red terry cloth. "Dry him off."

Certain the concern she could see in Jett's eyes was for his charges, she took the towel with a quiet "Sure" as he turned to unhook Empress's other lead. A moment later, he was wiping sweat from the mare's neck and flank with a plastic scraper and telling the horse what a good job she'd done.

He seemed as comfortable working with a thousand pounds of magnificent muscle, sinew and raw power as she imagined he would be with a thousand tons of earth moving equipment. He knew exactly what he was doing with these animals. And he looked perfectly natural doing it.

She, on the other hand, was doing a terrible job of holding back unwanted memories as she started to gently rub Empress's baby boy dry. She had never even seen a newborn foal before, and cleaning up twenty-five pounds of horse that was mostly soft little whinnies and spindly legs was an experience not a single one of her baby books had prepared her for.

Don't look back, she told herself silently, repeating the words like a mantra. *Don't look back.*

The foal's pink tongue lapped at her hand, then at her knee. A moment later, it had hoisted its head as high as her chin.

"Jett?" Annie stopped rubbing, surprise diluting everything but fascination. "I think he's trying to stand up."

"Sure hope so. It's going to be hard for him to nurse from down there."

At his dry tone, Annie shot him a look of pure indulgence and turned back to the foal. The sweet little thing had his front legs stretched out and was trying to get his back legs out from under him. Back end wobbling, he got his backside up, but by the time that end was even with the front, his hind legs were stretched too far out to balance. In the hay again, he blinked up at Annie, as if to ask what had gone wrong.

Reassuring him that he was all right, Annie stroked the newborn's head. As she did, Jett crouched down beside her and ran his big hand down the foal's speckled back. "Handsome little thing, isn't he?"

Annie's response was one of quiet agreement, though she doubted Jett paid any attention to what she'd said. He wasn't talking to her. He was talking to himself. Now that he'd done whatever it was he'd needed to do with Empress, he'd turned his attention to the foal. Like a new father checking to make sure all the parts were there, he ran his hand down one foreleg, feeling the slender bones, checking the colt over as if to assure himself that it was, indeed, all right.

The corner of his mouth kicked up as the little fellow struggled upright once again. She'd never seen him smile like that before. So easily, and with such little reservation.

"You're good with animals."

Though his focus remained on the wobbly foal, his smile faded with his shrug. "I grew up with them."

"Just because you grew up with them, doesn't mean you'd necessarily be good with them. That was a compliment, Jett."

There was chiding in her tone. But it was the admiration in her quiet expression that caught him completely off guard. No one had ever looked at him that way before. As if they actually... respected him.

"I guess I did like being around them," he admitted, though he'd all but forgotten that himself. Even when he was at the ranch last year, he'd just done the work and not thought much about the animals themselves. "Not that it makes any difference."

"It made a difference to that little guy," Annie countered, nodding toward the foal. "If it hadn't been for you, he might not have made it. He's lucky you were here."

From down the aisle came the muffled shuffling of hay as the other horses began to settle down in their stalls. The old building creaked with the cold. Jett hardly noticed. He barely even noticed that he was getting cold himself, since his jacket was still in the corner. The haunted look had nearly faded from Annie's eyes, and the healing warmth in her smile was like a balm to his soul. She had a way of making him feel better about himself than he ever had—though he hadn't realized until just then how good it felt to have actually been needed. Twice now, she'd told him he had been.

That he might need *her* was something he refused to consider.

That he wanted her was a foregone conclusion.

Even now—especially now—he wanted to cup her face in his hands and drink so deeply of her that she would be clinging to him when he bent her back to bury himself in her softness.

The curve of her mouth slowly vanished, the fullness of her lower lip even more tantalizing than the smile had been. Pulling his glance before she could look away, he curled his fingers into his palm.

The last time he deliberately touched her—when he came up behind her to open the door for Hank—she'd gone as stiff as starched steel. That hadn't made a lick of sense to him, either. Only moments before, she'd had her hand curled around his arm.

He had no idea why she retreated from him when he initiated the contact. She felt what he felt. He could see it in her eyes. That gut-tightening awareness was there now. Guarded, definitely. Unwanted, probably. But he never pushed a woman. Either she came to him without hesitation or not at all. He wasn't about to ruin his good feelings about the evening by having her pull back from him again.

The colt, struggling up again, blinked at the towel Annie had used to wipe it off. To keep him from getting tangled up in it, Jett tossed it aside. "He's just about got the hang of it."

The soft expulsion of Annie's breath wasn't audible over the rustle of straw and the colt's soft nickering. Feeling more disappointment than relief that Jett's attention had been diverted, she followed his lead and concentrated on the colt. He made it all the way up this time, only he didn't seem to know where to go from there.

Annie understood the feeling completely.

Thinking it was pretty pathetic that she could relate so well to a horse, she held her hand out to steady the teetering little critter.

"That won't help."

Jett was right. The foal took one step and down he went.

"He'll be fine," he assured Annie, hearing her sympathetic sigh. "The way his tongue's going, he wants a meal too badly to stay down for long." Hauling himself to his feet, he picked up his jacket to keep from offering her a hand up and headed for the stall's open gate. "Why don't you go on up to the house? I'll be another hour here."

"Can I help with anything?"

He shook his head, trying hard not to change his mind. It would be better for them both if she left. "I'm just going to change the bedding and make sure he gets up and nursing."

With a nod, Annie stood up, too, brushing straw from her pants and jacket as she did. He wanted her to leave. And she really should go, as late as it was. But he had been up longer today than he had all week, and he was far more tired than she. Fatigue had carved itself into every masculine crease and angle of his face, the lines etched more deeply than she had seen them in days.

"If you're going to be another hour, do you want me to bring you some coffee, or something to eat?"

She wouldn't have been surprised if he told her not to bother. Instead, looking as if he really appreciated the offer, he told her coffee would be great and that he wouldn't mind a sandwich, if it wasn't too much trouble. He disappeared a second later to get a pitchfork, which left her with nothing to do but head back to the house.

She really would have preferred to stay. The last thing in the world she wanted was to be alone with the thoughts the birth of the foal had brought. Despite her best efforts to keep them at bay, those thoughts were never far from the surface. Neither was the emptiness that was so acute it haunted even her sleep. She couldn't remember the last time she'd slept through a night without awakening to that dull, aching sensation in her chest.

Everything had turned out all right tonight, though. Needing to focus on that thought, she mentally pasted pictures of a wobbly newborn foal over memories of a nursery with an empty crib. The effort was wasted. Try as she might, as she hurried up the hill, she couldn't shake the memories of the times everything had gone all wrong.

Don't look back, Jett had said. *Put one foot in front of the other and don't look back.*

Recalling his advice, once more praying it would work, she shifted her focus completely—and tried instead to be grateful that Jett hadn't wanted her to stay. He made her feel too much, want too much. And what she wanted more than anything was for him to take her in his arms. Just to have him hold her. Just for a while. As a friend. Because, in some odd and indefinable way, it felt like that was what they were becoming.

That she found comfort in a thought so full of contradictions was something she felt certain only Jett could understand.

The foal was up and nursing when Annie returned to the stable with a sandwich and a thermal container of coffee, twenty minutes after she left. But she stayed only long enough to stroke Empress's sleek flank and smile at the foal noisily downing its first meal. As preoccupied as Jett seemed and as tired as he was, he looked as if he wanted only to be left alone. So she headed back to the house and to bed, thinking that he'd be returning soon himself. But he wasn't back when she went downstairs a little after 3:00 a.m., and he still hadn't returned when she got Michael and Amy up for school a few hours later. Wondering if Jett had fallen asleep in the stall, Annie filled another thermal container with coffee and headed down to the stables after she dropped the kids off at the bus stop.

She wasn't inside the building ten seconds before she wished she hadn't come.

Chapter Seven

Annie stood frozen inside the yawning entrance of the stable. It had been too dark last night for her to see that the building was also open at the other end. Or to notice the bridles and halters hanging along the wood-plank walls. She hadn't realized, either, how big the place actually was. She scarcely noticed now.

Except for the subdued voices coming from Empress's stall, not a sound came from inside the building. There were no whinnied greetings, no shuffling of hooves. There seemed to be no movement at all, other than the swirling of straw dust at her feet when the morning breeze swept through the tunnellike space.

The stall doors all stood open, their occupants having been turned out into the large rectangular corrals Annie had passed on her way. Empress and her foal hadn't been among them. Not that Annie had expected them to be. She'd just made a point of looking when she noticed the dozen other horses wandering the perimeter of the iron-pipe enclosures. From where she stood, a few feet outside Empress's stall, she could see her now, though. And something was terribly wrong. The beautiful horse lay on her side, her breathing shallow, her eyes glazed.

Hank must have returned after she'd left Jett last night.

"Damn shame," she heard him say in his gravelly drawl. "We were both checking, too. As fast as she went down, she must have been bleeding inside all along."

"How long before the vet gets here?" Jett replied.

"He said he was leaving as soon as I called. Reckon he should be here any minute now."

Annie couldn't hear what else Jett said, standing back as she was. But when she saw him crouch down beside the mare's back, the slump of his shoulders spoke volumes.

"Come on, partner," the gruff and grayed foreman muttered. "There's not a man here going to blame you for this. You saved the foal. If you hadn't been around, we'd have lost them both." Hank heaved a heavy sigh. "Nothing to do now but put her down. She'd have been useless, anyway. Couldn't breed her after she'd been damaged like that."

The old cowhand's words were filled with as much regret as practicality. He hated the thought of losing a good horse. As stunned as Annie was to find the scene she'd left so drastically altered, all she heard was the rationale behind his verdict.

The color draining from her face, she watched in sick silence as Jett looked up and saw her standing in the aisleway. He was on his feet an instant later.

Hesitation marked his tone. "How long have you been here?"

Annie heard him. She just couldn't respond. With her arms crossed over the anxiety burning her stomach, her focus remained fixed on the horse. Empress shuddered, her massive body jerked, then she quieted again.

What Hank had said still echoed in her ears as Annie took a faltering step back. "Do you really have to—?" She cut herself off, unable to say the words.

They weren't necessary, anyway. As stricken as she looked, Jett knew she'd heard what had to be done. He hated the thought of an animal having to be put down himself, but the mare was suffering, and there was no other way.

"Take the foal for us, will you?"

Annie's glance shifted to his face, twin lines forming between her troubled eyes.

"We had to let him nurse as much as he could. To get the colostrum," Jett explained, because her incomprehension seemed to question why they would still have the little guy in there. "But we need to move him now."

Her expression didn't change when she looked from him to the stall. What he had said didn't seem to make sense to her. That was something that surprised him a little. He'd have thought for sure that a woman who knew where labor pains started would know about the antibodies and nutrients a newborn needed from its mother's first milk.

The distress in Annie's eyes seemed to have magnified when she looked back up at him. "Why would she be useless just because she couldn't be bred? She could still be ridden, couldn't she?"

It was Jett's turn to look confused. But his incomprehension lasted only long enough for him to realize that she hadn't been thinking about the foal at all. She'd been thinking about what Hank had said.

"Logan doesn't keep horses just for riding, Annie. These are all part of his string. Horses he uses for handling cattle," he explained, wishing the vet would hurry up. "Empress was a brood mare."

"And because she can't breed, she's useless?"

"For God's sake, Annie," he growled, not knowing what to make of the pain in her voice, or why it mattered so much to her, anyway. "She's dying. It doesn't matter whether she could be bred again or not. I'm going to bring you the foal. Take it into an empty stall and just stay with it. Okay?"

Jett didn't wait for an answer. His impatience fueled by fatigue and agitation, he strode through the doorway behind him. A moment later, he was out again, the foal braced in his arms and his expression a study in stone.

It occurred vaguely to Annie that it was apparently quicker for him to carry the little colt than for him to show her how to lead it. Either that, or he didn't want to set him down and have him trot back in to his mom. With the foal's skinny legs dangling like crossed sticks and his nose sniffing the air, Jett packed the blinking bundle of curiosity the length of the long aisle.

Feeling as if she were on autopilot, Annie followed him to the last stall. Reluctantly slipping in behind him, she watched him settle the foal on the thin layer of straw and leaned against the wall. She didn't want to be here. All she wanted was to go home and curl up on her bed and wait for sleep to come and numb the ache she'd so desperately tried to stave off last night. But she didn't have a home of her own right now, her bed was in storage, and sleep only took the ache away for a little while.

Jett was already back at the doorway. "I'll bring you something to feed him in a few minutes," was all he said before he walked out, closing the gate behind him.

With nowhere else to go, Annie listened to the fading beat of his heavy footsteps. That dispirited sound was accompanied by a small but insistent nicker and the feel of something warm and wet moving from the back of her hand to her thumb.

Eyes the color of dark chocolate stared up at her. The foal had his little pink tongue going a mile a minute, determined to find something to nurse on.

"Vet's here," Annie heard Hank call over the distant rumble of an approaching truck.

Seconds passed before Jett's subdued voice drifted down the breezeway. "Might as well tell him to go on home." A stall door gave a forbidding creak. "There's nothing here for him to do."

Annie sank down in the straw. "Come here," she whispered, and put her arms around the orphaned foal's soft little neck.

Hank had set off for the hills with Empress and a backhoe by the time Jett made it back to the far end of the stable. Preoccupied with the loss of the mare, his ribs more sore than they'd been in two days from what he'd had to do last night, he clamped his hand over the top of the gate and started to pull it open. All he wanted was to finish up and get some sleep.

At least that was his thought before he looked inside the stall.

The morning sun streaked at an angle through the high, narrow window at the back of the enclosure, its brightness muted by rain-stained glass. The low rectangle of light landed in a far corner, illuminating a faded red water bucket suspended by a heavy hook and the particles of dust that danced on the shifting currents of air. Annie sat in the corner, wedged into the angle of the wall, her legs crossed Indian-style. The foal, its legs tucked beneath it, lay asleep at her knees.

With her head turned to the side, Annie didn't notice him standing there. The way she absently stroked along the foal's withers, Jett wasn't sure she was even aware of her own

motions. He could see only her profile, but there was a remoteness about her expression that made her look incredibly sad.

He wasn't particularly surprised by what he saw. As soft-
hearted as Annie was, she couldn't help being affected by
the events of the morning. What caught him totally un-
awares was the depth of the pain in her eyes when the groan
of the opening gate made her glance up.

Incredibly, concern for him shifted over her upturned
face. She was as pale as moonlight, and when she spoke, her
voice held the faintest tremor.

"Are you okay?" she asked, watching him set a tin pail
in the feed bin.

Ten seconds ago, he hadn't thought he was. Once he saw
the moisture glistening in her eyes, how he felt no longer
mattered.

"I've been worse," he returned, unwillingly touched that
she should think of him when she looked so troubled herself. "How about you?"

She gave a little nod, but if she'd meant it to indicate that
she was all right, there was pathetically little conviction in
the movement.

The woman was too sensitive for her own good. Wanting
the threatening tears to go away, having no idea what to do
if they fell, Jett crouched down by the wakening foal. "It
was an animal," he quietly reminded her, remembering how
concerned she'd been with Empress. "That doesn't mean it
wasn't valued. But these kinds of things happen on a
ranch."

His perspective was lost on her. "What about her baby?"

"It's a foal," he corrected. "Not a baby. And he'll be
fine. The animals around here aren't pets, Annie. You can't
let yourself get that attached."

"How can you avoid it?"

He'd seen that same plea in her eyes once before—the morning she asked how he could so easily pick up and move on when something set him back. He couldn't imagine being as vulnerable as she was. Like the foal now rooting around between them, she didn't seem to possess any natural defenses at all.

"You probably can't," he told her, giving up. She'd never be capable of steeling her emotions the way he'd learned to do. She cared too much. Even when she tried not to, she cared anyway. Though he hadn't a clue why, she even seemed to care about him.

"I'm talking about you."

"I know what you meant. But I told you before, Annie—you really don't want to be like me."

He had no idea what made her look at him the way she did, as if he had just taken away some unspoken hope. But a strange distance entered her expression as she looked away. It was almost as if she had shut down inside, as if whatever she was feeling was simply too much for her to bear.

Jett reached toward her, but before his hand made it past the foal, he caught himself and settled his palm on the animal's back. He'd never experienced the need to offer comfort before, so he wasn't really sure how to go about it. He'd just instinctively reached out to soothe her, the way she had once soothed him—until he remembered that she didn't want his touch the way he did hers.

Not knowing what else to do, he did nothing. She looked absolutely lost, and he had no idea why. He knew only that it had to be something beyond sympathy for a dead mare and an orphaned foal. The haunted look he'd seen last night once more shadowed her eyes.

"You never answered me, Annie. Are you all right?"

"I will be."

"But you're not now."

"No," she whispered. "Not really." Her chin edged up ever so slightly. "I just need to figure out how to be useful again. Once I do, everything will be fine."

The brave little smile she gave him faltered a little, but it was obvious that she was working hard to get past whatever she was dealing with. Yet all her response had done was confuse him even more.

"Useful?" The word was scarcely out of his mouth before caution entered his tone. *She's useless because she can't be bred?* Annie had asked, stricken, outside of Empress's stall. "How do you mean that?"

One slender shoulder lifted in a vaguely defensive shrug.

"It doesn't matter," she murmured, and reached for the restless foal.

She was shutting him out. Intimately familiar with the tactic, and refusing to let her use it on him, Jett immediately removed what distracted her and set the foal behind him.

That she didn't protest what he'd done might have worried him, had her strange detachment not served his purpose. With his body blocking the little animal from her view, he literally had her cornered. "It does matter," he countered. "Tell me what you're talking about."

Had anyone asked why he was pushing, Jett couldn't have answered with any certainty. Maybe he was doing it because he couldn't stand the thought of her feeling the way she did. Or maybe he was just being his usual callous self. He wanted an answer. Damn the consequences. More than one woman had pointed out that he was not the most sensitive man in the world. But then, he'd never cared enough to try to understand what was going on with any one of them, either.

That he cared now bothered him greatly. But not nearly as much as seeing Annie this way.

"Why were you so upset about what Hank said?" he insisted when she answered with nothing but silence. "About the mare," he went on, refusing to let her pretend she didn't know what he was talking about.

With that, he got what he wanted. Her eyes lifted to his, and the guilt and pain he saw there hit him like a blow.

"Annie?"

For a moment, she said nothing. She just sat with her arms crossed so tightly he didn't know how she could breathe. It was as if she were trying to hold something in. Or maybe she was just holding herself because there was no one else to do it.

"Do you ever want children, Jett?"

Had any other woman asked such a question, he'd have been a mile down the road by now. "The only thought I've ever given to kids was preventing them," he admitted, knowing her well enough to understand that he needn't feel threatened by her questions. "It's not something I've ever considered. Why?"

She hugged herself tighter in her protected little space, accepting his response as if it had been expected. "I... We," she corrected, the distance in her expression entering her voice, "spent nine years trying to get pregnant. We succeeded three times, but I was never able to carry a baby to term. The last time I miscarried, there were complications. I just didn't know how badly I was messed up until I had to have surgery six weeks ago." She swallowed, her voice dropping to a strangled whisper. "Now I can't get pregnant at all."

The quiet breath Jett sucked in had as much to do with his own feeling of unease as the complicated mix of emotions Annie held inside. Sorrow, blame and failure were all written in her eyes. He could see now why she'd been so upset about overhearing Hank, but Jett couldn't begin to relate to her losses. Watching her curl into herself, he had the feeling she mourned the children she hadn't borne as deeply as she would have a child she'd held in her arms. That, more than anything else, caused the heaviness to steal around his heart.

She was trying desperately to hold back the tears, and the struggle was more than he could bear to watch. When one crystalline drop leaked out to trail down her cheek, his thumb caught it before it even reached her jaw. But it was only when he felt the warmth of her skin beneath his fingers that he stopped to worry about how she would react to what he'd done. Yet she didn't pull away from him as he feared she would do. All she did was draw a breath that sounded strangely like a sob and duck her head toward his hand so he couldn't see the other tears that fell.

He had the feeling that the only time she cried was when no one could see her. And that meant, if she let herself cry at all, she did it all alone.

He hadn't cried since he was fifteen years old. He'd been alone then, too.

His fingers curled beneath her jaw, the heel of his thumb resting at the corner of her mouth. With her face cupped in his hand, he felt the dampness of her tears trail toward his wrist. It was as if his touch had unleashed them.

That made him feel even more helpless than he already did.

"Annie," he whispered. "What can I do?"

She lifted her head, her lashes spiky and wet. What she wanted was to stem the flow of tears. They never helped. But more than anything she just wanted the awful feelings to go away, so she wouldn't have to deal with them anymore. She didn't care what Jett said—she *did* want to be like him. Imperturbable. Pragmatic. Cynical. Only he wasn't as unfeeling as he sometimes seemed. Nor was he as hardened as he thought he was—and that was just another disappointment to add to the long list of things she'd counted on and were no longer there. His touch was tender, and his eyes were a shade uncertain. Yet he possessed a kind of strength she needed very badly. Almost as badly as she needed his arms around her.

Hating that she had to ask, unable to deny the need, she abandoned her pride. Her voice thick with tears, she whispered, "Would you hold me?"

She had no idea what thoughts went through Jett's mind in the moments before she felt his big hands draw her forward and he turned her into his lap. She concentrated only on the feel of his strong arms closing around her and the solid warmth of his chest when he pressed her head to his shoulder. With her face buried against his soft flannel shirt, she breathed in the scents of fresh air, horse, and something indefinably male. What she exhaled was a sob she couldn't hold back. It had been so long since she'd been held, and the feeling of being protected, cared for, was almost more than she could handle. That was exactly how Jett made her feel as he stroked her hair and told her to go ahead and cry.

So she did, quietly soaking the front of his shirt.

And Jett held her, not knowing what else to do or say.

He'd never before held a woman while she cried. It was far different from holding one he was planning to undress. Though he was definitely aware of how Annie's sweet, slender body curled into his, he was more concerned with what had put her in his arms than with what to do with her now that she was there.

"I'm sorry about what happened," he told her, still smoothing her hair. It was such a simple thing. The briefest brush of fingers over corn-silk softness. He meant to offer comfort, now that he had some idea how it was done. Yet he could almost feel the tension leaving his own body as he did it, the sensation of calmness vaguely, inexplicably familiar. "About what Hank said, and about all that's happened to you. But not being able to have kids doesn't have anything to do with being useful, Annie. You just keep doing what you've always done. You're still the same person."

She curled her hand on his chest. "I'm not that person anymore, Jett."

"Sure you are," he said soothingly, trailing his fingers over her forehead the way she had his. "People don't change that much."

He meant to encourage. For a few moments, as she quieted against him, he thought he had. Then he heard her say that she had to change. Somehow. She couldn't move on if she didn't.

"I spent my whole life wanting to be a wife and mother," she told him, her voice muffled with tears. "Now, I'm not a wife, because my husband left me to find someone who can give him the son I couldn't, and I'll never have a child of my own. I don't know who I am anymore, Jett. I don't even know what I'm supposed to want."

She didn't feel as if she had a solid grip on anything anymore. The future hung out there like some big black void waiting to be filled with plans and goals and dreams. But she didn't have any more dreams. Those dreams had suffered each time a month passed and she discovered she wasn't pregnant, and then they had died, one by one, with each child she lost. So she tried not to think about the future too much at all. All she knew for certain was that she needed roots somewhere. She couldn't stand being so unsettled.

She glanced up when she told him that, looking at him in the same unprotected way she always did when she turned to him for words of wisdom. That she thought him wise at all baffled him completely. But he had no advice, sage or otherwise, to share with her now.

"I don't know anything about dreams, Annie. I can't honestly say I've ever had any." He spoke the admission without defense or apology as he coaxed her head back to his shoulder. Right now, with her, none seemed needed. "I can't imagine being settled the way you want to be, either. But I do know what it's like to not think too far ahead. Sometimes it's the only way there is to get from one day to the next."

"But it's such a hard way to live."

"You're just not as comfortable with it as I am," he told her, not comfortable himself with the need he felt to hold on tighter and make her desolation go away. "It just takes time."

She felt good in his arms, nestled in as if she'd found the solace she needed there. In many ways, she seemed to him like a battle-weary soldier, one who had fought to the bitter end. But it was how part of that end had come about that had Jett's hand slowing its rhythm as he rubbed her arm.

"You said your husband left you to find someone who can give him a son. Is that why you and your husband split? Because you can't have children?"

With Annie's face buried against his chest, Jett couldn't see her expression. He didn't need to see it to sense her discomfort with the question. The tension in her slender body increased perceptibly in the moments before she drew back from him. Wiping at her tears when he let his arms fall, she slipped from his lap.

"That was one of the reasons." Looking as if she couldn't quite meet his eyes, she took another swipe at the moisture on her cheeks and cast a glance toward his chest. "I'm sorry," she murmured. "I got you all wet."

For a moment, Jett said nothing. The odd detachment Annie had suffered when he first came in was no longer apparent. Now, watching her struggle to compose herself as she sat back against the wall, he thought she looked more embarrassed than anything else. That distress had as much to do with the question he'd asked as with what had just happened. Not certain how he felt about what had just happened himself, he banked his curiosity about her evasive answer and settled for letting the colt distract them both.

The little fella wasn't going to let himself be ignored much longer, anyway.

"Stay put," Jett told Annie, feeling the foal bump at his back again. Like most newborns, he didn't want to do anything but sleep and eat. "You can feed him."

Sucking in an unsteady breath, Annie tried to ignore the tension she felt in Jett when he rose to pour milky liquid from the tin bucket he'd brought into a shallow plastic bowl. She didn't know if she should thank him for what he'd done, or resent him for what he'd caused her to admit. She had been so busy reassuring everyone else that she was all right that she hadn't allowed herself to fully face how completely her world had changed. It had been as if, by not saying the words out loud, she could keep the situation from being quite as irretrievable as it was. But with Jett the words had come tumbling out. He was a man who knew nothing of what she had wanted. He'd even admitted he'd never had any dreams of his own. So why she felt any kinship at all with him was as much a mystery to her as the overwhelming sense of security she'd felt in his arms. For those few precious moments, she had actually felt safe.

The reminder that she'd actually *asked* him to hold her had the color moving back into her cheeks. What he thought of the request was anyone's guess. He was acting as if it hadn't happened at all.

"Wet your fingers with it."

Annie felt her unease shift focus. Looking at the yellowish liquid in the bowl he'd set between her and the foal, her nose wrinkled. "Why?"

"So he can get the taste of it. He'll suck it from your fingers like he would a teat. Keep your fingers in the milk, and once he's got the hang of it he'll drink from the pan."

"Wouldn't it be easier to give it to him in a bottle?"

Indulgence marked his tone. "If you take your turns feeding him from a bottle, he'll want the same thing from Hank or anyone else who feeds him. No one around here has time to hand nurse an orphan a half-dozen times a day unless he won't eat any other way. This is faster."

The foal, now quite vocal about his hunger, poked his head between them. "My turns?" Annie inquired, taking one last swipe at her cheeks.

"I told Hank I didn't think you'd mind helping out," she heard Jett say, as she dubiously dipped the tip of her index finger up to her knuckle and lifted it toward the foal's mouth. "A newborn foal has to be fed every few hours, and Hank's already spending half his day checking on the men and the herds and the other half tending chores up here. There aren't any spare hands available."

The drop of formula disappeared into the straw. "What about you?"

"I'll spell Hank in the evenings and at night."

Concentrating on what she was doing, grateful for the diversion, Annie dipped her finger in the milk again. "I don't mind helping."

"Good. The supplement is in the supply room," he told her as the foal latched on to her finger and caught the second drop. "The proportions of powder to water are on the bag." A frown entered his voice. "It'll work better if you use two fingers and get them down into it. He'll never get the taste that way."

"Like this?"

"Yeah."

Her mouth curved softly as the foal latched on.

"Now put them in all the way."

With a shrug, she dipped them up to her knuckles.

"*All* the way," Jett muttered.

Reaching across the pan, he snagged Annie's wrist and submerged her fingers completely in the milk. His own fingers slipped down behind hers, the warm liquid easing the friction of calluses against soft skin. With her hand cradled in his, a faintly electric sensation raced the entire length of her arm. An instant later, she had gone still. So had Jett.

"I think I've got it," she said, appalled at the lack of strength in her voice.

A muscle in his jaw jerked. "We haven't even started. Relax your hand."

Not until she'd done what he said did he move. When he did, he nudged the animal forward and lifted her fingers toward it.

As soon as the colt caught the scent of the milk on her fingers, Jett drew Annie's hand closer to the pan so that the foal would follow them to the milk. It took three tries, every one of them made in nerve-stretching silence, but the little foal finally figured out that what he wanted was in the pan. How to get it was a problem Jett solved by slipping Annie's hand back in the liquid.

With his fingers still curved around her wrist, he angled the back of her hand against the bottom of the bowl so that her fingers would curl up above the surface. This time, as the foal sucked from them, Jett slowly drew her fingers down and away, so that the animal's curled tongue was pulling the liquid from the bowl.

Now that the foal was doing what he was supposed to do, there was no need for Jett to keep her hand in his. But he didn't let her go. With the foal occupied with his breakfast, Jett's eyes locked on hers, something dark and dangerous tightening his expression.

Annie's heart jerked against her ribs. Like a sensuous line of smoke, the tension in his big body seemed to curl around her, stroking, teasing—just like his thumb as he drew it over her palm. The slickness of the liquid made his touch unbelievably light, unbelievably sensual. He wanted it to feel that way. The motions were deliberate; the look in his eyes was an unnerving blend of heat and curiosity.

If he pulled her toward him, she would go. She had never felt so safe, so protected, as when she'd been in his arms. But safety wasn't being offered now, and the thought of how terribly she would disappoint him, and herself, had her easing away.

The curse Jett muttered as he rose like a monolith of stone was low and succinct.

Taking a clean handkerchief from his back pocket, he thrust it toward her. "Here. Wipe off your hand."

The unsteadiness of her quiet "Thank you" only brought another curse. Annie didn't hear that one, though. Jett muttered it to himself as he took the handkerchief back and wiped his own hand, then turned to swipe up the pail. He should never have gotten that close to her. Breathing in her scent and the feel of her skin slipping against his had him feeling as tight as an overwound spring. Knowing she'd felt that same awareness didn't help his frustration in the least.

He started for the gate. Two steps later, he'd wheeled back around.

"Why are you afraid of me?"

His question had her eyes widening. "I'm not."

He gave a low snort. "Yeah? Watch."

The pail hit the ground with a clatter, startling the foal and causing Annie to jump. There was less than three feet separating them. He covered the distance in one stride. It occurred to him, vaguely, that the response he'd get by bearing down on her wasn't a true test of what he wanted to prove. As far as he was concerned, it didn't matter. He could tiptoe up to her and get the same reaction.

With his body so close Annie could feel his heat, he reached down and picked up her hand. There was nothing at all threatening about the gesture. He simply cupped her fingers in his and lightly traced his thumb over the fading bruises on her wrist.

With the predictability of a sunrise, her glance fell to the middle of his shirt and she pulled back to cross her arms.

Frustration dissolved fatigue. He moved closer, only to have her step away.

Another step wasn't necessary. She had nowhere else to go.

Annie felt her back meet the wall, but Jett kept coming. He stopped a foot away, the space between them so thick with tension that she could have sworn she felt it pressing against her chest. He loomed over her, his big body blocking the sunlight.

"Why do you do that, if you're not afraid of me? I just touched your hand, Annie. That's all I did over there, too." His head jerked angrily toward the corner. "You didn't seem to have any problem with getting physical when I was sick. Your hands were all over me. And not five minutes ago you had no problem crawling into my arms. But when *I* touch *you,* you pull away. I want to know why."

Humiliation had her ducking her head. Jett's fingers under her chin lifted it right back up.

"Please, Jett," she whispered, and tried to slip past him.

He had no intention of letting her go. He wanted an answer, and he was going to get one. To keep her from evading it, or him, he planted his hands on either side of her head.

"'Please, Jett' is not an answer, Annie." To counter the way he'd trapped her, he deliberately softened his tone. "I want to know why I keep getting such mixed signals from you."

"They're not mixed signals," she said defensively. "It was different when you were sick. You needed someone to take care of you."

"And over there?" he prodded, jerking his head toward the corner where he'd held her while she wept. "Why was it okay for me to touch you then?"

Because I needed someone to take care of me, a voice inside her cried, but she forced back the words. Saying them aloud would make the need so much greater, and she couldn't let herself acknowledge how badly she was handling being alone. She could hardly admit that to herself, much less to a man she could grow to need far too much.

When her only response was withdrawn silence, Jett's hands slowly slid from the wall.

"Damn it, Annie."

"Please, Jett. It's not you. Really."

"Then what in the hell is it?"

"It's me," was all she could bring herself to admit. Guilt and self-doubt shadowing her face, she skirted Jett to pick up the foal's empty pan and leave the stall. "The problem is me."

Chapter Eight

Jett told Hank that afternoon that Annie had agreed to feed the foal during the day. The ranch foreman was properly grateful, conceding that he wouldn't have thought a city girl would be so willing to take on ranching chores—especially since she was the sister of Logan's wife, and Logan's wife tended to steer clear of anything bigger than a barn cat. Of course, he'd concluded, Mrs. Whitaker had plenty to take care of as it was, what with the house and the kids and her job in town. But as for "Miz Annie," he just hadn't really expected someone who looked as fragile as a hothouse flower to take to tending livestock.

Until yesterday, Jett wouldn't have, either. Yet Annie had apparently handled the task without incident. Hank had said she'd looked like she knew exactly what she was doing when he ran into her with the foal at three that afternoon. Hank had let her know then that he'd take the 6:00 and 9:00

p.m. feedings and that Jett was taking the feedings at midnight and 3:00 a.m.

"She didn't seem too happy about that," the old man had told him, speculation running rampant in his rheumy eyes. "Said you shouldn't be up at that hour, since you're just recovering. I told her it don't matter what shape a body's in when it comes to taking care of the stock. Any man born on a ranch knows chores got to be done one way or another."

Jett had just finished that particular chore. The 3:00 a.m. portion of it anyway. Letting himself back into the house, quietly, so as not to disturb its sleeping occupants, he hung up his jacket and hat in the mudroom and pulled off his boots. It was raining again. Not a downpour like the one he'd arrived in. Just the soft stuff that turned the fields green and unleashed the color in the millions of wildflower seeds that had been in hibernation. Still, mud was mud, and he didn't suppose he should leave it all over the floor.

Unbuttoning the shirt he hadn't bothered to tuck into his jeans, he stepped soundlessly into the kitchen.

The room was dark, but the yard lights leaked inside to create shapes and shadows.

"How is he?"

The hushed voice came from the long cushioned seat in the bay window. Annie sat in that cozy space, her knees drawn up beneath a long, pale gown and the curtains pulled back so that she could watch the rain. Or maybe she'd been watching him. She would have seen him coming up the road.

"Fine," he returned, wishing she wasn't there.

"Do you want some tea? It was probably cold out."

Having spent most of the afternoon trying to work off his frustration from the morning, and the better part of the night wrestling the sheets, he was in no mood for her graciousness or her concern. "I don't drink tea. I thought you were into hot milk this time of night, anyway."

"How did you know that?"

Flicking open the last shirt button, he lifted his shoulder in a dismissing shrug. "It's just something I'd noticed."

He noticed too much about her, he thought, heading for his room. He knew more about her than he wanted to know, too. The one thing he did not know was why she shied away from his touch.

The thought nagged at him like a festering splinter. Even now, he could remember how she'd buried her head against his chest and leaned into him, curling her whole body around his as if she couldn't get close enough. She'd *asked* him to hold her. Yet she didn't trust him to make any move at all.

He was halfway across the room when he heard her quietly call, "Jett?"

Grasping at patience, he drew to a halt. "What?"

"I'm sorry about this morning. About the way I fell apart on you."

"Forget it."

"If that's what you want."

At the lack of hesitation in her reply, he turned to face her. She was ten feet away, curled up at one end of the window seat, her eyes luminous in the pale light.

"I don't want you angry with me," she told him, tightening the hold she had on her mug. "Please?"

He could have denied that he was angry. He supposed he could even have told her he had no idea what she was talking about, and let her off easy. A gentleman probably would. But he knew exactly what she was referring to, and he'd never considered himself a gentleman. The fact that she wanted him to deny how she'd made him feel just because *she* didn't want him to be upset with her only salted the wounds to his pride and integrity.

The shadows receded when he stepped closer, revealing the plea in her upturned face.

"Sorry," he muttered, no trace of apology evident in his hard voice. "I tend to get that way with people who don't trust me. It was nice of you to take the blame by saying the problem was you," he added, holding up his hand to cut her off when her mouth flew open. "But I don't need protecting. And I sure as hell don't appreciate being lied to."

"I never lied to you," she breathed, the words rushing out as if the air had just been knocked from her lungs. "And I do trust you."

"Sure you do." He leaned down, planting his hands on the long cushion and bringing his face within inches of hers. The intimidation was deliberate. If she was going to fear him, he might as well give her a reason. "This morning," he began, wanting to make sure she knew the exact time he was talking about, "I asked if you were afraid of me. You said you weren't. But that isn't true, is it?"

"Jett..."

"Is it?" he insisted, crowding her. "Yes or no."

"Not exactly."

"Then if you're afraid of me," he concluded, ignoring her qualifier, "it means there's something about me you don't trust. I don't know what you thought I was going to do," he told her, his eyes glittering hard on her face. "But I sure as hell didn't have anything in mind that wouldn't have required cooperation. I don't take what isn't offered. Ever."

For a moment, Annie didn't move. She wasn't even sure she was breathing. His words had been little more than a fierce whisper. Yet they echoed in her ears as if he'd shouted them.

"It never occurred to me that you would. I do trust you," she insisted when he gave a snort and pulled back. "I'd never have told you the things I have if I didn't."

"If you aren't afraid of what I'll do, then why—?"

"I told you," she cut in. "The problem isn't you. It's me."

"Then explain 'the problem' so I can understand it."

She ducked her head. "I can't."

He wasn't going to settle for that. Reaching down, he took the mug she was strangling from between her hands and set it on the table. Seconds later, he'd pulled a chair around and was sitting in front of her. Not the way he had with Michael, with the back like a barrier between them. He was facing her with his elbows planted on his thighs and his hands clasped between his spread knees.

"Try," was all he said.

Without the mug to hang on to, Annie hugged her knees to her chest. She was grateful for the darkness. She was grateful, too, that the edge in Jett's voice wasn't quite so sharp. She just wished he would let the matter go.

"This is what you did this morning," he informed her, watching her avoid his eyes. When she pulled herself from his lap after he asked why her ex-husband had left her, Jett had thought that she looked more embarrassed than anything else. It was that same unease he sensed in her now.

A different sort of disquiet suddenly hit him. "This is about your ex, isn't it?" His voice went flat. "You're still in love with him."

It wouldn't have surprised Jett just then to hear her say that she was. It would certainly explain a lot about her. But Annie was already shaking her head.

"No," she said, her voice quiet with acceptance. "I think our feelings for each other had changed long before he said he couldn't take any more."

"Couldn't take what?"

Annie's arms tightened around her knees. "Tests and... things."

Tests? "Things?"

"Another round of fertility drugs, or looking for some new method to try," she explained weakly.

"To get you pregnant."

His bluntness made her hesitate. Or maybe it was the fact that he didn't appear to suffer any of the uneasiness she felt about discussing such an intimate matter with him that gave her pause. "To get me pregnant," she concluded, trying it his way.

"I thought he wanted a child, too. You said one of the reasons he left was because you couldn't have any."

"It was. But he also wanted a normal life, and a wife he could make love to when he was in the mood, not when a calendar or chart said it was time. Those aren't unreasonable things for a man to want," she had to admit. "But I guess you could say that pursuing what *we* wanted most wound up killing what we had."

Trying to have a child had consumed their lives. At least that was how it sounded to Jett as he watched her strangle her knees. It was what she'd said about the calender and the chart that had his attention, though. A man didn't spend much time on a ranch without learning about fertility cycles. What he knew about infertile couples, however, could be engraved on the head of a finishing nail.

It had never occurred to him that sex could become a chore. But it sounded very much to him as if the years of trying to conceive had turned the act into little more than a means to an end. Spontaneity had been lost. Passion and pleasure had become secondary—if, in the end, they had existed at all. If sex had become little more than a task to be performed, it was entirely possible that Annie blamed herself for not pleasing the husband who had left her.

After all, she had said that the problem was with her.

"If you're not still hung up on him," Jett began, over-looking his relief at that fact, "and if you trust me, then what is it you're afraid of?"

"Of what happens when you touch me," she whispered, the strain in her voice making her words barely audible. "Or of what won't."

Caution blanketed his features. The need to draw her to him was strong, a living, breathing force inside him. What *won't?* he wondered. But that wasn't what he asked. "Is what happens bad?"

"No. No," she repeated, almost wishing he was still up-set with her. Heaven knew she had few defenses when he wasn't. All he'd had to do was give her a nudge, and she'd told him things she hadn't even confided to her sisters. "It's . . . not."

It had just been such a long time since she'd experienced the longing he made her feel. She couldn't bring herself to tell him that, though. She couldn't tell him, either, how what he could make her feel probably wouldn't last, because then he would think her cold and unresponsive—like Rob had said she'd become.

Her head was bent, and her knees were still drawn up to her chest. Reaching across the two feet separating them, Jett slipped his hand beneath her chin and turned her face to him.

"That's a start," he whispered.

The movement was imperceptible in the darkness. But Jett felt her head move toward his hand, just like when he'd caught her tears.

He leaned closer, his breath feathering her cheek. "That's definitely a start."

His last words vibrated against the corner of her mouth, the feel of his lips so incredibly light that Annie wasn't sure he was even touching her. Like a wisp of silk trailed over skin, the absence of pressure seemed to sensitize her nerves, making her exquisitely aware of how slowly he carried that kiss to her bottom lip. Only it wasn't a kiss so much as it was a caress. And when Annie's lips parted and she felt the graze of his tongue, she couldn't remember ever having been touched in such a way.

His hand had fallen from her face. It pressed into the cushion by her hip, bearing his weight as he leaned forward. He held her there with nothing more than the gradually increasing pressure of his mouth, and the warmth he caused to pool low in her stomach.

A soft moan snagged in Annie's throat, half sob, half plea. Jett drank it in, slipping his tongue inside her mouth. She tasted as sweet as the rain, and the touch of her tongue to his when she leaned toward him sent a flood of pure heat racing through his body. Angling his head, he deepened the kiss, drawing her up by her arms until she was on her knees. His arms slid around her, roaming her back, her hips, as he bent to mold her to him. Beneath the soft flannel draping her body, he could feel her trembling. He could feel, too, the delicate shift of supple muscle as the tension slowly eased out of her and she lifted her arms to curve around his neck. She was kissing him back. Not with the passion he brutely held in check, but with a needy curiosity, as if she were afraid to trust what she felt, but more afraid to not feel it.

His heart was thundering. His breathing quickened, then turned shallow.

So did Annie's.

Jett was lifting her, easing her up so her head was above his, his lips trailing down her throat as he sought the tight bud of her breast. She couldn't believe how he made her feel. She couldn't believe he wanted her. But there was no denying he did. She'd felt the rigid length of his erection as he drew her up his body. But when he started to nuzzle aside the soft fabric of her gown, he stopped only an instant before she would have stopped him herself.

His body felt as hard as hammered steel when he turned her away from the window seat and lowered her feet to the ground. For several moments, he simply held her there, his arms loose around her and his breathing harsh in the otherwise quiet room.

"If anyone had a problem," he finally said, lifting his hand to trace from the curve of her jaw to the pulse pounding at the base of her throat, "I don't think it was you." His hand moved up again, and for one heartstopping moment, she thought he was going to kiss her again. All he did was touch her hair.

The tautness in his face seemed to ease. "You'd better go up to bed, Annie. It's not safe being down here this time of night."

The house was still quiet when Annie slipped out at six the next morning to feed the foal. It was Saturday, so the kids were sleeping in. She hoped Jett would sleep in, too. At least until she left to take Michael to his basketball game, drop Amy off at her 4-H meeting and meet Lindsey for lunch. He really had overdone it in the past twenty-four hours, and he could use the rest. And she could use the reprieve of not running into him just yet. In those same twenty-four hours, she had fallen apart in front of him, bared her soul, ticked him off and nearly admitted she thought she was frigid. Though Jett had proven to her that she wasn't quite as dead inside as she'd thought, she wasn't sure being around him was such a good idea. Not now. Not as badly as he confused her. All her life, she had been so levelheaded, so reasonable in her choices. She thought first, then acted. With Jett, she simply reacted.

The Fates, she had long ago discovered, could truly be perverse. She hadn't been back from feeding the foal for two minutes when, trying to be quiet about pouring water into the coffee maker, she heard Jett come in from the hall.

The old black sweatshirt he'd pulled on made his shoulders look impossibly wide, and the jeans molding his lean hips had a hole in one knee. His hair was combed, but he hadn't shaved, and there was a vaguely preoccupied look about him when he glanced toward her.

"Shouldn't you put that under the filter?"

From behind her came the spatter and hiss of liquid against a hot surface.

An instant later, she had the carafe in place and the rich, brown liquid was dripping into it. "What are you doing up so early?"

The preoccupation in his expression was echoed in his voice as he reached for something atop the refrigerator. Or maybe, she thought, it was distance. "I have things to do."

"I already fed the foal."

"Other things," he enigmatically expanded. "What are you doing today?"

The question sounded so innocuous. So normal. Glancing up from where she'd picked up the dishcloth, she saw Jett set the yellowed roll of paper she'd seen him with yesterday on the counter. Leaning against the counter himself, he crossed his arms over his chest and his feet at the ankles and waited to see what she had to say.

She might almost have described his stance as casual.

Almost.

"I have to take the kids into town, and I'm meeting my sister for lunch. Why?"

"Just wondered. How long before the coffee's ready?"

She could have sworn he had something specific on his mind. Whatever he was doing apparently had something to do with the paper he'd taken from Logan's office. Whatever he'd wanted with her, however, had been dismissed in the instant it took him to glance toward the sputtering coffee maker.

"Just a couple of minutes," she told him.

"Mind if I take some with me?"

She would have told him she didn't mind at all, but even as he spoke he was untangling himself to get a thermos. Seconds after taking it from one of the lower cabinets, he disappeared into the pantry.

He emerged with a fistful of granola bars and a loaf of bread. Looking as if he'd done this all before, he set those items near the breadboard, then opened the refrigerator to pull out the sandwich meat.

He was accustomed to fending for himself. He even seemed to prefer it.

"I could make you something hot, if you want."

"This is fine."

As if he were playing cards, he dealt out four pieces of bread on the breadboard, tossed meat over them all and reached for the bread again.

Wondering if he was going to put anything between the slices, suspecting he wasn't, she leaned back against the counter herself. "Where do you go when you leave here?"

"Wherever there's work. As long as it's dry."

"I meant during the day," she explained, finding his response more telling than he could have imagined. For him to have replied in such a manner so quickly, leaving the ranch had to be uppermost in his mind.

She was unprepared for the tug of loss she felt at that thought. Wanting to avoid it, she made herself concentrate instead on Jett's hands as he slapped the remaining pieces of bread over the meat. He had beautiful hands. Broad and strong, yet capable of such gentleness.

That diversion was no help. "There's somewhere you go every day. I just wondered where it was."

"Out to the homestead," he said over the crackle of paper as he rewrapped the meat.

"What's the homestead?"

"My maternal grandparents' home. It's where my mom was born. It's quiet out there," he added, clearly more interested in putting his lunch or breakfast or whatever it was together than in what he was saying.

Annie frowned at his profile. While she worried about him being gone so much instead of resting, he'd been spending his days at his grandparents' house? "They still live there?"

He finally spared her a glance. "Who?"

"Your grandparents. You just said you'd been going out to their place. I've never known anyone who lived in one house as long as they must have."

"Nobody's lived there for at least thirty-five years. They both died long before I was born."

Opening the drawer next to him, he pulled out two sandwich bags and proceeded to stuff his creations into them. Annie scarcely noticed how familiar he'd made himself with the kitchen. She was too busy thinking that by "quiet," he must have meant there were no people around.

"How far is it from here?"

"A couple of miles, give or take."

"Doesn't riding that far bother you? With sore ribs, I mean?"

"Not as much as it did the first day."

His cryptic response left Annie with only one conclusion: He must have felt that the pain he endured getting there was worth the solitude he sought.

The coffee maker sputtered to silence. Wondering how a person could come to need to be so alone, she turned to the task of filling his thermos and her mug. Thinking he might be in a hurry to be on his way, she asked if he wanted a cup now, too.

He was apparently in a bigger hurry than she'd thought. Instead of answering, he came up behind her to take the insulated container the moment it was full and screwed on the lid himself. He didn't put it with the rest of his things, though. Taking the carafe from her, he slid it back on the burner. A moment later, his hands settled on her shoulders and he turned her around.

"What I want," he said, caution in his touch, "is for you to come with me. But I'd forgotten the kids would be around today."

It was his caution that made it impossible for Annie to move as she felt his hands slip slowly toward her nape, his fingers drawing small circles over the muscles in her shoulders. The motion was meant to soothe, to relax. To let her know she had nothing to fear. Now that she knew how those hands felt roaming her body, she'd never be able to relax with them on her. Ever.

"It's Saturday," she explained, never questioning whether or not she'd go.

"I'd figured that out."

An indulgent smile lifted one corner of his mouth. There was a faintly teasing quality to it, something she would have found rather remarkable, had she not been so busy wondering at how susceptible she was to him.

The fingers of one hand slowly curved around the back of her neck. "Maybe some other time," he suggested, drawing her closer.

His head bent then, blocking the light, blocking everything but the taste and the feel of him when his mouth covered hers. The kiss was slow, thorough, and filled with a familiarity that shouldn't have been there. He'd kissed her only once before. Yet, just like last night, he immediately angled her head the way he wanted it, aligning her to him as if he already knew exactly how to get the most contact out of her body.

Annie's breathing had altered. So had his. Jett became aware of that about the time he realized he was going to be in real pain if he didn't get out of there. Even if he hadn't already decided that whatever they did was completely up to her, because he would be moving on no matter what happened, with the kids upstairs, there was no sense starting something he had no hope of finishing.

Taking her by the shoulders, he set her back. She looked beautiful with her mouth damp and swollen from his kiss. She also looked as if she hadn't quite been ready for it to end.

"Hold that thought," he told her, and gathered up thermos, sandwiches and granola bars to stuff into the pockets of the jacket hanging in the mudroom.

The sound of water running in pipes indicated one of the kids was up. Knowing that whoever it was would be stumbling into the kitchen any moment, wanting something to eat, Annie took a breath that did little to calm the chaotic beating of her heart and watched him go.

The feeling of being completely upended was still with her when she joined her youngest sister at The Café a few hours later. Annie would have thought she'd be accustomed to the feeling by now. But Jett had added a totally new dimension to it.

Apparently it showed.

"That's the ketchup, sis."

Annie glanced across the flamingo-pink Formica table at the back of the 1940s-vintage restaurant. Apart from the steak house out on the highway, The Café was the only place

in town that regularly served gossip along with what the lo-
cals called a sit-down meal. Or so Annie had been informed by the loquacious waitress in the frosted bouffant
and the eye-popping coral lipstick behind the counter.

A very pretty, very pregnant Lindsey wiggled the sugar at
her.

"I think you want this."

Looking like the epitome of calm, which Lindsey Hayes
Whitaker usually was not, she traded bottle for jar and dubiously eyed Annie. With her willowy height, thick, wheat-
colored hair and great cheekbones, Annie always thought
Lindsey looked more like a model than the owner of a dress
shop in a truly obscure little ranching community. Right
now, she reminded her of their mom.

"What?" she asked flatly, dumping the sugar into her
iced tea.

"Are you all right?"

"I'm fine," she returned, the automatic response sounding suspiciously like an echo of Jett. Not sure she was all
that pleased with the similarity, she smiled anyway and met
her sister's assessing scrutiny. Pregnancy agreed with Lindsey. For that, Annie was truly grateful. But she'd already
told her that. "What makes you think I'm not?"

Carefully arched eyebrows rose in disbelief. "Gee, I don't
know, Annie. Maybe it's because you've said, 'That's great'
to everything I've said in the past five minutes. It worked for
the dress sale I told you I'm having this weekend and for the
contract Cal got to restore the library, but it really didn't
quite cut it on the question I just asked."

True chagrin washed over Annie's face. "I'm sorry,
Linds. I really am. It is great that the sale is going so well."
She really had heard that. "And I am pleased that Cal has
so much business." She'd heard that, too. "I guess I just
didn't hear that last part."

"I asked about the house hunt," she reminded her, smiling at the waitress, who slid their BLTs in front of them before hurrying off to get orders from the three old men bickering among themselves at the end of the counter. "How's it going?"

"It's temporarily on hold. I told you the other day about the places I've already seen, but I won't be able to look at any more until Sam and Logan get back."

"They don't get back for another week. Why can't you look before then?"

"Because a new foal was born at the ranch yesterday, and I have to feed it every few hours."

Lindsey had just lifted a french fry from her plate. Hanging in midair, it formed an inverted U as she glanced across the table at her sister. "*You're* feeding it? Why?"

"Because Jett said there aren't that many men working there this time of year and there's no one to handle an extra job. We're both feeding it. And Hank. Logan's foreman is taking a shift, too."

The fry joined the others. "They've got you in the barn?"

"It's a stable. The horses are kept in the stable. The bulls are in the barn."

"Whatever," Lindsey replied, clearly puzzled that her sister cared to note the difference. "I just can't picture you anywhere near something that isn't on a leash or in a bowl."

"Why not?"

"Because you're the person I called for advice on how to do a proper ladies' tea, remember? The one who knows place settings and how to look graceful under fire. Sam and I both look up to you as the Emily Post of the family. Being around all that... smelly stuff just doesn't sound like something you'd even want to do."

There had been a time when Annie wouldn't have thought so, either. But at the moment, watching her sister frown at her, she was thinking only how a person wasn't supposed to stray too far from the image other people had of her. People liked to know what they could expect. What they could count on. She could appreciate that. But when people pigeonholed a person that way, it made change even more difficult. And sometimes they didn't even notice a change had already occurred.

"The only reason I knew how to do a proper tea," she told her sister, "was because an officer's wife hosts and attends enough of the blasted things to float the Seventh Fleet. But I'm not an officer's wife anymore, Lindsey. I'm just me."

Annie had deliberately lowered her voice. Doc Weger had been the first to tell her that The Café was where a person could pick up gossip. The last thing she wanted to do was add grist to the mill before she'd even unpacked.

Lindsey's voice lowered, too. "I hate to disagree with you, Annie, but you're not being you. It's not like you to be so defensive. I thought everything was going all right with you."

"It is."

"Right."

Annie scowled. "So things are taking a little longer to fall into place than I hoped they would," she conceded. "I'll be fine once I get my own place."

"Which you've just delayed so you can baby-sit a horse."

"Jett said it needs to be done."

"Jett did, huh?" Lindsey cocked her head, her expression a little too curious. "Is he still as strong and as silent as he was at the wedding?"

"Strong, yes. Silent, no."

Speculation turned to concern. "Annie? What's going on?"

Annie wished she knew. She had known Jett for only one week, but in some ways she felt closer to him than she did to people she'd known most of her life. That made no sense at all to her. How could he understand her when he couldn't relate to anything she needed? He had no more desire for roots than she had to continue living the untethered existence she'd lived for the past year. He'd even told her he never had any dreams—and she found that lack far sadder than having lost her own. But what should have held her back was how he kept a part of himself so securely locked away. From her. From everyone.

It was that part she wanted to reach. That she needed to understand him would have worried her, had it not felt so necessary.

The mom-to-be looked as if she were about to repeat her question. To save her the trouble Annie murmured, "Nothing is going on, Lindsey. Really. We're just…friends. He's all wrong for me. And I'm all wrong for him."

At the protective disclaimer, a knowing look entered Lindsey's eyes. "The Whitaker men tend to make women feel that way about them."

Affection warmed Annie's words. "Do I detect a sisterly warning coming on?"

"Not from me." Lindsey shoved her plate forward, leaning into the space she'd created. "In case you've forgotten," she said, her voice barely above a whisper, "Sam didn't want me to have a thing to do with Cal at first. I'm the last person who will warn you off a Whitaker. I married the rebel, remember? Just be careful."

There was as much sympathy as encouragement in Lindsey's words, but Annie found precious little help in them. Jett *was* all wrong for her. She didn't even know how long he planned to stick around.

Still, when she was with him, she wasn't quite so aware of the hollow feeling inside her. And when he touched her, he made her feel something she hadn't felt in a very long time. He made her feel desired, feminine. More importantly, he made stepping beyond the familiar so much easier than she'd thought it would be, and he didn't seem surprised that she enjoyed it. That was what made it impossible for her to hear the warnings of her heart when she saw him ride into the stable Sunday evening.

Chapter Nine

Annie had just rinsed out the tin pail when the syncopated beat of a horse's hooves told her someone was approaching the stable. The beat slowed from a canter to a walk. Just outside where she was working in the storage room, they slowed to a stop.

Jett didn't notice her step into the doorway when he swung off the big bay. Nor did he pay any attention to the children's voices drifting from the foal's stall. His focus was on the horse as he dug a sugar cube from the front pocket of his jeans and held it beneath the horse's soft muzzle, crooning to the huge animal the way men have sweet-talked their horses for centuries. Moments later, still preoccupied, he was unbuckling saddle straps.

His side still bothered him. That was obvious to Annie from the way he winced when he hoisted saddle and blanket in one sweep from the horse's back and carried it to a saddle horse. Yet, uncomfortable as he was, he still insisted on handling the heavy tack and riding to and from the homestead every day.

Annie dried out the pail and rehung the towel. She had wondered before at the strength of Jett's need for solitude. She wondered now at how easily he handled the animal and all its accoutrements. By his own admission, he had spent little time on the ranch in the past several years. Yet he was as comfortable with all of its demands as someone whose entire life was devoted to it.

"Hi."

At her quiet greeting, Jett looked up from clipping a lead to the horse's harness. She could tell that he'd been in the sun again. The squint lines fanning from his blue eyes were shades paler than the pinked bronze of his face. Unlike Logan and Hank, Jett didn't always wear a hat outdoors. When the air was balmy, he seemed to prefer the feel of the wind in his hair.

His need for freedom underscored nearly everything about him.

"Hi," he returned, letting go of the harness. Ducking beneath the rope, he wiped his brow with the sleeve of his forearm and stopped in front of her. "Feeding time?"

"We're just finishing up. How about you? Are you hungry?"

The cool blue of Jett's eyes drifted to her mouth before returning to lock on hers, turning molten somewhere along the way. "For what?"

The sounds surrounding them suddenly became muffled, the shuffle of hooves and the lilt of Amy's voice subdued by the pounding in Annie's ears. With Jett less than an arm's length away, she was no longer aware of the scents of horse and hay and leather—only of the fresh air permeating Jett's work shirt and scent of musky male clinging to him.

She stepped back, though what she really wanted was to ease herself into his arms. "For supper," she told him, hoping the tremor she felt inside wasn't audible in her voice. "It's ready, if you want to join us. I know Michael wants you to. He was hoping you'd show up before we went in."

Jett had heard the kids. But the mention of them had him stepping back, too. "Thanks, but I have things I need to do out here."

"You have to eat, Jett."

"Just leave me a plate."

"Can we help you with whatever needs to be done?"

She was sure from his slowly forming scowl that he was about to tell her he could manage just fine on his own. But the gate on the foal's stall had already opened to release a grinning Michael. The expectant-looking child was now right behind them.

"I'll help, Uncle Jett. Do you want me to brush down Firelight for you? I do it for Dad sometimes. I can stand on that stool over there."

Annie had no idea what Jett thought of the suggestion. She was too busy watching the little cocoa-colored colt follow a pigtailed Amy down the wide center aisle. Amy, who had just picked up one of the numerous barn cats that wandered the complex, didn't even notice that she had a shadow. She was too busy animatedly explaining to her aunt that the cat had once been hers, but now it lived in the stable and its job was to catch mice.

"That's really nice, honey," Annie said, distractedly patting the little girl's head on her way to stop the foal. "But you left the gate open. We're supposed to make sure the latch is pulled down tight, remember?"

It wasn't apparent whether Amy remembered or not. The huge fur ball in her arms might have once been her pet, but it no longer liked being snuggled and squeezed. The child had no sooner turned to see how close the foal was when the ten-pound tabby vaulted for freedom. Had Amy not turned, there wouldn't have been a problem. Because she had, the cat landed inches from the little colt's white-stockinged forelegs.

Startled, brown eyes wide, the colt darted toward the open stable entrance. Annie lunged for him—only to promptly lose her footing on loose straw. A bone-jarring jolt later, resting on one hip and the heel of one hand, she found herself nose-to-muzzle with the animal she'd thought to rescue. The foal had turned around and trotted right back.

Jett stood over her, holding out his hand.

"Are you okay?"

Annie glanced from his dusty boots to the frayed hole in the thigh of his faded jeans. Suffering nothing but a slight loss of dignity, she started to tip her head farther back, then decided she'd didn't want to see his expression after all. After brushing her hand off on her jeans, she slipped her hand into Jett's palm. "I was afraid it would run away."

"Foals don't bolt like a horse would when something scares it. They'll startle, but they'll come right back."

"More trusting, obviously."

"More naive," he corrected, and hauled her up. "The instincts a horse develops to avoid danger are its best defense."

Jett had pulled her to her feet directly in front of him, so close that all she could see were the buttons on his shirt. So close that, when she looked up, she could see the chips of silver in the eyes so steadily holding hers.

Is that what you've done, Jett? Developed instincts to avoid danger?

If I have, they're not working.

A muscle in his jaw tightened. With the brush of his thumb over her wrist, the motion skimming the bruises he'd so unwittingly left there, he released her hand and coaxed the foal into the stall.

"You and Amy go on up and have your supper," he said over the metallic click of the gate being latched. "Michael and I will be up later."

Michael, hearing his uncle's agreement that he could stay, pulled down a chunk of air with his fist and hissed a quiet "Yes!"

The boy had been completely bored with her and Amy. But it wasn't Michael's pleasure over spending time with his uncle that surprised Annie. It was Jett's capitulation. From the way he balked when she mentioned that Michael would like him to come to dinner, she'd had the impression he didn't want to get any more involved than he was with the child.

"Amy and I can wait until you two are through. It's just a pot roast, so it'll—"

"Don't," Jett cut in, his stance suddenly as rigid as his tone. He drew a deep breath, forcing patience as he let it out. "There's no need for you to wait. I said Michael and I will eat later."

He turned away then, heading for the feed bin in the storage room. Calling Michael over to scoop oats for the stalls, he handed the boy a bucket and reached for a curry-comb to start working on the horse waiting patiently in the middle of the aisle.

"When's his bedtime?" Annie heard Jett ask her when she and Amy walked past him.

His unyielding manner was cloaked now, the gruffness missing from both his voice and his expression. All that remained was a strange sort of agitation that he seemed intent on masking.

"Eight o'clock," she said, unable to imagine what had made him so defensive.

"I'll have him back to the house soon."

"That will be fine," was all Annie could think to stay before he gave her a tight little nod and went on with his task.

Jett was true to his word. He had Michael back to the house within the hour. Annie was on her knees next to the bathtub, rinsing from Amy's hair the soap the little girl had missed, when she heard them down in the kitchen. By the time she got Amy's hair dried, though, Jett had left again.

"He went down to the trailer to tell Hank we did all the stable chores for him," Michael told her when she asked where Jett had gone. "He sure knows a lot about horses and cows. Did you know when he was my age he wanted to be a veterinarian?"

Annie shook her head, marveling more at the child's worshipful tone than his revelation. That Jett had wanted to be a vet came as no particular surprise. Not as good as he was with animals. "I didn't know that."

"Well, he did. He said that was what Dad wanted to be, too, but he had to drop out of college."

"Jett did?"

The freckles on Michael's nose merged when he frowned. "No. Dad. Jett said he only got his GE something in the army. But that's what Trevor's going to school for now. To be a vet. So he said at least one Whitaker will finally make it. It sounds neat. But I want to operate big cranes like Uncle Jett and use dynamite to blow holes in mountains and make dams and stuff." His expression turned wheedling. "Do I hafta take a bath?"

"After working in the stables," she prefaced, thinking Jett would consider himself a most unlikely hero, "you bet you do."

That wasn't what Michael had wanted to hear. But he went off under only mild duress, while Annie headed downstairs to finish the supper dishes.

The news that Jett had acquired a GED in the army was all but forgotten when she entered the kitchen. She had left places neatly set at the table for Michael and Jett. But that wasn't where they'd eaten. Though the dishes themselves were by the sink, the bread plate, their milk glasses and the salt and pepper shakers sat around spaces made by missing plates on the end of the breakfast bar.

The thought was fleeting, but as she picked up the glasses, it occurred to her that she'd never seen Jett sit at the table. That thought nudged another. In the short time she'd known him, he'd come up with every excuse short of needing to do his nails to avoid sitting down to a meal with her and the kids.

"Auntie Annie! Michael's gonna get me wet!"

"Of course he is," Annie muttered, and told herself she had no business being disappointed to discover that Jett couldn't handle even that much domesticity.

It was Annie's need for the very thing Jett so studiously avoided that had her at that same kitchen table the next morning. She'd told Lindsey she'd have to put her search for a house off for a week, but that didn't mean she'd forgotten about it. As preoccupied as she was with the thought, she didn't notice Jett in the kitchen until she heard him at the coffee maker.

"You're late this morning," she observed, her glance skimming up the row of buttons on his collarless denim shirt to the shaving nick on his chin. "You usually leave while I'm taking the kids to the bus stop."

"Different plans this morning." He nodded toward the paper spread out in front of her. "Still looking for a house?"

The classified section from Sunday's paper lay open on the table. Red circles delineated possibilities. Black lines ruled out the rest. There was one circle on the page.

"More like looking for a needle in a haystack."

"Slim pickings? Or are you being too picky?"

Refusing to consider the latter a possibility, she frowned at the page. As badly as she wanted a place of her own, there had to be something she was missing. "Slim pickings," she muttered, watching steam curl from his mug as he took a sip of coffee. "There's only one house in here that wasn't listed last week."

"What'll you do if you can't find a place?"

"Stay in the apartment over Lindsey's store until I do find one," she returned with a shrug. "There won't be much else I can do."

"Does that mean you're not going anywhere today?"

She should, she thought. She should ask him to take the noon feeding for her, go to the phone right now and call the Realtor to see if the woman had listed anything else in the past week. But if the woman had anything to show her, she would have called herself.

Having indulged in that bit of rationalization, Annie gave up. "I don't have any plans."

"Want to come with me?"

Jett posed the question casually, as if he really didn't care whether she went with him or not. There was something he wanted her to see, but he didn't care to mention that. Nor did he care to consider why he wanted her to see it. All he considered was that he felt better when he was with her—and that she probably had no idea what she did to a man when she smiled like that.

"Where?"

The warmth of that smile spread through him. She didn't even know where he wanted to take her, yet she was ready to go. "The only place I ever go around here. Out to the homestead."

Her anticipation faltered ever so slightly. "On a horse?"

"Yeah." He smiled back. He couldn't help it. "Do you know how to ride?"

"Not yet."

Jett liked her game reply. Better yet, he liked the fact that she was willing to try something that intimidated the day-lights out of her. Annie had never been on a horse before. Not even on a pony when she was a child. Her sisters had at a fair once, she told him when he saddled up their mounts a few minutes later. But she had stayed back with their mom because she'd been frightened by the animals.

She didn't appear terribly trusting of them now, either. The bay Jett had been riding for the past several days and the smaller sorrel he saddled for her, were a far cry from children's ponies. These were working animals. Big, quick and powerful. But they'd been broken by the best horse-man in West Texas. No one knew horses better than Lo-gan, he told her. Unless it was his son. Trevor was a master with them, too. And a horse broken and trained by a Whi-taker could be ridden by just about anyone.

"Did you ever break any horses yourself?" Annie asked, certainly hoping he was right.

"Never got the chance."

Annie didn't get to ask Jett why he hadn't. It seemed to her that he would have had plenty of opportunity to work with the horses while he'd been growing up on the ranch. It even seemed a little odd that he would have missed the op-portunity. But Jett was already diverting her attention by explaining how to hold the reins to guide the lean steed's

movements. Then he was boosting her up into the saddle
and she wasn't thinking of anything but the hundreds of
pounds of quivering muscle snorting under her.

"You'll be fine," Jett assured her, soothing both her and
the horse. Moments after that, he was astride his big cin-
namon-colored mount and leading her through the yard of
the main complex, the morning sun at their backs and their
shadows preceding them on the hard-packed earth.

It helped enormously that Jett led them at a walk, letting
her become accustomed to the feel of the horse moving under her. It helped, too, that the sorrel automatically followed the bay's every move. Because it did, the nervousness
Annie had bravely masked gradually receded as they headed
down a rutted road leading to an endless open field, and she
relaxed enough to move with the horse the way Jett did so
easily.

Until a week ago, Annie could no more have imagined
herself on a horse than she could have envisioned herself
painting her body purple. It simply wasn't something she'd
had any desire to do. As an adult, she hadn't even given
horses much thought until a few days ago, when she found
herself helping deliver one. It was just that she needed to
move ahead now, and moving ahead meant new experi-
ences. With Jett leading the way, trying something she'd
never done before didn't seem quite so daunting.

She had never been on range land. Because of that, she
wasn't prepared for the vast distances or the variations in the
terrain that stretched out all around them. They traveled
across rolling hills and what Jett called "flats" while he explained that Logan used that particular land for spring and
summer grazing. Then they rode past a huge granite bald
and a canyonlike depression carved by the waters that filled
the ponds in Logan's winter ranges. They crossed a creek
and a stream—the difference, she learned, being that the

latter was wider and deeper, though she couldn't much tell the difference herself. And all that in just two miles. It was nearly incomprehensible to her that they could ride for another forty-eight and still not reach the RW Ranch's western boundary.

She had just mentioned that to Jett when he reined his horse to a halt. The sorrel stopped, too, aided in part by Annie's newly learned but definitely novice skills. They had reached an oasis of budding live oak trees and the small creek that flowed through it. Unlike the brown and rocky flats, the ground here sported clumps of ankle-high grass, bright green from the rains. Much of the land they had crossed was showing signs of rebirth. But here, except for the winter-dead tumbleweeds tangled around a skeletal snag, it looked as if spring had already arrived.

With the creak of leather, Jett swung from his saddle. Still holding his reins, his horse clomping behind him in the dirt, he came up beside her.

"Can you make it down by yourself?" he asked, looking as if he were prepared to lift her off if she looked less than confident.

"One way or another," she muttered. Not wanting him to hurt himself by lifting her, she started to swing her leg behind her, as she'd seen Jett do.

"Hold on to the saddle horn."

Right, she thought, and gave it another try.

She did great, until she realized she had to press straight down toward the ground with her other leg to keep it from swinging foward. But she corrected that, too, and managed to slide down between the very forgiving horse and Jett without injury to any of them.

She had no idea why that made her smile. But it did. Even as she rubbed her backside, she was grinning.

So was Jett. At least his eyes were. "Sore?"

"Numb. I think I understand now why Hank walks the way he does."

"It takes some getting used to."

What it took was calluses, but she didn't mention that. She was too busy wondering at how much younger Jett looked when he smiled. The expression had a rusty edge, as if it didn't get used very often. But the difference it made in his features was truly remarkable.

"So," he began, his voice hushed by the riotous twitter of birds calling to each other from the trees. "What do you think?"

It was hard for her to think at all when he looked at her that way. His glance had fixed on her mouth, the glint in his eyes looking like a spark of heated memory.

"About what?" she ventured, stealing her hand over her heart.

For a moment, she thought he might close the gap between them. For one insane instant, she even thought about doing it herself. She craved the strength of his arms, the security she'd felt when he held her. It was an illusion, that security, something as insubstantial as smoke. She wanted it anyway.

But Jett wasn't offering even the illusion right now. Instead of drawing her closer when his hand closed over hers, he merely slipped her reins from her fingers and turned to tie the horses under a tree by the creek.

"The old homestead. This is it."

Annie wasn't sure what she'd expected. Something out of "Little House on the Prairie," she supposed. Or maybe something quaint and white, with a little picket fence. There was no fence. She couldn't even see much of the building. The place where Jett had been spending all his time was set back in the trees, and so overgrown with tumbleweeds and briars that she would have missed it had he not pointed out where it was.

"It didn't always look like this," he told her, the edge in his voice hiding his disappointment at her less-than-enthusiastic reaction. "When I used to come here, the porch didn't sag and the roof was in better shape. That pile of tumbleweeds out there is what I pulled off the porch. There used to be a stand of poplars over there to block the wind, but it looks like spider mites got 'em."

She had followed him through the clumps of grass to where the bushes opened up. She could see the weather-grayed building better now, and its sad and withered beauty. The house was small and L-shaped, with three turned posts holding up the precariously dipping porch roof. Shutters with missing slats still held a few stubborn flecks of peeling blue paint, and someone had spent hours carving the lace-like wood panels that embellished the eaves. Those panels were warped now, cracked and peeling, too. And the same weathered gray as everything else.

The most telling feature of all was the ancient power line that slumped from beneath the pitch of the roof to a nearby pole that had no other lines leading anywhere.

"You came here a lot when you were a boy?"

"Yeah," he muttered, the planks on the porch groaning when he stepped up on it. "I used to come here to hide from Ben." The rusty knob rattled when he pushed the door open. Its oval window was gone. "Want to look around?"

Caught off guard by the scope of his response, Annie hesitated for a moment before giving him a quick nod. Just as it had the day he so matter-of-factly mentioned that it was his father who used to beat him, his tone now had been as casual as a shrug.

He'd said he'd been about Michael's age when it happened. But it could have gone on for years. Michael was ten now. Her heart snagged painfully. Was that when he'd learned to prefer being by himself? she wondered. He must have felt safer here, alone.

"Did he beat your brothers, too?"

Jett had just stepped inside, the dim light casting his face in shadow when he turned. "What?"

"Your father," she clarified, hoping Jett wouldn't be upset with her for asking. "Did he hit them, too?"

His lips thinned, more in concentration than annoyance. "I think Logan was already gone when Ben started drinking so much. But he'd take after Cal once in a while. At least he did until the night Cal laid him out on the living room floor. I don't know if he tried anything after that. I wasn't around."

"You weren't?"

"That was the night I split."

Jett walked into the ramshackle house then, his boots making hollow thuds on the floor of the open and empty room. With the protesting squeal of a latch in need of oil, he opened a set of interior shutters to let in the light. Some of the panes were missing from the window, and he'd washed the ones that remained so the sun could illuminate the surprisingly open space. But Jett wasn't thinking of the hours he'd spent cleaning out the inside of the old place. He was thinking about how Cal had protected him, as he'd done so many times before that wet and miserable night. His brother had even given him what little money he had.

Get the hell out of here before he comes to, he remembered Cal saying while Jett, scrawny as a starved calf, shoved his clothes in a bag with tears running down his face. *I might not be around the next time something sets him off, so get as far away from here as you can.*

What about you?

Don't worry about me. I'm bigger than you are. I can take care of myself.

Jett shook his head, shoving the thoughts back in the dark hole where so many other memories were buried. He and Cal had both escaped, though he had no idea what Cal had gone through or when he'd made it out himself. They never spoke of it. It didn't matter now, anyway. None of it did.

Annie had remained just inside the door, her back pressed to the frame as she watched him across the dim and empty room. There was as much caution as concern in her quiet question. "How old were you?"

"Fifteen."

Another latch squeaked.

"Where did you go?"

His arms stretching wide, he opened the shutters securing the window next to the wide gray stone fireplace. "Austin," he muttered, wishing he could let it go at that. His sense of self-preservation wouldn't let him, though. He wanted Annie so badly that he ached just looking at her. But he needed her to know just how different from each other they really were. If she had a problem with that, then she was free to back away. If she had the brains God gave a grasshopper, that was exactly what she would do.

He almost wished she would, before he had to do it himself.

Maybe, he thought, turning to face her with his hands on his hips and the weight of something unbearably heavy pressing down on his shoulders, that was why he'd brought her here. He hadn't yet shown her what he'd wanted her to see. But maybe this was why it had felt so important to him that she come. He wanted her to know that he hadn't come from a world that was at all familiar to her, and why it was that he knew nothing of the world she lived in.

So he very deliberately told her that after he escaped a home where he'd been jerked around by the hair and slammed into walls, he'd lived on the streets and slept in alleys and stolen to survive. He'd become a very good thief, actually. But he'd never taken anything he didn't need—until he turned seventeen. By then he'd became so good at avoiding the cops that he stole a car. He'd thought that if he could just get up to Idaho or Montana, somewhere where there was no chance of running into anyone who'd ever worked for his father, he could work on a ranch up north. He was big enough then. Big enough that no one would laugh at him, anyway. But that time he got caught.

"The juvenile authorities called here, but Ben had died," he said, his voice as devoid of feeling as it had been since he'd first spoken. "Logan had dropped out of college and was running the ranch, so he drove up and talked the judge into having me go into the army instead of jail."

"How long were you in the military?"

He wasn't surprised by the caution in her voice. Now that she was privy to his less-than-illustrious background, a little reticence was the least of of what he expected.

"Six years. Never made it past specialist," he said flatly, speaking of his rank. She'd been married to a major. A jet jockey, to boot. Her father had been career military, too. Hard telling what she'd think of a mere enlisted man. "I was as far removed from officer material as you can get without spending an entire enlistment in the stockade."

If he sounded defensive, it was because he wasn't going to apologize for failing to be one of the elite. He'd gone from living completely on his own to being blocked in on all sides by rules, regulations, and sergeants who saw it as their solemn duty to break him. But he'd been bullied all his life, and he'd refused to be broken. In the interests of his own survival, he'd flirted with conformity enough to live within the system. He'd even learned to appreciate certain aspects of it. But he'd never felt as if he were part of the team. He'd never felt as if he were part of anything. Except for his brothers, no one had ever given a damn about him. Even then, they weren't that close.

Jett mentioned none of that. Aware of Annie's quiet approach, he considered only that it had been a very long time since he'd recalled any of this. He wished to heaven he hadn't found it necessary now. He hated the empty, sick feeling the memories put in his gut.

Pulling up the window, he sucked in a breath of the sweet morning air. But it didn't have the stabilizing effect he'd sought. The breath hit his lungs with a jolt. The air smelled like Annie. Not sure what to make of the phenomenon, he glanced back toward her. It wasn't her scent he'd caught. The breeze was blowing into the room, and she had only now stopped in the beam of light filtering through the window.

Though the scowl creasing Jett's forehead seemed to change quality, it kept Annie from moving any closer. He wore his defensiveness like a shield. Its hard edges defied anyone to get past, much less get in.

"The reason I asked how long you were in," she explained, "is because Michael said that was where you finished school. I just wondered if that was where you learned to handle that huge machinery you work with, too."

He was trying to push her away. She felt certain of that. Just as she felt certain he believed she was judging him for being a different sort of man from the others in her life. She thought that decidedly unfair of him. But all that mattered at the moment was how odd it seemed that he'd become agitated only when she asked how long he'd been in the service. When he spoke of his father and brothers and of the years he'd lived on the streets, he'd exhibited no emotion at all.

He flicked a piece of peeling yellow paint from the window ledge. "Yeah," he muttered, distraction causing his defensiveness to subside. "It was."

"Michael also said you'd wanted to be a veterinarian."

"Yeah, well, there isn't a lot of call for veterinarians in the military, so they don't pay to train many of 'em."

"Ever think of going back to school and becoming one now?"

The look he gave her was tolerant at best. "Look," he said in the flat tone of the truly exasperated, "I've got a GED and a total of three college courses under my belt. It would take years to get the education I'd need for something like that."

"Those years are going to pass anyway," she pointed out, only now appreciating that there might be a bit of a chip on those broad shoulders. "If it's something you want, you should do it."

"What makes you think it's something I want?"

"You told Michael you did."

"That was a long time ago, Annie. I was a kid. I knew then that it wasn't going to happen. Every time Ben would catch me trying to fix up some stray, I'd get my ears boxed. I lost my desire to work with animals long before I left."

He turned back to the window and jammed a stick between it and the windowsill to keep it from closing. He'd sounded disgusted with her, as if she'd had no business suggesting such an off-the-wall idea. But Annie had the feeling he was more upset with himself than with her. She didn't doubt for a moment that what he told her about his past had been more of a warning than evidence of any desire on his part for her to know him better. But he'd revealed far more than he planned.

He'd practically had the sensitivity beaten out of him as a child. What had remained had been buried in order for him to survive the years he'd lived on the streets, then driven deeper as the military toughened him further. He worked now in a profession that was rugged and rootless, and he had convinced himself he needed nothing and no one.

Yet, somehow, a spark of his sensitivity had survived. She'd seen it. Felt it. It was evident even in this room.

"This place needs a lot of work," Jett said, sounding determined to change the subject, "but it's better than it was. At least I've got all the trash hauled out."

"That's what you've been doing here? Cleaning it up?"

"Cleaning it out is more like it. The first couple of days, I didn't do anything but pull the tumbleweeds off the porch so I could sleep in the old chair out there." He pushed his hand through his hair, his frown still in place as he contemplated something outside the window. "I've cleaned the birds' nests out of the fireplace and chimney and knocked the cobwebs from the ceiling beams and walls in here. But I haven't done anything to the kitchen or bedrooms."

The floor had been swept clean, too. Though it was dulled by years of neglect, the sunlight revealed a surface that had been painstakingly constructed of matching lengths of wood held in place by smooth wooden plugs. As big as the room was, it would have taken whoever laid this floor forever to get everything to match.

"You said your grandfather built this?"

"That's what I was told. This and all the land from here to the Pedernales merged with the Whitaker ranch when Mom married Ben. This was the old Rutlidge place. That's how it became the RW."

He'd said he'd never met either of his grandparents. He'd said, too, that his mother had been born here. As young as he'd been when she died, he probably had precious few memories of her.

"Jett?" Annie began, studying his profile as he frowned at something outside the window. "Why are you doing all this?"

His shoulder lifted in a dismissing shrug. "I thought about doing it last time I was here, but I was busy helping Logan move his cattle. I left before I could do anything about it." His tone was dismissive, distracted. "It's just a way to kill time."

The casualness of his response shouldn't have surprised her, she supposed. But she wasn't given a chance to wonder how convinced he was of his reasoning when he glanced back at her.

"What's the matter?" she asked, wondering why he looked so odd.

"What's the perfume you wear?"

Her eyebrows slowly rose. "My perfume?"

"Yeah. What's it made of?"

"I imagine it's lots of things. Why?"

For a moment, Jett said nothing. Still studying her, he cautiously reached out and touched the hair feathering above her ear. The parallel lines in his forehead deepened for a moment. Then, strangely, they disappeared as he slowly shook his head.

"Just curious," he murmured, lowering his hand to grasp hers. "Come on." With one last glance toward the bush blooming outside the window, he gave her hand a gentle tug. "There's something I want you to see."

Chapter Ten

The back porch of the house was long, shallow, and lined with a splintered wood railing. Like the porch at the front of the house, it begged for repair—and rocking chairs and pots of geraniums. All that occupied it now were the vines that had grown through the slats.

It was the view beyond the house that saved the place from feeling completely desolate. Drawn by it, Annie could feel Jett's eyes on her back as she moved across the worn planks and slowly descended the step.

The meadow hadn't been visible as they rode up, protected as it was by the dense ring of cottonwood and pecan trees surrounding it. But the back of the old wood-beam and limestone house opened onto an enormous field covered with more wildflowers than Annie had ever seen in her life. Pink, white and lavender, they carpeted the field, so thick in places that it looked as if someone had spilled acres of pastel paint over a bed of clover and grass.

Yet it wasn't the flowers Jett wanted her to see.

"I've seen a doe with her fawn out here a couple of times. The fawn doesn't look more than a few days old."

Annie turned from where she'd stopped in the dirt a few feet beyond the porch. Jett leaned idly against one of the posts supporting the sagging shingled roof, his thumbs hooked in the front pockets of his jeans.

"It looked to me as if it might have been born about the same time as the foal," he added. "Thought you might like to see 'em. They usually come out from behind those pecans right over there."

The creek meandered along the far edge of the meadow. Jett dipped his head toward it, the breeze lifting his dark hair from his forehead. He hadn't worn a hat today. Or a jacket, either. His denim shirt was open at the throat and its sleeves were rolled to the elbows. The lack of protection wasn't an act of defiance, for the air was warm. Yet, to Annie, he looked a little defiant anyway. Or maybe it was defensive. Despite his casual stance, his jaw was working.

The man was just like the land surrounding him—unpredictable, untamed, and ruggedly beautiful. "You wanted me to see a fawn?"

"And the doe," he repeated, shouldering himself away from the post. "I don't even know if they're around right now."

In the time it had taken for her to release his hand and walk to the spot where she stood watching him, Jett had clearly become uncomfortable with his reason for bringing her here. He was trying to minimize the gift he was giving her, too. But the very fact that he didn't seem to know what she would think of his gesture made it all the more precious to her.

Annie could think of only one reason he would want to share his discovery. The first time he mentioned having her come to the homestead with him had been the morning after the mare died. He'd wanted her to know of another birth that hadn't ended so badly.

If his intention was to keep her off guard today, he was definitely succeeding. "Thank you, Jett," she murmured, her chest feeling a little too full.

His shoulder lifted in a dismissing shrug. "You haven't seen them yet. You have to look through there."

She didn't tell him she didn't need to see them. Or how touched she was by the gesture. He wouldn't have wanted to hear it. Letting the sweetly scented breeze blow her hair away from her face, she turned in the direction he indicated.

Anchoring one hand on the opposite shoulder as if to protect her heart, she looked out on the meadow. "I can't believe all these flowers."

"I don't ever remember seeing them this early in the year before," he said, coming up behind her. "But I don't know that I ever paid much attention to what was blooming when I came here, either. Except for berries. They grow wild all through that thicket," he pointed out, lifting his hand over her shoulder to indicate a sweep of land to their right. There was space where a garden had once grown, overtaken now with weeds. A rusted harrow lay drunkenly on its side, not far away. "I used to eat so many I'd wind up with a bellyache."

It actually sounded like a good memory to Annie. One of the few she imagined Jett had of the years he'd spent on the ranch.

"What else did you do when you were here?" she asked, hoping there were more. "Did you ever climb these trees?"

"Lots of times."

His favorite had been the huge live oak rooted over by the old cypress water tank. He would scale its sprawling branches and watch the herds move in the valley below. The raccoons chattered constantly and, in the summer, the cicadas would make every bush and shrub sing. It would be hot then, too, he told her, and so dry that the creek turned to dust—until the thunderstorms came in July and August and the creek and the washes would run in torrents.

She could feel him behind her, close but not touching her as he spoke. Yet, as he spoke, she began to sense the security this place had once offered him—and to understand why a young boy would have found refuge here. He had been able to watch the animals. Or play with them, if he chose, without being punished for taking pleasure in their company. Here, he'd been free to be a little boy.

She didn't know who she was protecting by not looking at him, but she didn't trust herself to meet his eyes as he shared his memories. He touched her in too many vulnerable places.

This place touched her, too. "You've never lived anywhere in particular, have you?"

There had been no question in her words, and the silence coming from behind her had a distinctly defensive quality to it.

"I'm not criticizing. I haven't, either," she told him, wondering if he'd realized they had that in common. "I think I've lived in every state and foreign country with a U.S. naval base. But I've never been anywhere like this." She cupped her other shoulder, hugging her arms to herself. "If I ever had to imagine a perfect place to raise children, this would be it."

She didn't expect Jett to respond. There was nothing for him to say, after all. She just wanted him to know how special she found this place. To her, there could be no place more wonderful than a piece of paradise where children could have the freedom to run and explore the way he had when he'd come here. Just because she would never have those children . . .

Light as the brush of a butterfly's wing, Jett's fingers skimmed the hair at her nape. "You'll never put it behind you if you don't stop thinking about it."

Annie shook her head, her voice as soft as a sigh. He'd come to know her a little too well. "It's hard to stop thinking certain ways when something has been on your mind for so long. But I'm working on it," she insisted as his hand settled in the space between hers and her neck. "I really am."

He knew she was. But he'd never wanted anything as badly as she'd wanted children, so he had no idea how long it would take for the sadness to leave her eyes. He didn't have to see her face to know he would find it there.

"What is Logan going to do with all this?" she asked, sounding very much as if she wanted to change the subject.

"It isn't his."

Annie turned slightly, her head tilting back to look up at him. Even narrowed in confusion, her eyes held traces of the sadness he'd known would be there.

"I thought Logan owned the ranch."

"He does. He and Cal. I was disinherited. Logan wanted to put me on the title when he took over," he added, turning her back to face his meadow. He wished things could have been different for her. That he wished he could make them better for her himself was as foolish a thought as he'd ever had. "But all I wanted was this. The homestead and a third of its stake are the only parts of the ranch that are mine."

"What are you going to do with it?"

"Clean it up a little."

"Then what?"

"Nothing."

His breath feathered the hair at the top of her head. Annie could have sworn she felt him press a kiss there, too. But when she turned to look at him, her arms still crossed protectively, she forgot whatever it was she'd been about to say.

Jett was reaching for her. Lowering her arms, he pulled her toward him. A moment later, his head bent, shadowing her face. His lips grazed hers. "You sure ask a lot of questions."

She would have asked if he minded, but his mouth closed over hers then, cutting off the thought completely. The only thought in her mind when he folded her in his arms was that he was making it impossible for her to think at all. That almost seemed to be his intent. From the way he slowly skimmed his hands over her back to align her soft curves with his harder angles, it was as if he were deliberately trying to make her forget everything but the feel of his mouth and his body. What he made her feel was good. He knew that. She had all but told him so.

What she hadn't known then, before that first time he kissed her, was how the stroke of his hand could electrify, or how the feel of his tongue sipping against hers could make her knees go weak.

Jett felt her sag against him, her response trapping a moan deep in his chest. If his intention had been to divert her, that reason had vanished like smoke in a high wind. He wasn't being altruistic, anyway. He was just doing what he'd wanted to do all morning, what he'd ached to do all night. What he wanted now was to feel more of her. All of her.

At the thought, heat raced through him like a spark hitting dry tinder. A heartbeat later, he was trailing his lips along her jaw to tease the shell of her ear. Then he was stealing her breath with a kiss that had her hands clutching his shirt. But when his hand moved over her ribs, seeking her breast, he felt her fingers curl around his wrists the moment he cupped its slight fullness.

He felt her tense, and heard her drag in an unsteady breath. But he didn't move his hand. He kept it cupped over the firm little mound straining beneath the soft cotton of her blouse and waited for her to decide what she wanted him to do. All he felt was the clench of her fingers, the movement filled with uncertainty. All he heard was the soft shudder of her breath when she lowered her forehead to his chest.

Though neither of them moved, it seemed to Jett that Annie suddenly was as skittish as the doe he'd brought her here to see. Knowing what he knew of her now, he had a strong suspicion he knew why, too. He'd wondered before why she hid herself beneath such baggy shirts and sweaters. Now that he thought about it, he realized she tended to keep her arms crossed over herself when he was around, too. In some ways, the posture was definitely protective. It was also concealing. But this was the first time it had occurred to him just how inadequate she thought she was as a woman.

Physical need warred with the bruised sensation squeezing his heart. He didn't know what the feeling was. Tenderness, perhaps, though he wasn't sure, because he'd never felt it before. He just knew that he hated that she thought of herself as undesirable, hated that she'd been made to feel less than the woman she was.

He touched his lips to the lobe of her ear. "All you have to do is take my hand away if you don't want it there," he whispered. "That's all you have to do, Annie. If I do something you don't like or don't want, all you need to do is let me know."

The breeze lifted her hair, tickling his temple. Annie's forehead was still pressed to his chest, but he felt her give a little nod just before her fingers uncurled and her hand fell away.

Jett wasn't sure what it was he felt just then. But when he nudged her cheek, seeking her mouth, he knew his kiss wasn't as insistent as it wanted to become. Neither was his touch when he slowly explored her shape. Her breasts were small, delicate, like the rest of her. And he couldn't help but wonder if the nipple blooming at his touch would taste as sweet as her mouth. But there was something more going on between him and Annie than sex. This was about trust.

And she did trust him. She'd told him so.

"You're perfect," he whispered, circling the taut bud with his thumb. "Don't ever think otherwise."

His breath was warm on her face, his kiss so gentle it made her chest hurt. He wasn't only making her want, he was making her crave. He was making her believe him, even though she knew his words weren't true. But that didn't matter. He seemed to believe them, and that was all she cared about. He told her she was beautiful. Then he told her again. And when he kissed her that way, as if she were something infinitely precious, that was how he made her feel.

There was no reason that should make her want to cry.

Her tears had been choked back, but her luminous eyes were huge in her face when he drew back. She looked confused and dismayed. But, mostly, she looked as if she didn't want him to notice.

"I'm sorry," she whispered.

"Don't be." Anchoring his hand at the back of her neck, Jett nudged her chin up with his thumb. "You don't have anything to apologize for." The tips of his fingers grazed her jaw, moving to her cheek as if he were memorizing the shape of her face, the texture of her skin. "Just remember what I said." His head bent, his mouth feathering over hers. "Okay?"

She wasn't sure what she was supposed to remember. The part about being beautiful or the part about telling him if she didn't like how he touched her. All she could think of at that moment was how he was making her want. Making her need. And she didn't know if it was gratitude she felt, or despair.

He would be gone soon.

"Okay," she returned, wondering at the intimacy of a relationship that shouldn't have developed at all.

Jett's hands were on her shoulders. Twisting his wrist, he darted a glance to his watch. His lips thinned.

"I've got to get you back to feed the foal," he said, digging his hands into his pockets as if to keep them to himself. "But while I've got you here, would you mind helping me lift something?"

Annie dropped her fingers from her lips. Doing something physical was probably an excellent idea. "What?"

"The back door. I need to take it off so I can level it. It won't close."

She'd noticed that. She also noticed that Jett wasn't waiting for an answer. As he tended to do with her, he just assumed she'd help. He was already heading back into the house.

"If that's the sort of thing you want to do around here, why don't you ask Cal to help you? He's the carpenter in the family."

"I know Cal's a carpenter. I just want to do it myself."

It was *his* property, the only thing in this world Jett felt the least bit proprietary about. The thought that he was also beginning to feel that way about Annie would have bothered him a lot more if he'd planned to be around much longer.

"By the way," Annie told him on their way through what had once been the kitchen, "he wants you to call him when you're feeling up to getting together. I ran into him the other day, while I was having lunch with Lindsey. She wanted to have you over for dinner, but Cal said he'd leave that up to you. He just wants to make sure he sees you while you're here.''

''I'll meet him for a beer,'' Jett muttered, walking through the front door to get the tools he needed out of his saddlebag.

He was back moments later, frowning at rusted hinges.

''Is this all you need help with?'' she asked, though she was thinking more about how Jett had groaned at the thought of going to his brother's house for a meal. ''Taking off the door?''

''That and finding the boundaries to the original stake. I brought the plat map, but that's something I can do later.''

It didn't take Jett long to pound the doornails from the hinges and remove the old paneled door. The thing was more awkward than heavy, and if Annie realized that what he'd wanted wasn't her help so much as her company, he wasn't able to tell from her silence. Ever since he'd mentioned finding the homestead's boundaries, she'd seemed preoccupied. She'd asked a couple of questions about it, but that was all. That was all right, though. With her so near, he was preoccupied himself. By the time they had covered the two miles back to the ranch, they hadn't spoken half a dozen words that weren't absolutely necessary.

Even when they reached the stable, they didn't do much more than trade glances before they dismounted. Coming up beside him, Annie handed him the reins so he could take care of her horse. In turn, he handed her the pail she'd earlier left to dry in the sun.

''Jett?'' she called, just as he started for the corral.

The preoccupation had slipped from her expression. Now she just looked a little hesitant.

"I'd like to ask Sandy...the newspaper's editor," she clarified, speaking of her boss-to-be, "if he'd be interested in an article about the homestead. Would you mind?"

His eyebrows merged. "What kind of an article?"

"About the people who lived there. What the cabin was like that was there before the house was built. How long it was the Rutlidge place before it became part of the RW. That sort of thing. There must be other ranches around here with old homes on them," she added, the possibilities multiplying. "If he likes what I do, maybe I could do a series."

"Getting into your new job, huh?"

She was certainly trying. He was the one who'd detected her lack of enthusiasm for it, after all. "If I can get an okay, will you help me with it?"

Annie really thought Jett might not go for the idea, which was why she'd taken so long mulling over whether or not to ask. The homestead was very personal to him, and the last thing she wanted to do was invade his privacy. If he'd shown the least bit of hesitation, she'd have backed off in an instant.

All he did was shrug, the motion belying the pleasure it gave him to see the animation creeping into her eyes. "I suppose so." Behind him, their mounts danced at the ends of the reins he held. "I don't know that I can tell you that much, but it's all right with me.

"I'll be back by six," he said then, steeling himself against the temptation of her mouth. An empty stall beckoned behind her. Cool. Dim. Strewn with fresh, sweet straw. One taste of her and he'd be backing her in there. "If Michael wants to help me with the stable chores, send him down around then. You and I can talk when we're finished."

A gentle smile curved her mouth, blooming brighter when she heard the foal begin to whinny in earnest. "Guess I'd better feed him. He sounds hungry."

Jett could appreciate the feeling. But there was nothing he could do about the hunger he felt at the moment except unsaddle the sorrel and work his frustrations out on a door.

They didn't get a chance to talk about the homestead that evening. Jett needed to help Hank with another mare that was about to foal.

He sent Michael up to the house at six, and showed up himself about an hour later to grab something to eat and head back down to the stable. First, though, he stopped at the breakfast bar, where Annie was frosting cupcakes with Amy.

"I don't know how late I'll be," he told her while she buttered a yellow cupcake with chocolate icing. "Why don't you just come out with me in the morning?"

"Because I have to take Amy and forty cupcakes to school. She can't handle them on the bus."

"Then come out after you get back. There's an old road to the homestead. I'll leave you a map and a set of keys to one of the Jeeps. Can you drive a stick shift?"

It had been a point of principle with Annie's father that his daughters learn how to drive a "real" car. With her attention divided between Jett, the little girl wearing more frosting than the cupcakes and what she was doing herself, all Annie said to him was, "I think I can manage."

Jett stood on the opposite side of the breakfast bar, the closest he would allow himself to get with the kids around. His glance bounced from the math papers on the table, which Annie had helped Michael with before she sent him up for a bath, to the cupcakes she and Amy were having to frost because Sam was homeroom mom and it was Morgan Something-or-Other's birthday.

"I don't doubt that."

There was a compliment somewhere in that laconic comment. Annie might even have seen it in Jett's eyes, had she dared to meet them for more than an instant. There was something about knowing that he wanted her that had her stomach jumping and her brain feeling as scrambled as the wiggly white lines of frosting Amy was looping over the cupcakes. Knowing he would never push didn't help. Knowing she wanted him to need her the way she feared she needed him didn't help, either.

Annie turned to the little girl at her elbow. "I think we're finished, honey. Run on into the bathroom now and wash your hands. And your face," she added, smiling at a telltale smear of chocolate at the corner of her mouth.

Amy eyed the last two undecorated cupcakes. "I want to do them, too."

"I'll save them for you. Go get the frosting off your face."

The dubious logic of her aunt's request stalled the little girl's protest. Suddenly looking as if she'd just caught on, the little girl's eyes darted from the big man towering across the counter to the woman with her mom's smile. "You're going to talk about big-people stuff, aren't you?" she said flatly.

"Yes. Now scoot."

With a heavy sigh and a last lick of chocolate frosting from the bowl, the too-wise six-year-old jumped off the stool and unhappily removed herself from the room.

"Big-people stuff?" Jett echoed, frowning.

"I wanted to talk about Michael," Annie returned, her voice low. "Did he mention if anything happened at school today between him and Billy?"

"He said Billy wasn't there."

Jett expected relief to soften the troubled look that had so suddenly entered Annie's eyes. Instead, the concern remained.

"I asked Lindsey if she knew anything about this Billy," Annie said, because she hadn't been able to just sit back and wait, as Jett had said they should do. "She'd never heard of him, but she asked Louella—she's the waitress at The Café—and Louella said that Billy is a foster child who's been getting in and out of trouble quite a bit lately."

"And?" Jett coaxed, clearly thinking there must be more.

"Well, I just think that might explain why he's been picking on Michael."

"Why would he pick on Michael just because he's a foster child?"

"That's not what I mean," she muttered. "I think he might be picking on him because Michael has what he doesn't. Billy told Michael that he couldn't call Logan 'Dad' because he wasn't his real father, remember? That wouldn't make any difference to Billy at all, unless he was craving someone to be his dad, too."

Comprehension was shadowed by something that looked suspiciously like recognition. That shadow flattened his voice. "So you're saying the kid's jealous."

"He could be. Jealous and hurting."

Jett's eyes narrowed, his glance not critical of her conclusion so much as curious about the sympathy in her voice. "You were calling the kid a brat the other day."

That was before she'd learned that he had no home of his own. "Well, he shouldn't have hit Michael," she defended, because the circumstances didn't excuse the action. "But maybe if Michael understood what Billy's problem was, he could deal with him better."

"What's understanding him going to do? When someone belts you, it doesn't matter if they're just in a bad mood or raging at the inequities of their own life. The end result is the same."

For a moment, Annie said nothing. Jett's guard had come up. She could see it in the faint tensing of his muscles.

"I just thought he could invite Billy out to the ranch," she said, aware from the sounds of little footsteps hurrying toward the kitchen that they were about to be interrupted. "It sounds to me like Billy needs a friend, and if they were friends, he wouldn't beat up on Michael anymore."

It was impossible to know what thoughts went through Jett's mind as he slowly shook his head at her. Annie suspected, however, that he found her solution hopelessly naive. Aside from that, Sam and Logan would be home in five days. Michael could tough it out until then.

Having reached those uncomfortable conclusions, she said nothing else and handed him a cupcake.

"You'd better go," she told him, since he looked as if he were about to leave anyway. "Good luck tonight."

With a muttered "Thanks," he accepted her offering, gave her one last inscrutable glance and headed for the door.

"Jett?" she called, just as he reached it. "If you can drive out to the homestead, why do you always ride?"

"Because it's the only chance I get to do it."

His response was accompanied by an indifferent shrug as he disappeared through the mudroom. But Jett's penchant for underplaying what mattered to him was becoming more apparent to her all the time. His seeming indifference about certain things now seemed more like a shield, as much a defense as the remoteness that sometimes entered his eyes. He was denying himself a great deal by staying away from the ranch as much as he did. As she listened to the door closing behind him, it was obvious to her that he missed the place.

* * *

Jett was nowhere to be seen when Annie bounced the dented gray Jeep with the interlocking *RW* on its doors to a stop near the pile of dirt-brown tumbleweeds just before noon. She knew he was there somewhere, though. The massive bay he rode was tied beneath the sprawling arms of the oak by the creek, helping himself to a snack of newly budded leaves.

Hauling a basket off the passenger seat, Annie headed for the house at the same pace she'd maintained since 6:00 a.m. Erin had called last night, needing an outfit she hadn't taken with her. So Annie had dropped the outfit off at Lindsey's, dropped the kids and the cupcakes off at school, then met Lindsey for a quick cup of coffee at The Café. Afterward, she'd stopped by the newspaper office for a chat with the affable Sandy, then raced back to the ranch to feed the foal again and see the new one. According to Hank, that birth had gone without a hitch.

Since Jett didn't answer when she ducked her head inside the house and called his name, she continued through to the back, leaving the basket on the drainboard on the way. She didn't know whether she was excited or nervous, or how much of which had to do with the high she was riding because the editor had liked her idea. Jett could make her feel that same way.

He wasn't out back, either.

More puzzled than concerned, she headed around the side of the house, her pace unconsciously slowing. Though it wasn't deliberate, each step she took was slower than the last, her shoulders seeming to relax by inches. She hadn't even realized they'd stored that much tension until then. Nor had she realized, until that moment, what it was that had affected her so about this place.

If peace had a sound, she could hear it there. It was in the rustle of leaves and the breeze sweeping knee-high grass. It was in the soft rushing of the creek and the looping note of a lone sparrow. If serenity had a scent, it was in the sweetness of a million wildflowers, and the soft pink blossoms climbing the chimney she faced. Wild roses. The enormous bush nearly obliterated the stones and completely framed one of the windows Jett had opened when they were there yesterday.

The movement she caught from the corner of her eye pulled her glance toward the meadow.

Jett stepped from the copse of trees twenty yards away. He had the long roll of yellowed paper in one hand and was wearing a white T-shirt that stretched snugly over his impossibly broad chest. From the power in his long-legged stride, it was hard to imagine that his strength had not fully returned. The way he pushed himself, it was a miracle it had managed to return at all.

He was an arm's length away before she greeted him with a quiet "Hi."

Her smile was soft, a little hesitant, and, to Jett, as healing as rain after a drought. She wore a loose blouse tucked into jeans that revealed the slimness of her hips and her slender waist. The blouse was the same pale pink as the roses beside her.

Until he noticed them blooming this morning, he hadn't realized what it was about her scent that had been so familiar. He couldn't help wondering if she'd noticed, too.

"I was beginning to think you weren't going to show up."

"I stopped by the newspaper office to talk to Sandy."

"What did he say?"

She had to restrain her smile. "He liked the idea. He just has to see the story first before he'll commit to anything."

"Sounds reasonable enough." His expression curiously distant, Jett blew out a long breath. "I'm not the one you should be talking to about this, Annie. You need to talk to Cal or Logan. They'd have more information than I do. You should clear it with them, anyway."

He saw the question enter her eyes, confusion blotting the light from her eyes like a cloud covering the sun. He'd told her he'd help her with her story. But that had been before he considered what helping her would mean.

His mouth pressed in a grim line. He didn't want to dig deeply enough to recall all he knew of the homestead's past. If he answered her questions about the family who had lived in this house, he would be reminded of too many things he didn't care to recall. He could tell her what Logan had told him about how Grandpa Rutlidge had started with a hundred Mexican longhorns, and how he'd built the house as a present to his wife when they finally had their long-awaited and only child. But then he'd have to remember who that child was, and he wouldn't be able to avoid the memories of how he'd hidden in the back bedroom, staring at the picture of his mother he'd kept under a floorboard. Cal had said she used to sing to them, and that she'd smelled pretty. But Jett couldn't remember anything other than how she looked in that picture. That was all he had of her. That and the china teacups that had once sat on a ledge in the kitchen. He'd taken them from the main house and hidden them with the photograph so Ben wouldn't smash them during one of his rampages. Cal had told him that the teacups had been their mom's.

He's jealous and hurting, Annie had said of Billy—and Jett hadn't doubted for a moment that she was absolutely right. He didn't have to know a thing about the kid to understand that not having what other kids seemed to take for granted could fill a person with a certain kind of rage.

No, he thought, dragging in a breath of warm, sweet air. He had no intention of resurrecting any of that. He could skim the surface, but he wasn't about to dig beneath it. The very thought had him wanting to get on the first plane to whatever job he could find. He would have right then, but his body couldn't yet stand the physical demands of a construction job. Now that Annie was here, the agitation he'd been dealing with all morning wasn't quite so bad, anyway.

Without thinking, he reached out to touch the hair feathering above her ear. The gesture was becoming familiar. So was the odd calming effect it had on him when he did it. She no longer pulled away when he touched her. Instead, her head shifted ever so slightly toward his hand, seeking its warmth.

Annie wasn't aware of what she'd done. She was thinking only of Jett.

"The story was a bad idea," she admitted, wishing she could take the bleakness from his eyes. She could see hurt there, too. And pain. He couldn't know it was so visible. The way he protected himself, he'd never willingly allow himself to expose such vulnerability. "I shouldn't have asked."

"There's nothing wrong with the idea." He lowered his hand, control slipping firmly into place. "I just don't know enough to do you any good."

Annie watched him step back, closing himself off, closing in. It was entirely possible that he didn't know much of the ranch's history, given the lack of closeness in his family. But there was more to why he'd changed his mind than limited knowledge. He was repressing how he felt about what he did know, blocking it the way he blocked everything else he didn't want to deal with. She'd seen him do it when he talked about what his father had done to him, and when he told her of coming to this place to hide.

"Come on," he said, stuffing the tube of paper under his arm and pushing his hands into his pockets. The need to touch her again was too strong, felt too necessary. It was one thing to want her. Needing what he felt when he touched her felt far too dangerous. "I'll walk you back to the Jeep."

"I don't have to go just because I'm not doing the story. Do you need help with what you're doing? Finding your boundaries?"

"You offering?"

She held his eyes, unable to hide the concern he kept telling himself he didn't want.

"If you want me."

The sensual jolt he felt at her words had Jett gritting his teeth. Wanting had never been in question.

His frame dwarfed hers. Hot as a brand, his eyes caressed her lips, the need to touch her electrifying the air. Behind him, the bay whinnied to have him pay attention to her. The distant bark of a coyote drifted in from the hills. All Jett noticed was how the delicate muscles in Annie's throat convulsed when she swallowed.

"You know I do," he murmured, drawing one hand from his pocket. He tilted her face to his, torturing himself with the memory of how she had opened to him. "But if you stay, it won't be the boundaries on this map I'll want to find."

Chapter Eleven

The air felt still, like the calm before a storm. Annie couldn't hear a single bird. The creek was silent. Not a blade of grass moved. It felt as if her heart had even stopped beating as Jett stood tilting her face to his. Then she felt her heart jerk hard in her chest, and the rush of blood in her ears cleared the way for the return of other sounds.

Jett's eyes were locked on hers. He was waiting. Just as he had yesterday, he was leaving the next move up to her.

Or so she thought before his thumb grazed her mouth and regret entered his eyes. "You'd better go, Annie. We both know what's going to happen if you stay." His jaw tightened at the thought. "And I can't promise it won't go farther than you want. I can't promise you anything."

She should have felt hurt. She should have felt disappointment. There was more than one meaning in his last words. But he was only saying what she already knew. He could offer her nothing. And he wouldn't ruin what they did have with pledges he couldn't honor.

The fact that what they shared was that important to him was all Annie needed to know.

She curled her fingers around his wrist, stilling the movement of his hand when he would have pulled away. "I'm not asking for promises."

"I'm not going to be around long, Annie."

"I know," she whispered, her voice tightening around the words. "As soon as you can, you're going to work. Someplace where it doesn't rain much," she added, because he'd mentioned it so often himself. "I know you've been making calls. It's hard not to hear you when you leave Logan's office door open." Her soft smile was forgiving, and bittersweet. "But you're here now."

"You're not making this any easier," he growled.

"I don't think I'm trying to."

Heat flared in his eyes as he searched her face. He wanted to do the the right thing. For her. He could walk away and not look back. Heaven knew he'd been doing it all his life. But she wasn't as good at closing doors as he'd become. He could hurt her. The thought made him feel as powerful as it did humble. Hurting her was the last thing in the world he wanted to do.

"Annie," he began, taking one last stab at nobility, "if you were anyone else, I'd—"

"You'd what?" she coaxed when he cut himself off.

He shook his head, tracing her lower lip once more. He'd started to say that if she were anyone else, he wouldn't hesitate to take what she was offering. But that wasn't true. He didn't want anyone else. He only wanted her.

"If you were anyone else," he amended, the truth feeling just as grim, "I'd walk away." An honorable man would. But he wasn't all that honorable. He was just a man. A man who had wanted her from the moment he awakened to find her hand clasped against his chest. "But I can't."

The end of the rolled map hit the ground. It had barely tipped over before he was hauling her into his arms, doing what he shouldn't do, what he had to do and what he couldn't not do if his life depended on it.

Annie felt her breath snag in her throat. Jett had no sooner pulled her to him than his mouth, hot and hard, came down on hers. She hadn't been prepared for his hunger. Or her own response to it. The impact stunned like lightning, rooting her in place before electricity radiated through every cell and pore. Raw and urgent, his hunger filled her as he drank from her lips, searching her mouth with his tongue, her body with his hands. She didn't remember reaching for him. Yet she must have. Her fingers bit into his shirt, bunching the soft cotton in her fists as she sagged against his chest. Then the pressure of his mouth was easing and the dizzying assault ended with his ragged intake of breath.

She'd scarcely managed a full breath herself before his hand found hers and he was leading her into the trees.

The creek was near. She could hear its gentle sound when Jett pulled her back into his arms. It was cooler here, too, beneath the wide low branches. But all she really noticed in the moment before he captured her lips once more was the raw need carved into the rugged lines of his face.

"Annie." Her name was a brush of breath against her mouth. "Make me go slow."

"Why?" she whispered back, clinging to him as they sank to their knees in the bed of sweet grass.

She heard him groan, the sound vibrating against her cheek as he sought the curve of her ear. "Because I want to know every inch of you." With the tip of his tongue, he traced the shape of her lobe, the moist heat sending sensation shivering through her. "Every inch."

Before she tasted his hunger, she hadn't realized how he'd held himself back each other time he kissed her. He was holding himself back now. The hard muscles of his body fairly vibrated with restraint as he pulled her blouse from her jeans and undid the buttons, one by one. She didn't want him to hold back. She wanted his passion, his heat. His hunger fueled her own. His need became her need. But he kept himself in check as he opened her blouse and slowly turned her blood to steam.

He wouldn't let her be shy. Her instinct to cover herself when he separated the front clasp of her bra and smoothed it aside was immediately countered. His fingers slipped beneath hers, covering the gentle mounds first with his hands while his mouth played intimate games with hers, and then with his lips when he pressed her back into the soft, cool grass. She felt warm where he touched her, until he laved her nipple with his tongue and gently blew over the taut bud. Then she felt the coolness tightening her more, and, again, the warmth. Sensations intensified, turning hot and liquid, tensing her in some places, loosening her in others.

She reached for him, needing more, wanting to give what he gave her. Sliding her hands down his back, she gripped the edge of his shirt, tugging it from his jeans. His skin felt warm and smooth, the muscles in his back coiled and hard. He tensed at her touch the same way she had tensed when the flat of his hand first skimmed over her bare skin. If he felt what she felt, then she wanted him to feel more.

She followed his lead, touching him as he touched her. After he slipped her blouse from her shoulders, she pulled off his shirt to splay her hands over the rippling muscles of his chest. After he skimmed denim and lace down her legs, she reached for his buckle. Fingers trembling, hands bumping, briefs and jeans joined the scattered clothes. Then he was kissing her breasts, and she, in turn, kissed the faint bruises on his collarbone and the angrier bruise at his side. His caresses were tender, torturous and wickedly clever; her own were far more uncertain, until his groans of pleasure encouraged her to be bolder. He was teaching her what pleased him, what pleased her and, ultimately, how to let go.

It occurred to her, dimly, that she should have taken another lesson from Jett and used the debris of the past to build defenses to protect herself. Instead, she had thrown away the precious few she had. Not that she'd had that many where he was concerned. She needed what she felt when she was with him too badly. There would be time later to deal with the consequences of having fallen in love with him. She might never again feel what she felt when she was in his arms. And what she felt was strangely free. When he held her, he blocked out all her doubts and inadequacies. He simply wouldn't allow them to be. It was as if she had nothing to fear from him, or herself, when she was with him.

Her bare skin sought his heated flesh. Her softer curves melded to his harder angles. Every place he touched her, she felt his heat.

And every place she touched him, he burned. Jett had ached for the feel of her hands on his body. Now he found her touch to be the purest form of torture. Small, soft, hesitant, her hands skimmed up his back, urging him closer. The exquisite sensations she elicited would have had him buried inside her already, had he not told her he would take his time. But this was Annie, and until he met her he'd never known how patient he could be.

He clenched his jaw, bearing the sound of her surprised little moans and sweet caresses until he could feel the sweat beading at the base of his spine. The need to make her feel pleasure, to drive every thought but thoughts of him from her mind, felt as essential to him as his next breath—until he felt her hand slip down his belly. When her hand closed around him, his control nearly vaporized.

He had wanted to take his time with her. But the need to possess her was too demanding, too urgent. The desire to go slowly had been a rational decision. What he felt now was the primal need to mate. Yet a core of that rationality speared the white-hot heat of need as he eased his weight over her. Drinking in her taste, her scent, he knew he'd needed to communicate to her how he felt. With every touch, he was telling her with his hands and body all the things he'd never let himself say. He was thanking her for the times she'd let him feel needed, and for being there for him when he was sick. He was letting her know how he desired her, and how he would miss her when he was gone. And when he slipped inside her, gritting his teeth as her sweet heat enveloped him, that was the most insistent thought of all.

Annie didn't want to leave this place. Ever. She lay cradled in Jett's arms, her head on his chest while his fingers smoothed the hair near her temple. He'd covered her with his shirt, but the rest of their clothing still lay scattered around them—except for the jeans he'd rolled up and stuck under his head for a pillow. Protected as they were beneath the low and sweeping branches of the tree, she could see out without being seen. Not even by the deer nibbling at the tender shoots of a sapling across the flower-covered meadow.

It was spring, a time of renewal. And renewed was how Jett made her feel. Her response to him had shown her how wrong she'd been to believe herself cold. But the feeling it gave her to know she had pleased him was even more precious. As precious as the peace she felt in his arms.

"I don't think I ever would have imagined wanting to be so far from everything," she admitted, lulled by the steady beat of his heart. "But it's so beautiful here. It must be hard for you to leave it."

"I guess I just don't think about it that much."

"This place? Or how hard it is to go?"

The muscles in his shoulder contracted with an instinctive shrug. "Either."

She wasn't surprised by the admission. "Isn't it hard moving around so much? I mean, don't you ever miss some of the places you leave behind?"

"I've never stayed in one place long enough to let it get that familiar." His fingers strayed toward her brow. "Do you have any place you miss?"

The hair on his chest tickled her cheek as she shook her head. "Not really. There are people I miss. But not places. I just miss not having a home of my own. It must feel nice to have a place like the RW to come back to."

He kept toying with her hair. Ever since he'd moved his weight off her and tucked her into his side, he'd kept up the rhythmic, hypnotic movement. She couldn't tell who the motion was meant to soothe—her, or him. Or if it was meant to soothe at all. She wasn't sure Jett even knew he was doing it.

"The only reason I come back is to see my brothers. But I don't belong here," he told her, needing her to know that. He could never be here very long before the restlessness set in. A few days. A week. He never knew how long it would take to hit, but, inevitably, it did. "The longest I've been here since I first left was the month I stayed after Logan's wedding. I wouldn't have stayed that long if it hadn't been so busy around here."

His warning hadn't been necessary. All she was trying to do was understand him. She raised her head, needing to see his face. "Why do you feel that way?"

He wished he knew. The restlessness would hit, and he would feel as if he were being driven away yet again. At the moment, though, what he wished even more was that he understood why he couldn't seem to get enough of this woman. "Did anyone ever tell you you ask an awful lot of questions?"

"Yeah," she murmured, knowing from the glint in his eyes that he was tired of talking. "You."

Sifting his fingers through her hair, he drew her closer. "How about being quiet for a while?"

It was almost time to go. For her, anyway. But the thought immediately vanished under the tender assault of Jett's mouth. She couldn't think when he touched her. Didn't want to. All too soon, the thought that she had to leave would return—and when it did, nearly an hour later, she was filled with regret at not being able to stay with him in this wonderful place. The only thing that made it bearable was the kiss Jett placed on her lips when he leaned through the window of the Jeep before he stood watching as she drove away.

He wouldn't return early with her. Their routine wouldn't change. He didn't need to say anything for her to know that. As that afternoon melded into evening, and one day followed the next, the only difference was their unspoken agreement to meet for a few hours each day at the homestead. She helped him find the markers that delineated his land and burn the dried-up brush around the old house. But Jett never joined her and the children for a meal, and he never asked her to come to his bed. They never spoke of when he would leave, either, or of any plans for the future that included the other. And each time he made love to her in the meadow, she denied the dreams that wanted to grow from the joy of just being with him.

She loved him. With all her heart. Yet she knew she couldn't hold him. He was instinctively a loner. That was how he survived. Anything that threatened that survival was kept at arm's length. Which was, in the ways that counted most, exactly where he was keeping her.

She just didn't realize how impossible that distance would be to breach until that weekend, when Sam and Logan returned home.

Sam and Logan had returned to the RW late Saturday night. Glad to be home, happy but exhausted, they'd peeked in at the sleeping children and turned in themselves. Annie, who'd greeted them at the front door in her bathrobe, had mentioned that Logan's brother was there, but it wasn't until the next morning that they connected. Logan and Jett, anyway. Always the first up, no matter what time he'd gone to bed, Logan had been doing a slam-dunk with a cup of coffee when Jett walked in seconds ahead of Annie.

Neither of the men noticed her, so she stayed by the refrigerator, watching pleasure and curiosity wash over Logan's handsome features. Dark-haired, tall and powerfully built, the resemblance he bore to his brother was strong. Jett was a little leaner, a little hungrier-looking, his eyes bluer. But she stopped drawing comparisons when she saw Jett hold out his hand. She wondered only if he was smiling, too. She couldn't tell. All she could see was his broad back while Logan grabbed his hand, hauled him in to slap him on the shoulder, then stepped away. Moments after that, Logan handed him a cup of coffee and motioned toward the back door.

"I was sure surprised when Annie said you were here. Come on down to the barns with me and tell me what's going on. It was nice to get away,'' he muttered gruffly. ''Nice for Sam, anyway. But I'll take a horse and a herd of long-horns over deck chairs any day.''

''You enjoyed yourself and you know it.''

At the sound of the gently chiding feminine voice, both brothers glanced behind them.

Sam had come up beside Annie. Unlike Annie, who'd pulled on jeans and a sweatshirt because she intended to feed the foal, Sam was in a bathrobe that looked like an over-grown baseball shirt.

Tucking a wisp of pale blond hair into the low ponytail at her nape, she smiled at her brother-in-law. ''He did have a good time,'' she insisted, looking as if she would have greeted him with a hug but she knew he wouldn't be com-fortable with the gesture. ''Don't believe him if he says oth-erwise.'' She cocked her head, moving toward the coffeepot herself. ''You're looking good, Jett. It's great to see you again. All Annie told us last night is that you were here. When did you arrive?''

Jett hadn't followed Sam's progress across the cozy kitchen. His attention remained on the woman standing quietly by the refrigerator.

Annie could practically feel her sister's eyes lock on her. In the moments before Jett spoke, even Logan seemed to sense the shift in current between the two people watching each other across the room.

''Annie can tell you about it.''

Sam, looking more curious by the second, darted a glance back to her sister.

Pulling her glance from Jett's, Annie summoned a smile. ''Just give me twenty minutes first, Sam. I've got a foal to feed.''

Sam's eyebrow shot up at precisely the same instant Lo-gan said, ''What foal?''

Annie's eyes locked on Jett's again. Only this time, more than just an odd sense of uncertainty passed between them. Empress had been one of Logan's favorites.

Sympathy, and a whole host of emotions Annie didn't care to identify, twisted inside her. "Your brother can tell you about it," she said to Logan.

Jett's jaw clenched. "You don't need to take care of the foal this morning, Annie. I'll do it."

"You sure?"

"Yeah. I'm sure."

He turned then, giving his brother a look that had him turning, too. Moments later, Logan had brushed a good-bye kiss over Sam's mouth—much as Jett had done with Annie the past few mornings—and headed to the door. Jett didn't come anywhere near Annie now, though. Either he was just being his reticent self with their siblings around or he didn't want to stake a claim to her in front of them.

With the awful feeling that he might not want their siblings to know how close they'd become, Annie watched through the window as the men headed down the road to the main complex, their way lit by the glow of yellow vapor lights and a faint ribbon of pink on the horizon.

It was literally the crack of dawn.

"Annie?" Sam quietly inquired. "What's going on?"

Annie and Jett had never discussed what they would do when Sam and Logan returned. Discussing it would have forced them to define whatever it was they had. What they shared was precious to Annie. But she wouldn't have hesitated to acknowledge her feelings about him to anyone. Family or otherwise. Just making feelings known was a form of commitment, though. From the way Jett had just acted, she had the feeling he wasn't sure he even wanted to acknowledge that he was attracted to her. The thought that he might not want anyone to know he cared about her hurt.

"I'm not exactly sure," was all she could say as she headed for the rack of mugs under the cabinet. "But I have the feeling I'm going to find out."

"How long has he been here?"

"Two weeks."

Sam's eyes went wide. "You've been with him here for two weeks?"

"That's not very long, is it?"

Two mugs hit the counter.

"I guess that depends on how you felt about him being here. I was thinking just the opposite."

Eyes the color of aged brandy searched eyes of golden brown. "Oh, Annie," Sam whispered, recognizing all too well the awful push-pull of emotions in her sister's eyes. She'd gone through it. Lindsey had gone through it. "You, too?"

Annie's shoulder lifted in a shrug. "I don't know that it much matters. He's probably not going to be here much longer, anyway."

"Did he say when he was leaving?"

Annie shook her head. "No. But it shouldn't be too long now. He wasn't feeling well when he got here," she told her sister, understating the matter a tad. "He's just been waiting to get well." He'd stopped favoring his left side. She'd noticed that yesterday. "I think he's just about there."

A smile suddenly lit Sam's face. "I don't think you have anything to worry about for a while. Considering what time of year it is, I'd be willing to bet that Logan isn't going to let him get away without a struggle. He's going to want him to stick around and help. He got him to stay for a month last time. Who knows?" she added with a wink. "The way he was looking at you, maybe you can convince him to stay longer... if that's what you want."

As Annie turned to smile at the little girl who'd just wandered in to give her mom a sleepy-eyed hug, Annie knew it was very much what she wanted. She was just afraid to want it too much. If she let herself admit how badly she wanted Jett to stay, she would start dreaming again, start creating a future with him in it. The past couple of weeks, all that occupied the nebulous hazy space she thought of as "the future" had been finding a house, planting a garden and starting work at the paper. Now Jett kept slipping into that space, too. Only, when she pictured him in it, she could see that house becoming a home.

It was dangerous, that dream. It was dangerous *to* dream. And loving a man like Jett was the most dangerous risk of all. She would never know when his restlessness would hit and he would be gone. Still, the thought that he might be around for another month was enough to stave off all the warnings her once-logical mind was trying to give her heart—until Sam tried to get everyone to the table for dinner.

"We'll eat in a few minutes, Amy," Sam said, pulling her daughter's hand away from an olive she was trying to snitch. "If you've finished putting the napkins on the table, go tell Erin to get off the phone and ask Daddy and your uncles to come on. Would you hit this with the paprika, Lindsey?" she asked, setting a bowl of steaming mashed potatoes in front of her youngest sister.

Lindsey, in one of Sam's aprons, added the last garnish of parsley to the roast and gave her oldest sister a nod. Annie, next to her pouring gravy into a boat, had no idea how someone could look smashing with Kiss the Cook emblazoned over her basketball belly, but Lindsey managed the feat somehow.

"I can't believe they're still in there talking about cows," Lindsey muttered, truly amazed at the topic that had kept the three brothers occupied with their drinks in Logan's office for the past hour. "Cal hasn't been around a cow since he was seventeen, but you wouldn't know it from the sound of him now."

A lid clattered when Sam set it in the sink. "It's just something they have in common to talk about. It's like sports and politics anywhere else. Around here, it's politics and livestock. I'm just glad they're talking. This is the first time in over twenty years that the three of them have been together at the same time. I can't imagine how good that has to make Logan feel."

There was a wealth of understanding in the glance Sam and Lindsey exchanged. That same empathy was in Annie's eyes when they looked toward her.

The three sisters had never discussed Logan's, Cal's and Jett's backgrounds, but it was clear at that moment that those men had chosen to confide that part of themselves to their respective mate. That Jett had opened up to Annie seemed to tell both of her sisters far more than Annie was prepared to believe—considering what she heard of the men's conversation just then.

Amy had delivered her message. The deep murmur of the brothers' voices became more distinct as they moved into the hall, stopping in the spacious entry before heading into the dining room. Their conversation was about the herds being moved for the start of calving season. Spring had started easing into itself with the arrival of the two foals Jett had helped deliver, and a dozen or so cows had apparently dropped calves just today. According to what Logan said, in another week there would be hundreds of births a day and no one would get any rest. He had already hired on six more men and was thinking about adding a couple more. All that mattered to Annie at the moment was that he wanted to know if Jett would like to stick around for a while.

"You're worth two of any other man," she heard him say, making his feelings about what had happened with Empress obvious to her. "You haven't committed to that job in Melbourne, so why don't you stay for a while? At least until the calves are worked."

Annie didn't realize she'd stopped stacking hot rolls into their basket, until she noticed that Sam wasn't moving, either. Sam stood by the stove, steam curling up from the carrots she'd just uncovered and her ear cocked toward the entry. Lindsey, sensing she'd missed something already and not wanting to miss more, paused with the small jar of paprika in midair. Since her sisters were blatantly eavesdropping, so would she.

Not one of them, though, heard Jett's reply. All they caught was Logan's "Just think about it" before one of the kids turned up the volume on the television and their attention was forced back to each other.

With both her sisters sending looks of apology her way, Annie could only lift her shoulders in the shrug Jett so often used when he wanted it to appear he wasn't bothered by something, and finish up with the rolls. She hoped she could do justice to the meal they'd put together. With a knot the size of a fist already filling her stomach, she rather doubted that she would. Jett had come back with Logan a couple of hours ago, cleaned up and then, with Cal's arrival, joined his brothers for a drink. In that time, he hadn't said a single word to her.

Carrying in the gravy and rolls, she couldn't help but wonder if he planned to ignore her all through dinner, too.

"Where do you want to sit, Annie?"

It was Logan who asked the question as the last of the serving dishes were set amid bone-white china on mauve damask. The kids had already grabbed their places, including Erin, who looked upset but in no mood to talk about it. Cal, as big as his brothers, his eyes just as blue and his dark sable hair pulled back in a neat low ponytail, was holding a chair out for his very pregnant wife. Annie's only choice was one of the two chairs in front of her, which left one remaining for Jett, who was hanging back by the buffet looking as if he'd rather not sit down at all.

"Sit by me, Uncle Jett," Michael coaxed, catching the rung of the chair next to him with the toe of his boot and pushing it back. "We can play tic-tac-toe with the salt."

Annie's eyes jerked to the man standing stiffly behind her.

"So that's why there's always salt all over when you two finish eating."

Defense flashed in guarded blue eyes, though she didn't think it had much to do with the mess he and Michael had made on the counter. "I thought we cleaned it up."

"You forgot the floor."

"Come on, you guys," Erin muttered, too busy being unhappy about Trevor's failure to make it home, yet again, to notice anyone else's unease. "Let's eat, huh?"

Since she and Jett were the ones holding things up, there was nothing for Annie to do but take her chair and breathe a sigh of relief when Jett finally slid in next to her. As stubborn as he'd been about sitting down to a meal, she'd halfway suspected that he wouldn't now. Her relief, however, was short-lived.

As attuned to him as she'd become, she picked up his tension as a magnet would metal. That tension coiled the muscles in his body, tightened the knot in her stomach, and when she glimpsed the hard set of his jaw she thought he looked the way a martyr might on his way to the stake. No one seemed to pick up on the strain but her. Least of all the little boy sitting next to him.

Michael immediately reached for the rolls.

"Hold it," Sam said, her quiet voice stilling Michael's hand on the napkin-covered basket. "Aren't we forgetting something?"

"Oh, yeah," he muttered, and gave his dad a sheepish grin.

Giving the boy a wink, Logan took his hand, then grasped Erin's; she in turn joined hands with Lindsey, who was already holding her husband's. Jett seemed to notice that Cal and Sam were holding hands, too, and that Sam had Annie's. Since Michael had simply picked up Jett's other hand without thinking that his uncle might not know what was going on, Jett didn't get a chance to decide whether or not he wanted to participate. He hesitantly slipped his hand around Annie's while Logan said the blessing.

It was clear to Annie that Jett hadn't known what was going on at first. As uncomfortable as he already was with the idea of a family meal, she fully expected him to let go of her the moment everyone said, "Amen."

Only Jett didn't. When everyone else dropped hands and started reaching for bowls to pass and commenting on how good everything smelled, he drew her hand under the tablecloth and rested it on his thigh. Immediately she felt his grip tighten, the motion seeming more to draw something from her than to offer anything himself. But when he reluctantly released her so she could take the bowl of carrots Sam was holding out, Annie felt better than she had all day.

At least she would have, if Jett had relaxed a little. She knew he had a good appetite. He usually ate as much himself as she and the two younger kids combined. Yet he hardly touched his meal. While everyone else talked about Sam and Logan's cruise, Cal's restoration of the library and Michael's black eye—since it was pretty hard to ignore the pea-green-and-purple shiner, Jett sat there as if the centerpiece were a time bomb and he was just waiting for it to explode.

Finally, when Sam lifted a bowl and asked if anyone cared for a second helping, it became apparent to Annie that he couldn't take whatever it was anymore. His body taut as a trip wire, he pushed his chair back, laid his napkin by his half-eaten dinner and muttered, "Excuse me."

He was on his way out of the room before Annie could lay her fork on her plate.

Had Erin not just found her uncle's departure the perfect opportunity to make her own escape, Jett's absence might have been regarded as unusual by the people remaining behind. But Erin excused herself, too, and Amy followed suit, so it just felt as if the meal were winding down. To everyone but Annie.

"I'll be back in a minute, Sam," she murmured. Placing her napkin on Jett's, she slid back from the table and turned in the direction he had gone when he left the room.

He'd headed into the kitchen. But he wasn't in there. The yard lights were just coming on, and when Annie looked out the window, she saw him out by the hitching rail that edged the backyard lawn. Grabbing her jacket from the mudroom peg, she tossed it over her shoulders on the way out the door and made herself walk instead of run.

Jett was leaning against the rail, his arms crossed over his chest, his legs crossed at the ankles. With his head tipped back to the fading evening sky, it looked to her as if he were searching the heavens for an answer. But when he heard her and dropped his chin to blow out a long breath, she had the feeling he hadn't found what he was looking for.

"What happened in there?"

Jett shook his head, the breeze lifting the strands tumbling over his forehead. "It would sound stupid."

"Try me."

There had been a couple of things going on, actually. But thoughts of how much his brothers had changed, how much less he now had in common with them, paled compared to the memories that had made his stomach feel on fire the entire time he was at that table. They were like old movie tapes. Ancient relics of a time that no longer existed. Yet, since he'd been at the ranch this time, he hadn't been able to get them out of his head.

"When we were growing up, we never sat down to a meal anybody could ever enjoy. The minute we'd get to the table, Ben would start picking on who hadn't done what chore, or who hadn't done what chore right, or why in the hell whoever'd heated the beans that night hadn't made 'em hotter or had burned 'em or some damn thing. It just felt like, any minute, somebody was going to criticize something and there'd—"

He cut himself off, jerked himself away from the rail and jammed his fingers through his hair. "I told you it was stupid. Just forget it, okay?"

Jett's agitation warned her. Always before, when he talked about Ben and how he'd treated him and his brothers, he'd maintained an attitude that almost seemed like indifference. And always before, Annie would have pursued the opening he'd given her. With him so clearly struggling to dam the feelings that had leaked past his guard, she wasn't about to deny his request.

Her only response was to catch his hand when it fell.

The day had faded, the artificial light coming from behind them casting harsher shadows than the gentler light of evening. Still, it seemed to her that some of the shadows in Jett's eyes lifted when he curled his fingers through hers.

"I want to talk to you, Annie. But not here." His glance searching her face, he reached out and smoothed the hair over her ear. "At the homestead. Can you come with me now?"

Chapter Twelve

The homestead was different at night, the stillness quieter, the space more vast. With evening giving way to night, Annie couldn't see the old house at all after Jett killed the lights on the Jeep. Its shadow blended with the trees, leaving nothing but black silhouettes against a backdrop of darkened sky. A silver half-moon crept over those treetops. Above, the heavens already glittered with greath swaths of stars.

The slam of the vehicle's doors echoed like gunshots in that stillness. But the night immediately settled back to silence, allowing Annie to hear the crickets, the distant burble of the creek and the brush of Jett's boots in the grass as he walked to the front of the Jeep. She met him there, wondering as she had for the past ten minutes what it was that kept him so inexplicably quiet.

He'd said little since she'd returned from telling Sam that

they would be back in a while. Now, snagging her hand as he leaned against the Jeep, all he said was, "Come here."

He tugged her into his arms, the motion seeming as natural as the feel of his lips meeting hers. Relief swamped anxiety and she flowed into him, their bodies seeking each other like old lovers, rather than two people who'd known each other's secrets only a matter of days. Yet it wasn't hunger Annie sensed in Jett when he tightened his hold, drawing her into the long, slow kiss. As his hands moved over her, what she felt in him was something more like . . . desperation. Cupping her hips to him, driving his tongue deeper into her mouth, he was as close as he could be without being inside her. Nearly crushed in his arms, it felt almost as if he were trying to blot out some tormenting thought by losing himself in her. Or maybe as if he were hanging on as long as he could before he had to let her go.

Annie's thudding heart jerked painfully at that thought. She pulled her head back, her hands clutching his waist as she searched his shadowed features.

In the pale blue light of the moon, she saw bleakness in the hard lines of his face, and the same agitation that had been with him all evening. He hadn't managed to escape it this time. Still, he sought to deny it was there.

"I've wanted to do that all day," he told her, grazing his fingers along her cheek. "But whenever I saw you, there were other people around."

"That didn't mean you couldn't talk to me."

His eyebrows drew together at the hurt she hadn't intended to let him see.

"How could I? Every time I saw you, you were with your sisters."

His logic was dubious, but the conviction in his tone made her feel foolish for being so sensitive. Foolish and relieved. It hadn't occurred to her that he might have been intimidated by a group of females bonding in a kitchen. Now that she did think about it, she couldn't envision too many males voluntarily venturing into that scenario. Especially one who had a thing about domesticity to begin with.

She rested her forehead on his chest, apology in her voice. "I guess I didn't think about that," she admitted, knowing some of the tension she felt was her own. "I was afraid you were avoiding me."

He tipped her chin right back up, his eyes glittering over her face. "Why would I want to do that?"

"I just thought you might not want anyone to know there was something going on between us." She hesitated. "We never talked about Sam and Logan coming back."

"No," he whispered, as aware as she that they had avoided what would amount to the beginning of the end. "We didn't."

She felt his arms loosen. But it was the way his eyes darted from hers that kicked her insecurities squarely into place.

"My brothers already know something's going on. I didn't say anything about anything that's…happened…." he decided to say, his discomfort with defining what they shared as apparent as his scruples about not sharing the details with anyone else. "But I talked to Cal this afternoon about what it would take to make this place livable. And to Logan about separating out the house and an acre or two of land. That's why I wanted you to come out here."

Annie went still. "I don't understand."

"I wanted to be with you when you saw it at night," he explained, dropping his hands from her waist. "I know you like it here during the day, but I always thought it was prettiest when the stars were out. Like they are now." He hesitated, then lifted his shoulder in that damnable shrug. "I want you to have it."

Annie didn't realize she'd stepped away until she saw Jett push his hands into his pockets. He looked very much like a man who wasn't sure how his gift was going to be accepted, and she had no idea how to feel about it herself. On the one hand, his generosity stunned her. On the other, she felt as if she were standing on a frozen lake with a huge crack racing toward her. He was giving the homestead to her. Not offering to share it.

Torn by ambivalence, all she could do was whisper, "Why?"

"Because you need a place of your own. This needs a lot of work, but you can stay in the apartment until it's finished. Cal said he'd hire a couple of guys to get started on it next week, if you want. It's all I can give you, Annie. It's all I've got."

The constriction in her throat made it impossible to speak just then. She didn't know what to say, anyway. All she could do was stare up at the sincerity in his night-shadowed face and wonder why she hadn't prepared herself better for this moment. He cared enough about her to give her the only thing that mattered to him. But there was something he had that was more important to her than all the land in the state of Texas. And he wasn't offering her that.

It's all I can give you.

What about your heart?

"You don't have to give me anything, Jett."

He knew that. And she could tell from the grim line of his mouth that her reaction wasn't the one he'd wanted.

"You're leaving, aren't you?"

Her quiet words held no inquiry. She already knew.

"The day after tomorrow. I found a dam to work on in Australia."

She didn't ask if where he was going was dry. She didn't ask, either, if he'd chosen that particular continent because it was as far away as he could get. "I thought Logan asked you to stay."

"I have to tell him I can't."

He was feeling it again. That awful anxiousness that demanded he move on. This was more than the boredom that made him move from one job to the next. It was the awful restlessness that pushed him to leave. The only place that particular feeling plagued him was the ranch. That was why he so seldom visited there. When it hit, the only thing he could do was go.

But, before he did, he'd wanted to give Annie something to make her smile. At the moment, seeing the tight hold she had on herself, he'd settle for just getting this over with.

He was already defensive, and the knowledge that he was hurting her made him even more so.

"Don't do this, Annie. You knew I was leaving. I never led you to believe otherwise."

"I never said you did," she said defensively, refusing to let him shift fault to her. "All I'm doing is asking about your plans to leave. I'm not asking you to change them."

She couldn't. Not only wouldn't it do any good, but when he refused, she'd be left with the memory of that rejection. She already had too many things she didn't want to look back on to include that in the ever-lengthening list.

She pulled her glance from the tight line of his jaw.

"I can't accept your gift, Jett. But I do thank you for offering it. I know what this place means to you, so that makes it—" Cutting herself off, she hugged her arms over the ache in her heart. "We'd better get back," she concluded, and started for her door. "I told Sam I'd help her with the dishes."

Jett turned her right back around. "Why can't you accept it?"

"Because it's your home," she told him, since it was one of the more obvious reasons she had to turn it down. "When you come back to the ranch, this is what you come back to. I can't take that from you."

"That's ridiculous. If I had a 'home' it was the place where Logan lives with his family. That's his home now. Not mine. This is just the homestead."

She didn't believe for a moment that he truly felt such indifference for this place. But something was pushing at him. The same thing that he hadn't been able to shake all night. Considering what he'd just said about the main house being Logan's, she suspected he felt like he didn't belong anywhere anymore.

Much as he must have felt when he had to leave at fifteen.

The thought had her reaching for him. It was no wonder he never wanted to stay when he came to the ranch.

She curled her fingers over his forearm, the need to touch as strong as the need to get past the protective wall he'd built around his heart. "Giving this to me isn't going to make the hurt go away, Jett. It won't change what happened while you were growing up."

"I'm not trying to change anything." Dismissal joined denial. "None of that matters, anyway."

"How can you say that? Jett, you can't even sit down and enjoy a meal with your family because of—"

"Don't." He shook off her touch, disgust sweeping his features when he turned from her. "I should never have told you that."

She'd wanted to breach his wall. Instead, he was erecting more, closing her out, closing himself in. She hated what he was doing to her. But what he was doing to himself was worse.

"Do you even know what you're running from?"

"How can I be running from anything? There's nothing here."

"You have *everything* here," she countered, her voice constricted by the sting of his dismissal. But this wasn't just about her. "Or you could have, if you'd just let yourself take it. You have a home here. People who care about you, who need you. And you walk away as if it means nothing. Ben isn't here anymore, Jett. There's no one making you leave but you."

His response was nothing but silence.

"I thought you had the secret to not giving the past too much power," she admitted, her voice sagging with defeat, "but you have no more control over its influence than I did. There's a difference between not looking back and simply not dealing with something. Pretending it doesn't matter doesn't mean it's not there."

She knew he'd heard her. She'd seen his back stiffen at the mention of his father, and his fists had clenched when she exposed his lack of control over the influence of his past. But when he turned to face her, it was apparent that he'd discounted everything she'd said.

"I offered this to you," he said calmly. "That had nothing to do with anything but you and me. I wanted you to have it, Annie, and you might as well take it. I'm not coming back."

His expression was as unshakably certain as his tone. She'd known before that he was a man who didn't want strings, that he cut himself off completely when he walked away. She had just never realized until now the lengths to which he'd go to accomplish that goal.

"Is that how you do it?" she asked, the revelation filling her with as much awe as pity. "Is that how ruthless you have to be when you say, 'Don't look back'?"

She would have felt better had she sensed incomprehension in him. That wasn't what she saw at all. Jett stood as rigid as the granite hills masked by the night, looking very much as if he wanted to tell her it wasn't her that he wanted to forget along with everything else. But she was very much a part of what he was putting behind him even now. He wasn't just ridding himself of unwanted memories by leaving. This time, he was cutting himself off from the only place that had mattered to him in order to forget about her.

"Clean breaks heal the fastest, Annie."

"I'm sure they do," she agreed, only pity remaining. "And I think you've been right all along. I don't want to be like you, Jett. I think it would hurt far too much."

The muscle in his jaw jerked. "I didn't want it to end like this."

She hadn't, either, and the fact that it had made her sound as sorry as she felt. "I guess we don't always get what we want, do we?"

There probably wasn't anyone around who knew that better than she. But before Jett could let that thought make him feel any more defensive than he did, he muttered, "I'd better get you back."

With a tight nod, Annie headed for her door while Jett headed for his. There was little to say that wouldn't lead to more hurt, and she didn't want to argue with him about ghosts he wouldn't even admit he was still fighting. Jett had decided he was leaving the day after tomorrow, and nothing was going to stop him. Not that she would even have tried. He didn't want her. That was all she needed to know.

Still, as they rode back in uneasy silence, closed in by the dark and their own agitated thoughts, she wished she could understand how someone so wrong for her could have come to mean so much. Their differences should have kept them poles apart. Yet what they had in common had somehow spanned that gap. He had become her friend before he became her lover. Though she already ached at the thought of never being held in his arms again, it was the loss of that friendship that made the pain so hard to take.

She needed to tell him that. She needed to tell him, too, that she wished him well. But Logan was walking toward them when they pulled into the yard, so now was not the time. The moment Jett cut the engine, he told her he was going to help Logan with the evening chores and was out of the vehicle before she could even say she'd see him later.

She didn't see him later, though. He didn't return to the house until after she went to bed. And when she came down the next morning, not nearly as enthusiastic as she should have been for her first day of work at the newspaper, he was already gone. Sam, looking as if she could cheerfully throttle both brothers for leaving her to bear the message, said Logan had just told her Jett had left at 5:00 a.m. for the airport.

The job Annie had regarded with such interest proved to be a godsend—in some respects. Though she felt more unsettled than ever starting something new, having to concentrate on telephones and typing and meeting new people spared her having to face the hole Jett's absence left in her life. For a while, anyway.

Now that Sam and Logan were back, Annie's presence wasn't required at the ranch. She would have been welcome had she wanted to stay longer, but she knew Sam's family needed their privacy as much as Annie wanted hers. So she went "home" that night to the little apartment over Lindsey's boutique in Leesburg and spent the entire evening unpacking the few boxes of things that would fit in the tiny place and hanging pictures and curtains to make it feel like home.

She would move on, because that was what she had to do. She'd try not to look back too much, either, but if she did, she wasn't going to worry about it. There were things she needed to remember even about the stuff that hurt. And though it hurt like the devil to think of Jett, she couldn't forget what he had done for her. He'd shown her that she could step beyond the world she'd known and find pleasure in the unfamiliar. And he'd made her feel good about herself again. Just because she would feel so much better if he were still there to share her day was something she'd simply have to learn to live with.

But she could do that. She'd learned to live with a lot that wouldn't ever be. The trick was getting what *could* be to happen. It seemed to Annie that, if she could get a place of her own and stop missing Jett quite so much, everything would be just fine. Unfortunately, there were some things that didn't want to fall into place, no matter how hard she tried.

She looked at three houses that weekend. Only one the weekend after that. Then, there wasn't a single new listing for the following fourteen days. Since part of her job was to set up the classified ads, she would have been the first to know if anything came up.

By the time the first of May rolled around, she was getting desperate.

This is the only place I've seen in six weeks that's even close to what I want, Lindsey. If I can get the loan, I'm buying it.''

"But, Annie—it's *orange*.''

Annie blinked at the house her very pregnant sister was frowning at. From where she and Lindsey stood at the edge of the road by Annie's little white sedan, and with the noonday sun shining directly on it, the color of the old Victorian did bear a striking resemblance to citrus fruit. 'The Realtor called it salmon, but I'll paint it.''

"That'll cost you a fortune. This place is huge. What would you do with five bedrooms, anyway?"

"I thought maybe I could rent some out."

Lindsey caught her long wheat-colored hair at her nape and arched a delicate eyebrow. "You've actually thought about doing that?"

"Sure." Crossing her arms over her white cotton sundress, Annie glanced back at the house. "It would help me make the payments."

"Are you going to serve sherry in the parlor? And collect cats? If you want, I think Sam might be able to spare one or two from their barns."

"You're not helping," Annie muttered, unable to see why her sister was having such a hard time with the concept. She'd have thought her sister would go off the deep end over decorating possibilities instead of finding flaws. Lindsey loved a new project. "This is the only place I've seen that's even close to what I want."

"This heat is definitely getting to you." Lindsey held up her hand, ticking off her fingers one by one. "The house has five bedrooms. You said you wanted two. You wanted a nice little yard with room for a garden. This place comes with half a dozen acres, a pecan grove and part of a river."

"It's one acre, six pecan trees and a tiny little brook. Stop exaggerating."

Her sister *was* exaggerating. But Lindsey had just picked up on what Annie regarded as the house's best selling features—the field behind the house and the creek that ran through it. Not caring to explain why the setting appealed so much, because she didn't want to consider it too much herself, Annie focused on her sister's odd disapproval.

"Why don't you like this house?"

"I didn't say I didn't like it. I just think you should keep looking." Arching her back to relieve the strain of what she was carrying in front, she let out a long, beleaguered breath. "Let's go get something cold to drink. It's a beast out here."

If Lindsey hadn't looked so uncomfortable, Annie would have been even more exasperated with her sister's unusually negative response. There were a lot of very nice things about the house. And if it was a little bigger than she'd wanted, well, she didn't think taking in boarders was such a bad idea. She didn't like living alone anyway.

She told her sister that, too, then added that she'd take her home so she could get off her feet. With only two weeks to go until the baby was due, she didn't need to be tagging along with her anymore. Not that it would be necessary, anyway.

"I want this house," she said on her way around the car. "After I drop you off, I'm calling the Realtor."

Across the white metal roof, Annie saw an odd look of panic cross Lindsey's face. "Don't you want to think about it for a while?"

"I have thought about it."

"Maybe you should think about it a little longer. Or wait to see what comes on the market in the next week or two. There's no need to rush into it."

"Rush into it? I've been looking for a house ever since I got here. I want to buy this, Lindsey."

"You can't."

Incredulous, Annie gaped at the eight-and-a-half-months-pregnant lady standing with her chin set and one hand at the small of her back.

"Why not?"

"Annie, don't do this."

"Don't do what?"

"Don't make me mess this up. I promised Cal I wouldn't say anything."

"What's your husband got to do with me buying a house?"

"He doesn't have anything to do with it." Exasperation turned to pleading. "Just give me a break here, will you? Hold off on this place for a while."

"Not without a reason."

For a moment, Annie actually felt sorry for her inexplicably unreasonable sibling. The woman looked truly torn between some promise she'd obviously made to her husband and the need to justify her truly odd objections.

Finally, when she was convinced that Annie was dead serious, resignation slowly stole through Lindsey's eyes. "If you're that set on doing this, then just do one thing first. Take a drive out to the RW. To the place the guys call the homestead."

"Why?"

"Just do it, Annie. Then, if you still want this place, great. With a coat of paint, it really would be lovely."

"Lindsey..."

"I'm not saying anything else, so don't ask."

With that, Lindsey eased herself into the seat, flatly refusing to say anything more on the subject—which Annie thought peculiar in itself, considering that her sister clearly had a lot more on her mind. All the way back to Lindsey's house, she kept glancing at Annie as if there were something she herself wanted to ask but didn't dare. That only added confusion to Annie's curiosity.

She had to admit to a little anxiety, too. The moment Lindsey mentioned the homestead, Annie had become aware of the too-familiar hollow sensation in the pit of her stomach. She hadn't been to the homestead since the night Jett had tried to give it to her, something both of her sisters now knew about. From her and from their husbands. Given Lindsey's truly weird behavior, Annie had the sneaking suspicion that Jett had gone ahead and asked Cal to fix up the place for her anyway. Cal had been spending a lot of time on the weekends out at the RW, which was why Lindsey had always been available on Sundays to go house-hunting with Annie.

She truly hoped that was not what Jett had done. If it was, she'd just have to turn it down again. At least this time, with him halfway around the world, she could do it in a letter.

Annie saw signs of construction even before the old house came into view. The overgrown cowpath that had served as access from the old ranch road had been bladed smooth, and new lumber was piled by the dead snag. Plastic-wrapped rolls of insulation were stacked a few feet away. Closer to the road was a large pile of shingles that bore a strong resemblance to those she'd seen on the sagging old roof.

Sure enough, as she pulled her car to a stop near the lumber, Annie could see that the roof was gone. So were the broken shutters and warped gingerbread that had decorated the eaves. New trusses, their golden-brown color clear against the pale blue of a hot May sky, sat atop a house that had been scraped free of paint.

The high-pitched buzz of a power saw drowned out the slam of her car door. That sound was constant, the electricity apparently supplied by the new power line running back toward the main road.

She'd have thought Cal was running that saw. Except his truck wasn't anywhere around. The new blue pickup parked at the far side of the house didn't look at all familiar to her. Thinking it must belong to one of the men Cal had working for him—specifically, whoever was wielding the saw—Annie picked her way through the wood scraps and stepped up onto the newly laid porch.

The front door was open. Walking in, she looked up at the sky through the angled and crisscrossing pattern of wooden supports, then glanced down at the tarp covering most of the beautiful old hand-laid floor.

The tug of memory was bittersweet. The first time Jett had brought her here, she'd noticed that floor and thought of the hours that had gone into fitting it just so. When Jett had told her how his grandfather had built the house for his wife and their long-awaited child, she'd thought that the placement of every plank in that floor must have been a labor of love.

She wondered now if Jett had ever thought of it that way, then told herself it was best she didn't think of him at all. Hugging her arms to herself, not knowing how that would be possible here, she continued across the room. She'd been telling herself to get over him since the day he'd left. Maybe, someday, her heart would get the message.

A man's white T-shirt hung over a ladder in the kitchen doorway. Following the deafening sound of the saw, she wandered into the kitchen herself. The old counters were gone, the foundations for new ones set in place but the tiles not yet laid. It was the window over the hole where the new sink would go that had her attention, however. Through it she could see a shirtless man in jeans working out back at a pair of sawhorses.

The saw had just wound down from its scream, and he'd bent to set it on a low box. Even before he straightened to strip off his clear safety glasses, Annie's heart slammed against her ribs.

It jerked again when Jett hoisted the long length of wood to his shoulder and turned around. Corded muscle tensed and shifted beneath tanned, sweat-glistened skin, and his dark hair fell over his forehead. His jeans hugged his hips, and his boots were covered with sawdust.

Swallowing around the knot beating in her throat, Annie's only thought was to wonder when he had returned.

Seconds later, with her still rooted by the window, he stepped through the door with an eight-foot length of four-by-four on his shoulder and went as still as the sweltering air.

It was impossible for Annie to tell whether Jett was dismayed or just surprised to find her there. As his cool blue eyes jerked from her face to her shoes, skimming the loose white cotton shift in between, she was afraid to speculate.

All she could think to say was, "When did you get back?"

Muscle shifted as Jett leaned the end of the pantry support against the wall. "A couple of weeks ago." He glanced at her again, his expression totally guarded, and pulled the T-shirt from the ladder to wipe it over his face. After taking a swipe at his chest with it, too, he tossed it back over a rung. "What are you doing out here?"

"I found a house I wanted to buy, and Lindsey—" Annie cut herself off. Her reasons for being here didn't seem nearly as important as the fact that no one had told her he'd been back for so long. Even that didn't matter, when she considered that he hadn't bothered to let her know he was back himself.

"You found a place to buy?"

She gave him a nod, not at all sure what his frown meant. "It's a little bigger than I wanted, but it'll do." She swallowed past the knot again, forcing it down. "Why are you doing all this?"

"I'm going to live here."

"You are?"

She'd called it his home. Jett had never thought of the homestead that way before, but she had been right. If home was where a person felt safe, then this had been the place.

"I'm going into ranching with Logan. Seemed like the logical thing to do when I found myself working cattle in the outback."

"I thought you were working on a project outside of Melbourne."

"I was. For a couple of days. Then some kid who didn't know a steam shovel from a snowplow drove a grader into my crane and I got to thinking that if I was going to get my neck broken, I might as well do it wrestling a steer." He liked being around animals. He knew them, knew what to expect. So it didn't make any sense not to work with them. He just hadn't realized how much he missed being around them until she pointed it out to him. "If I was going to work with them," he concluded, "I figured I might as well do it here. I can take over a lot of what Hank's getting too old to do."

"Is that fair to Logan? Having him count on you like that?"

"I want him to count on me," he countered, scowling. "He's all for the idea."

"But what will he do when you leave again?"

There was no accusation in her question, just honest concern. She knew him well. She just didn't know that, because of her, a few things had changed.

"I'm not going anywhere, Annie." His lips pressed together, and he shoved his fingers through his hair. "I think you might have been right about Ben. About how I was letting what had happened get to me, I mean. I asked Cal if he'd ever felt the way I did, and he said his feelings about all that went on back then had a lot to do with why he'd stayed away for so long. Until Lindsey got him out here to talk to Logan last spring, he hadn't set foot on this place in seventeen years." His hair fell back over his forehead when he dropped his hand. "There's too much I like about this place to stay away anymore."

Uneasy, afraid it showed, Annie watched him watch her across six feet of sawdust and bent nails. He looked uncertain, which wasn't like him. And defensive, which was.

"Why didn't you want me to know you were back?"

"Because I wasn't ready."

She sucked in a shuddering breath. She'd asked. Now she knew.

"I'll let you get back to work. I wouldn't have come, except my sister thought I should." She managed a faltering smile. If he was going to be around, she'd have to get used to seeing him. With her sisters married to his brothers, they'd have holidays in common, at the very least. "Take care of yourself. Okay?"

He moved before she could, blocking her way. "I didn't mean that the way it sounded, Annie." He lifted a hand toward her. Then, not knowing if she'd welcome his touch, he let it fall to his side. "I meant I didn't want you to know because this wasn't ready... and I guess I needed it to be."

The uncertainty in his expression was mirrored in hers. "Jett, I can't stand this." More than anything, she wanted to have him put his arms around her. She didn't care that he was sweaty and dirty and smelled of hard work. She just wanted him to hold her, and to ask if he was all right, and if he'd been hurt when the kid graded his crane or whatever it was that had happened. But he looked as wary of her as she felt of him. "What's going on?"

The muscle in his jaw bunched as he searched her face. He looked uneasy, and clearly unprepared to talk to her now. But he must have decided that, as long as she was here, he might as well get it over with.

"I guess a lot of that depends on you," he said, reaching toward her again. "On whether or not you're willing to give me a chance.'' His fingers hovered at the side of her head, hesitating before he touched them to the fawn-colored hair feathering from her temple. "Do we have a chance, Annie? I won't push for anything. I'd just like to know if we could start over, or something.''

The warm air suddenly seemed hard to breathe. Or maybe it was the apprehension in his eyes that caught her breath in her throat. "Or something?"

"Yeah," he muttered. "I have an idea, but there's no sense going into it if I've screwed things up too badly for you to want to consider it."

Annie felt the smile form even before it touched her mouth. "You come back after a month and expect me to just take up where we left off?"

"Where we left off wasn't so good. I was sort of hoping we could back up to the day before. Then, maybe, after a while..."

"After a while...?" she prompted when he said nothing else.

A faint frown touched his forehead, his voice becoming quieter as he carried his touch behind her ear. "Do you remember the first time I brought you out here?"

Of course she did. She remembered every moment they'd spent together. "Sure."

"Do you remember asking me why I didn't go back to school to be a vet? I told you then," he went on, the question clearly rhetorical, "that I really hadn't wanted that for a long time. But what you said after that, about how the time would pass anyway, even if I didn't go back to school, that got me thinking about where I'd be this time next year...or five years from now. Then I started thinking about Michael and the kid that belted him."

If the confusion in Annie's expression was any indication, the sequence of his thoughts didn't make any more sense to her than it had to Jett. He was pretty sure he wasn't going to make a whole lot of sense with the rest of what he had to say, either. But he didn't know any other way to explain to her how the events of the two weeks they'd shared had brought him to the conclusion that had drawn him back here.

All he could do was give it his best shot. So, calmed by the simple act of stroking her hair, he told her how good it had made him feel to know he'd helped Michael, and how he'd really enjoyed spending time with him. He told her, too, how he liked watching her with the children, and how the compassion she had for Billy had given him an idea he hadn't been able to shake.

"You told me once that Logan had filled a gap in Michael's life by being his dad. I'd like to fill a gap in somebody's life someday, too, Annie.

"You said this place was perfect for kids," he went on, leaping forward even though he suspected he should ease her into the idea. "And I know you wanted children of your own. But since that's not possible, maybe we could take in someone like Billy. Or a whole houseful of Billys, and maybe a little girl who doesn't have a home of her own."

"You want foster children?"

"Or we could adopt. Or both. Or after we get married, it could just be us." He knew now what had caused his restlessness. In a way, he *had* been running. But he'd been searching for something, too. "I just need to be with you. Here."

Jett made himself be quiet. He was blowing it big-time, he could tell.

Annie didn't say a word. She just stood staring up at him, her brown eyes wide and filled with something he wasn't sure he understood and was afraid to question. He knew he should have waited. In another week, he would have had the house together enough to bring her out here and he could have shown her how comfortable it would be. He'd been working day and night to get it finished. Then, when she saw that he was serious about staying put, he would have taken his time about easing himself back into her life and laid this all out a little at a time.

"Say something."

Annie shook her head. He cared enough about her to accept her as she was, and he wanted them to give the home he'd never had himself as a child to children who needed it. He was offering her everything she could ever hope to want, could ever dare to dream, and she simply couldn't speak just then. Instead, she reached up on tiptoe, curved her arms around his neck and hung on as tightly as she could.

Jett's immediate instinct was to wrap his arms around her and pull her even closer. The fact that he'd been working in the heat and he had sawdust sticking to his sweat kept his hands curved lightly on her shoulders.

"You're wearing white," he told her, aware of yet another reason he should have waited. "I'll get you all dirty."

"I don't care."

If she didn't, neither did he. In the space of a heartbeat, he had her in his arms, holding her as close as he could get her and breathing in the scent of wild roses clinging to her hair. Needing badly to know what she thought of all this, daring to hope, he whispered, "What does this mean?"

"It means I love you."

Jett felt himself go still. Then he felt himself smile as he kissed the top of her head and drew her closer yet. He could think of several times he'd expressed that feeling to her in similar silent ways.

"That's good," he whispered, skimming his palm over the back of her head. "Because I love you, too." He had loved her from the moment he wakened to find her holding his hand. He just hadn't realized it until he tried to leave her behind.

He tipped her face to his, blocking out the sun shining through the roof when he kissed her. He loved her, that kiss said. He cherished her. And he'd missed her more than he'd ever thought he could possibly miss another human being.

Though there was so much more she needed to say, at that moment, that was exactly what Annie's kiss told him, too.

Epilogue

"I was so afraid I'd messed this up," Lindsey said as she fastened the long row of tiny satin buttons at the back of Annie's wedding gown. "I never did tell you how mad Cal was when I told him I'd sent you out here. He said that was exactly why he hadn't told me sooner that Jett had come back. He knew I'd let it slip."

Annie smiled into the oak cheval mirror in the corner of the homestead's newly decorated master bedroom. Over the shoulder of her long white silk sheath, she could see her statuesque sister's frown of contrition. Both her sisters were behind her. Sam in beige silk. Lindsey, thin again, in peach.

"You did tell me. And stop feeling guilty about it, please? You didn't mess up anything."

"Well, Sam didn't say anything to you," Lindsey muttered, stepping back to eye the simple lines of the dress. "And she knew about it longer than I did. But then, she didn't say anything when she found out Cal wanted to marry me, either."

"Not because I didn't want to." Sam held out the elbow-length veil. "When I found out Jett was living out here in a trailer and working on this place, the first thing I wanted to do was tell you." Moving closer, she fluffed the filmy tulle while Annie secured the braided pearl headband into place. "But Logan didn't tell me he was fixing it up for you. He just said Jett was back and that he was going to work the ranch with him. I didn't want to create problems for either of you." She stepped back, checking her watch. "I just hoped it would work out. It can be tough on a girl falling in love with a Whitaker. But being married to one..."

Sam let her voice trail off, a smile forming as she glanced at her youngest sister.

Lindsey, meeting the glint in Sam's eyes, grinned. "Yeah," she said. "It sure is."

Annie, veiled and gowned, teardrop pearls dancing from her ears, turned to frown at her siblings. "It's what?"

Her sisters, still grinning, headed for the door. "You'll see," they chorused.

"You'd better hurry up," Sam added. "Mom's got everybody outside." Her expression turned soft. "You look beautiful, Annie."

Annie returned her smile. She felt beautiful, too. Not because of what she'd seen in the mirror, but because of the man waiting for her in the meadow behind the home they would now share.

"I'm right behind you."

Clutching her bouquet, Annie followed her sisters past the dining room table supporting a tiered cake and champagne punch, and out onto the back porch of the gleaming white house. Her heart felt a little too full for her chest as she glanced out at the knot of people standing on a carpet of pink and lavender wildflowers.

Jett had wanted the ceremony here. And she couldn't have imagined it being anyplace else.

She couldn't see Jett, though. At least she couldn't until the knot began to unravel when Amy pointed toward the three women coming toward them. Taking Michael by the shoulders, Annie's mom nudged him back to stand beside his grandfather. Cal, holding his four-week-old son—another dark-haired, blue-eyed future heartbreaker—stepped back to smile as his wife came up to his side. Even Trevor was there. The spitting image of his father, the young man kept enough distance between himself and Erin to let Annie know that her niece must have been right about him wanting to avoid her.

Annie's heart went out to the girl. She knew how hard it was to love someone who didn't return the feeling. Yet, seeing Jett turn from where he'd been talking with the black-robed minister, she also knew the joy of discovering that the feelings had actually been there all along. It just took some people time and distance to realize what they had.

Silk rustled as she moved closer, the breeze tugging at her veil. Sam and Logan moved into place, and the minister smiled. But all Annie really noticed just then was Jett. If she lived to be a million, she would never forget the look in his eyes when she stopped next to him. Possessive and proud, his glance slid over her, a smile entering his eyes when he saw what she was holding.

Locked in her double-fisted grip was a nosegay of baby's breath and pink wild roses.

He looked back to her, affection softening the rugged lines of his face.

"It's going to be good, Annie," he said, his deep voice low, as he touched his fingertips to the hair smoothed back from her temple. "No matter what happens, it's going to be good."

"We'll make sure it is," she promised. "I love you, Jett."

"I love you, too, Annie," he whispered. Then, knowing that, together, they finally had a home, Jett reached for the hand of his bride.

* * * * *

Silhouette

SPECIAL EDITION

That
Woman!

Do you take this man...?

A woman determined to stay single: Serena Fanon
A man with a proposal: Travis Holden

The last thing Serena Fanon expected on her return
home to Big Sky Country was an offer of marriage. Most
surprising was the man doing the asking—Travis Holden.
Serena thought she wasn't interested. But
how could she refuse Montana's best-lookin',
most heart-stoppin' man?

**Made in
MONTANA**

Find out this September in
MONTANA PASSION
(SE #1051, 9/96)
by
Jackie Merritt

Look us up on-line at: http://www.romance.net

TSW996

MILLION DOLLAR SWEEPSTAKES
AND EXTRA BONUS PRIZE DRAWING

SWP-ME96

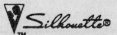

As seen on TV!
Free Gift Offer

With a Free Gift proof-of-purchase from any Silhouette® book,
you can receive a beautiful cubic zirconia pendant.

This gorgeous marquise-shaped stone is a genuine cubic
zirconia—accented by an 18" gold tone necklace.

(Approximate retail value $19.95)

Send for yours today...
compliments of ▼ *Silhouette*®
™

To receive your free gift, a cubic zirconia pendant, send us one original proof-of-
purchase, photocopies not accepted, from the back of any Silhouette Romance™,
Silhouette Desire®, Silhouette Special Edition®, Silhouette Intimate Moments®
or Silhouette Yours Truly™ title available in August, September or October at your favorite
retail outlet, together with the Free Gift Certificate, plus a check or money order for
$1.65 U.S./$2.15 CAN. (do not send cash) to cover postage and handling, payable
to Silhouette Free Gift Offer. We will send you the specified gift. Allow 6 to 8 weeks for
delivery. Offer good until October 31, 1996 or while quantities last. Offer valid in the
U.S. and Canada only.

Free Gift Certificate

Name: _____

Address: _____

City: _____ State/Province: _____ Zip/Postal Code: _____

Mail this certificate, one proof-of-purchase and a check or money order for postage
and handling to: SILHOUETTE FREE GIFT OFFER 1996. In the U.S.: 3010 Walden
Avenue, P.O. Box 9077, Buffalo NY 14269-9077. In Canada: P.O. Box 613, Fort Erie,
Ontario L2Z 5X3.

FREE GIFT OFFER
084-KMD

ONE PROOF-OF-PURCHASE

To collect your fabulous FREE GIFT, a cubic zirconia pendant, you must include this
original proof-of-purchase for each gift with the properly completed Free Gift Certificate.

084-KMD

FORTUNE'S Children™

Bestselling Author
MERLINE
LOVELACE

Continues the twelve-book series—FORTUNE'S CHILDREN
in September 1996 with Book Three

BEAUTY AND THE BODYGUARD

Ex-mercenary Rafe Stone was Fortune Cosmetics cover girl
Allie Fortune's best protection against an obsessed stalker. He
was also the one man this tempting beauty was willing to risk
her heart for....

MEET THE FORTUNES—a family whose legacy is greater than
riches. Because where there's a will...there's a *wedding!*

A CASTING CALL TO
ALL FORTUNE'S CHILDREN FANS!
If you are truly one of the fortunate
few, you may win a trip to
Los Angeles to audition for
Wheel of Fortune®. Look for
details in all retail Fortune's Children titles!

Look us up on-line at: http://www.romance.net

FC-3-C-R

The exciting new cross-line continuity series about love,
marriage—and Daddy's unexpected need for a baby carriage!

You loved

THE BABY NOTION by Dixie Browning (Desire #1011 7/96)
and
BABY IN A BASKET by Helen R. Myers
(Romance #1169 8/96)

Now the series continues with...

MARRIED...WITH TWINS! by Jennifer Mikels
(Special Edition #1054 9/96)

The soon-to-be separated Kincaids just found out they're
about to be parents. Will their newfound family grant them a
second chance at marriage?

Don't miss the next books in this wonderful series:

HOW TO HOOK A HUSBAND (AND A BABY)
by Carolyn Zane (Yours Truly #29 10/96)

DISCOVERED: DADDY
by Marilyn Pappano (Intimate Moments #746 11/96)

DADDY KNOWS LAST continues each month...
only from

▼ Silhouette®
TM

Look us up on-line at: http://www.romance.net

DKL-SE

You're About to Become a *Privileged Woman*

Reap the rewards of fabulous free gifts and benefits with proofs-of-purchase from Silhouette and Harlequin books

Pages & Privileges™

It's our way of thanking you for buying our books at your favorite retail stores.

**Harlequin and Silhouette—
the most privileged readers in the world!**

For more information about Harlequin and Silhouette's PAGES & PRIVILEGES program call the Pages & Privileges Benefits Desk: 1-503-794-2499

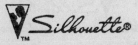

Silhouette®

SSE-PP175